PRAISE

"A cracking good read and a phenomenal start to a thriller series that has already electrified France and become a huge bestseller across Europe and beyond. Vivid characters, evocative international settings, and a history darker than midnight. I highly recommend this novel!"
—Douglas Preston, No. 1 bestselling coauthor of the famed Pendergast series of novels

"A superbly esoteric blend of history and adventure."
—Glenn Cooper, internationally bestselling thriller writer

"History, adventure and thrills."
—*L'Express*

"A fascinating tale with a tight-knit plot."
—*NVO*

"Masterfully written."
—*20 Minutes*

"A vivid story."
—*Metro*

"Giacometti and Ravenne's series kickoff has abundant visceral appeal."
—*Kirkus Reviews*

"European bestsellers Giacometti and Ravenne make their U.S. debut with this intrigue-filled thriller... those into Freemason lore and Nazi myths will be satisfied."
—*Publishers Weekly*

Shadow Ritual

Éric Giacometti
and
Jacques Ravenne

Translated by Anne Trager

LE FRENCH BOOK ▮

First published in France as
Le Rituel de l'Ombre
by Eric Giacometti and Jacques Ravenne

©2005, Editons Fleuve Noir, department d'Univers Poche
English translation ©2015 Anne Trager

First published in English in 2015
By Le French Book, Inc., New York
www.lefrenchbook.com

Translation editor: Amy Richards
Proofreader: Chris Gage
Cover designer: Jeroen ten Berge
Book design by Le French Book

ISBNs:
Trade paperback: 9781939474308
E-book: 9781939474292
Hardback: 9781939474215

This is a work of fiction. Any resemblance to actual persons, living or dead, is purely coincidental. The main characters are all imaginary. The authors did find inspiration in historical and Masonic documents and real science. The descriptions of the Masonic ceremonies are relatively accurate, but the novel does not represent the official beliefs of the Masonic jurisdictions mentioned.

"The urge to discover secrets is deeply ingrained in human nature; even the least curious mind is roused by the promise of sharing knowledge withheld from others."
—John Chadwick,
The Decipherment of Linear B

ULAM

The entryway

~~~

Question: What did you see as you entered?
Answer: Grief and distress.
Question: What is the reason for this?
Answer: The commemoration of a mournful event.
Question: What is that event?
Answer: The death of Master Hiram.

. . .

Question: What else was done?
Answer: The canvas covering the coffin representing the tomb was lifted with a sign of horror.
Question: Enact that sign, my brother. What word was pronounced?
Answer: Macbenac, which means the flesh falls from the bones.

—Master Freemason preparation

PROLOGUE

1945
BERLIN

The bombings had redoubled at dawn, and the ground trembled. The man's razor slipped a second time. Blood dribbled down his stubbly cheek. He clenched his jaw, grabbed a damp towel, and dabbed the cut.

Designed to last a thousand years, the bunker's foundations were showing signs of weakness.

He looked in the cracked mirror above the sink and barely recognized his face. The last six months of combat had left their mark, including two scars across his forehead, souvenirs of a skirmish with the Red Army in Pomerania. He would celebrate his twenty-fifth birthday in a week, but the mirror reflected someone a good ten years older.

The officer slipped on a shirt and his black jacket and shot a half smile at the portrait of the Führer, a mandatory fixture in all the rooms of the Third Reich Chancellery's air-raid shelter. He put on his black helmet, adjusted it, and buttoned his collar, fingering the two silver runes shaped like S's on the right.

His uniform had such power. When he wore it, he soaked up the fear and respect in the eyes of passersby. He reveled in the gazes that oozed submission. Even children too young to understand the meaning of his black uniform pulled away when he tried to be friendly. It reactivated some primitive fear. He liked that. Intensely. Without his beloved leader's national socialism, he would have been a nobody, just like the others, leading a mediocre life in an

3

ambitionless society. But fate had catapulted him to the inner circle of the SS.

Now, however, the tide was turning. Judeo-Masonic forces were triumphing again. The Bolsheviks were scampering, ready to take over like a swarm of rats. They would spare nothing. Of course, he hadn't either. He'd left no prisoners on the Eastern Front.

"Pity is all the weak can be proud of," Reichsführer Heinrich Himmler liked to tell his subordinates. That same man had given him—a Frenchman—the Iron Cross for his acts of bravery.

Another tremor shook the concrete walls. Gray dust fell from the ceiling. That explosion was close, maybe just above the bunker in what remained of the chancellery gardens.

Obersturmbannführer François Le Guermand brushed the dust from his lapels and examined himself again. Berlin would fall. They had known this since June, when the Allies invaded Normandy. But what a year it had been. A "heroic and brutal" dream, to borrow the words of José-Maria de Heredia, the Cuban-born French poet Le Guermand loved.

A dream for some and a nightmare for others.

It began after he'd joined the SS Sturmbrigade Frankreich and then the Charlemagne Division, swearing allegiance to Adolf Hitler. This came two years after he'd marched off with the Legion of French Volunteers Against Bolshevism. Marshal Pétain's spinelessness had disgusted him, and he had set his sights on the Waffen SS units that were taking foreign volunteers.

He had fought bravely, and one day a general invited him to dinner that changed his life. Anti-Christian comments filled the conversation. The guests praised old Nordic religious beliefs and championed racist doctrines. Le Guermand listened with fascination as they related the strange and cruel stories of the clever god Odin, the dragon slayer Siegfried, and mythic Thule, the ancestral homeland of supermen, the real masters of the human race.

Le Guermand was seated next to the general's liaison, a major from Munich who explained how SS officers with pure Germanic blood had received intensive historical and spiritual training. "The Aryan race has waged battle with degenerate barbarians for centuries," he said.

Before, Le Guermand would have mocked the words as the wild imaginings of indoctrinated minds, but in the candlelight, the magical stories were a powerful venom, a burning drug that flowed into his blood, slowly reaching his brain and cutting it off from reason. Le Guermand was caught in the maelstrom of a titanic combat against the Stalinist hordes, and at that moment, he understood the real reason he had joined this final battle between Germany and the rest of the world. He grasped the meaning of his life.

On that winter solstice in 1944, in a meadow lit up by torches, he was initiated into the rites of the Black Order. As he faced a makeshift altar covered with a dark gray sheet embroidered with two moon-colored runes, he heard the deep voices of soldiers chanting all around him: "*Halgadom, Halgadom, Halgadom.*"

"It's an ancestral Germanic invocation that means 'sacred cathedral,'" the major told him. "But it's nothing like a Christian cathedral. Think of it as a mystical grail." The major laughed. "In a Christian context, it's like a celestial Jerusalem."

An hour later, the torches were extinguished. As darkness swallowed the men in ceremonial uniforms, Le Guermand emerged a transformed man. His existence would never be the same. What would it matter if he died? Death was nothing but a passage to a more glorious world. François Le Guermand had joined his fate with that of this community. It was cursed by the rest of humanity, but he would receive sublime teachings promising new life, even if Germany lost the war.

The Red Army continued to advance. Le Guermand's division took a battering. Then, on a cold and wet morning in February 1945, when he was supposed to be leading a counterattack in East Prussia, Le Guermand received orders to report to the Führer's headquarters in Berlin. There was no explanation.

He bid good-bye to his division, only to learn later that his fellow soldiers, exhausted and underequipped, had been decimated that very day by the Second Shock Army's T-34 tanks.

The Führer had saved his life.

On his way to Berlin, Le Guermand passed countless German refugees fleeing the Russians. The radio broadcast Dr. Goebbels's propaganda: Soviet barbarians were pillaging houses and raping women. It made no mention of the atrocities committed by the Reich when they had marched victoriously on Russia.

The lines of frightened runaways went on for miles.

How ironic. In June 1940, his family had pulled a cart along a road in Compiègne, France, fleeing the arriving Germans. Now he was a German soldier, and he was retreating. From the backseat of his SS car, he contemplated the dead German women and children lying on both sides of the road, some in an advanced stage of decomposition. Many had had their clothing and shoes stolen. This depressing spectacle was nothing compared with what he would find when he arrived in the capital of the dying Third Reich.

Past the northern suburb of Wedding, he gazed at the burned and crumbling buildings, the victims of incessant Allied bombings. He had known Berlin when it was so arrogant and proud to be the new Rome. Now he gawked at the masses of silent inhabitants trudging through the ruins.

Flags bearing swastikas hung over what remained of the rooftops. His car came to a stop at an intersection on Wilhelmstrasse to let a convoy of Panzer Tiger tanks and a detachment of foot soldiers pass. Le Guermand watched as a man spit at the troops. Before, such behavior would have led to an arrest and a beating. On this day, the man just went on his way.

A banderole remained intact on the side of an intact building—an insurance company—that hadn't been destroyed. "We will vanquish or we will die," its large gothic letters read.

Arriving at the chancellery guard post, he found the bodies of two men hanging from streetlights. They hadn't been as lucky as the man who had spit at the troops. The dead men were wearing placards: "I betrayed my Führer." Probably deserters caught by the Gestapo and immediately executed, Le Guermand thought. Examples. No Germans could escape their destiny. The bodies, their faces nearly black from asphyxiation, swayed in the wind.

To his surprise, there was no officer to meet him at the bunker, but instead, an insignificant civilian. His threadbare jacket bore the insignia of the Nazi Party. The man told him that he and the other officers of his rank would be assigned to a special detachment under the direct orders of Reichsleiter Martin Bormann. His mission would be explained in due time.

The man led him to a tiny room. Other officers, all detached from three SS divisions—Wiking, Totenkopf, and Hohenstaufen—had received the same orders and were lodged in nearby rooms.

Two days after they arrived, Martin Bormann, secretary of the Nazi Party and one of the few dignitaries to still be in Adolf Hitler's good graces, called the Frenchman and his comrades together. With a cold, self-confident gaze on his bloated face, he looked at the fifteen men gathered in what remained of a chancellery meeting room. Then Hitler's dauphin spoke in a strangely shrill voice.

"Gentlemen, the Russians will be here in a few months. It is possible that we will lose the war, even though the Führer still believes in victory and has put his faith in new weapons even more destructive than our long-range V-2 rockets."

Bormann let his eyes drift over the group before continuing his monologue.

"We need to think about future generations and remain committed to final victory. Your superior officers chose you for your courage and loyalty to the Reich. I speak especially for our European friends from Sweden, Belgium, France, and Holland who have conducted themselves as true Germans. During the few weeks we have left, you will be trained to survive and perpetuate the work of Adolf Hitler. Our guide has decided to stay to the end, even if he must give his life, but you will leave in due time to ensure that his sacrifice is not in vain."

Le Guermand looked around. The other officers were murmuring and shifting in their chairs. Bormann continued.

"Each of you will receive orders that are vital for our work to continue. You are not alone. Other groups such as yours are being formed throughout German territory. Your training will begin at eight tomorrow morning and will last for several weeks. Good luck to all of you."

During the two months that followed, they were taught to live an entirely clandestine life. François Le Guermand admired the organization that persevered, despite the impending apocalypse. He felt detached from his French roots, from that nation of whiners that had prostrated itself at the feet of Charles de Gaulle and the Americans.

Le Guermand was cloistered in underground rooms and went days without seeing sunlight. A rodent's life. There was no rest between the lectures and coursework. Soldiers and civilians introduced him to a vast network that was especially active in South America, as well as Spain and Switzerland.

They were trained in covert bank transfers and identity management. Money didn't seem to be a concern. Each member of the group had a duty: to go to his assigned country and blend with the population under a new identity. Then wait—ready to act.

By mid-April, the Soviets were just six miles from Berlin. Three hundred French survivors of the Charlemagne Division were guarding the bunker. That was when the liaison officer from Munich arrived. Bormann deferred to the major, as though he were a superior officer. Le Guermand ate a quick lunch with the major, who called Hitler an evil madman and then held out a black card embossed with a white capital T.

"This card marks your membership to an ancient Aryan secret society, the Thule-Gesellschaft," the major explained. "It has existed since long before the birth of Nazism. You have been chosen for your courage and devotion. If you survive the war, other members of the Thule will contact you with new orders."

The cut on his cheek was now imperceptible.

It was finally time. It was April 25, and they were scheduled to leave on April 29.

Le Guermand polished the tips of his shiny boots. He wanted to be impeccable for this final meal with his comrades.

He stepped out of his small room, left the bunker, and took the long underground tunnel to the exit, emerging aboveground. He headed toward a large military building. The two soldiers on guard saluted him, and he hurried to the conference room.

Le Guermand walked through the door and looked around. Something was off. His companions were standing straight as fence posts and staring at a dark-haired man in a chair at the back of the room. The man's SS jacket was unbuttoned. Tears were rolling down his cheeks.

It was one of his comrades, a transmission specialist. Le Guermand stepped closer and stiffened when he saw two patches of dried blood where his ears had been. The man was groaning and mouthing a plea for help.

"Gentlemen." Martin Bormann's voice echoed in the room. "What you see here is a traitor. He was packing his bags to join Heinrich Himmler. The BBC announced this morning that our loyal Heinrich has offered the Allied troops unconditional capitulation. Our Führer was enraged and gave orders to execute anyone planning to join this betrayal, starting with his companion Eva Braun's own brother-in-law, Herr Fegelein."

The man was still groaning.

Bormann approached the prisoner calmly and touched his shoulder. He smiled and went on. "Our friend wanted out of his assignment. We cut off his ears and tongue so he couldn't converse with his master about our glorious Führer's decisions."

The party hierarch ran his fingers through the prisoner's hair, a distant look in his eyes. "You see, a German, and an SS at that, cannot turn on his own people and go unpunished. Learn that lesson. Never betray. Guards, take this piece of trash outside and shoot him."

Two guards seized the man's arms and dragged him out.

With the man gone, some of the tension in the room lifted. Everyone knew Bormann hated Himmler and was waiting for the occasion to discredit him as commander of the SS. Now it was done.

"Time is flying, men. Marshal Zhukov's first army is approaching, and his troops are already at the Tiergarten. You will leave sooner than planned. Heil Hitler."

The officers straightened and shot out their arms in response. "Heil Hitler."

An explosion shook the room.

François Le Guermand turned to leave with the other men. But Bormann grabbed his arm and gave him a harsh look. "You know your instructions. It is vital for the Reich that you follow them to the letter."

The room shuddered with another explosion, and the spasm spread through Bormann's hand. Le Guermand looked him straight in the eye.

"I will leave Berlin by the underground network and go to a point in the western suburbs that is still safe. I will lead a convoy of five trucks to Beelitz, nineteen miles from the capital. There, I will bury the crates we transported. But I must keep one briefcase."

"And then?"

"Then I will join our ninth army, which will fly me to the Swiss border. I will figure out how to cross the border and get to an apartment in Berne, where I will wait for further instructions."

Bormann's face relaxed a little.

Le Guermand cleared his throat and asked, "Sir, what's in the crates?"

"That is not for you to know. Just obey. Do not be undisciplined like your compatriot Frenchmen."

Bormann gave a weak smile, pursed his lips, and turned and walked away.

DACHAU CONCENTRATION CAMP

Sunlight seeped through the dirty window, lighting up the dust particles dancing in the air, the only animation in the ramshackle barracks. The place was rank with death. Two days earlier, on April 23, the kapos had locked the doors, not bothering to remove the corpses.

Among the dozens of emaciated bodies, only three men—all of them French—were still alive.

Henri, a neurologist from Paris arrested in 1941 and recently transferred from the Reich's medical research labs, had been delirious since nightfall. Deprivation, cold, and the long march ending at Dachau had depleted his strength. Leaning against a wall, he struggled to keep himself upright.

"We were wrong. The devil does exist. Evil is here, among us, lurking deep in our consciousness, waiting to be released. It's like a coiled snake or a malevolent brother bent on forcing out the password to a room filled with everything he's been lusting for."

The youngest of the three, twenty-year-old Marek, turned to the third, Fernand, a retired administrative worker deported from Montluçon, France. "He won't survive the night."

"I know. What can we do?"

Henri slumped to the floor. Panting, he continued. "They woke up the ancient snake, the source of all evil. It gave them the seeds of hell. The fruit of the tree of knowledge has dropped to the ground. The seeds have sprouted everywhere."

Fernand pulled a bowl from under a cot. He dipped his fingers in the gray water to wet Henri's lips.

"Other demons will rise tomorrow. We will worship them. Evil wears many masks. It takes over because we are full of pride."

"What are you saying, brother? I don't understand," Marek said.

Henri sniggered. "They went everywhere to find him, even the outer reaches of the deserts. But he was here the whole time. He was just waiting for us."

"His mind is going."

They heard boots stomping, and the barracks door swung open. Four men in green uniforms rushed toward them. All but one were wearing helmets. The one without the helmet brought down his heel and crushed Henri's hand. The dying man cried out.

"Take him away," the torturer shouted.

The soldiers grabbed Henri and lugged him out. The door slammed shut. The two remaining prisoners hurried to the grimy window.

Henri was forced to kneel in front of the SS officer. Brandishing a metal-tipped cane, the officer turned toward the barracks and smirked at the two Frenchmen. He twirled the cane and slammed it down on the kneeling man's shoulder.

Marek and Fernand heard something crack. Henri howled. The officer ordered his subordinates to lift the prisoner and turned toward the barracks again. Wearing the same look, he used the cane to slam the back of the prisoner's neck.

Henri fell to the ground, facedown.

The blood drained from Fernand's face. He turned to Marek.

"Do you understand?"

"Yes. He knows who we are. He's perverting the ritual. But why? We aren't a threat to him anymore. We're nothing!"

"Marek, if either of us survives, we must remember this murder and hold these people accountable, just as the three men who murdered the master were brought to justice."

The SS officer stretched and then leaned over Henri, whispering in his ear. The Frenchman shook his head.

The officer scowled and straightened. He raised the cane over his head and brought it down on the victim's head.

That was the last of the three blows—one to the shoulder, one to the back of the neck, and a final one to the head.

The torturer was well versed in Freemason ways.

The German nodded to the two prisoners and started walking toward the barracks.

Fernand and Marek watched in silence, holding onto each other as their final moment arrived.

The door flew open. Sunlight flowed into the room, illuminating every inch, as if to better accompany the return of darkness.

Southwest of Berlin

He had to get out of the truck. François Le Guermand shouted an order to lob grenades on the crates.

Outside, the enemy was gunning down the occupants of the five trucks, which were stopped on the road.

His command went unheeded. The soldier was already dead. Half his face had been blown away. It was too late to leave the truck now. Le Guermand pushed the body out of the vehicle and swerved off the road. Swearing, he headed toward a line of trees.

Everything had started so well. He had left Berlin without a hitch and taken command of the small convoy as planned. They were just six miles from the hiding spot when they drove around a bend and straight into a Russian roadblock.

What were the Ivans doing there? General Wenck's Ninth German Army, which was retreating westward toward American lines, was supposed to control this zone. Le Guermand realized that the rout had occurred more quickly than they had thought.

He had to get out of this mess.

A Russian soldier appeared from behind a bush. He took up position in front of the truck. Le Guermand accelerated and ran the man over. A concert of bullets whistled through the air. A projectile hit Le Guermand in the shoulder, and blood spurt all over the steering wheel. Le Guermand howled, and an acid taste filled his mouth.

He glanced in the rearview mirror to check on the rest of the convoy three hundred yards behind him. One vehicle was on fire, and Russian soldiers were already climbing into the others.

He bit his lip. The crates couldn't fall into enemy hands. He pressed hard on the gas pedal, and the truck sped along a muddy lane toward the dark forest.

His heart was pounding. He didn't have much time. The Reds would catch up and kill him slowly, making him pay for all the atrocities the Germans had committed.

One of the trucks exploded, giving him some breathing room.

He raced along, hit a rut, and swerved, nearly losing control. But he managed to right the vehicle. He would need at least a minute to reach the woods. He allowed himself a bit of hope. No one was behind him.

He let out a yelp of victory when he reached the first trees standing guard over the forest. The truck bounced over another rut, and Le Guermand grimaced in pain. The blood was pounding in his head, but there was no stopping. Those damned Ruskies would never take him alive.

The truck careened past the trees, no Russians in sight. Le Guermand chanted to himself as the sunlight disappeared behind the thick branches. Maybe he would get out of this alive.

Then he saw it. A gigantic tree trunk was blocking the track just yards in front of him. He slammed on the brakes, skidding and slipping on the mud until the weight of his cargo shifted and the vehicle tipped over. The truck started rolling down a hill covered with emerald-colored ferns.

The descent seemed to last an eternity.

Helpless, Obersturmbannführer Le Guermand gazed at the branches slapping against the windshield like wild animals clawing the vehicle.

Then, by some miracle, the slope flattened out, and the battered truck came to a stop in what looked like a muddy creek.

Le Guermand's head hit the steering wheel, but he didn't feel any pain. He had slipped into a kind of trance on the edge of madness. Everything around him was dark. The truck had slammed into a rocky bank covered with blackish moss. Only a few rays of sunlight could make their way into this dark chasm.

There was no noise. Nothing but a heavy, wet silence.

He managed to climb out of the cab, his head spinning and his legs shaking. Blood was spurting in fits from his temple and dripping down his face and neck. He was slipping in and out of consciousness, but he was still standing, and a survival instinct was deeply embedded in his muscles.

He walked around the truck and climbed into the back. If he was going to die here, he wanted to know why. What was in those damned crates?

And what was that sickly sweet smell? He looked down and saw that bullets had ripped open a can of motor oil, and the dark liquid was spilling between the crates. He took two steps to retrieve the can and slipped. He reached out to keep himself from falling. He felt something hard, but soft too. And sticky. It was a bullet-ridden face. He pulled his hand away and retched.

Gathering his last strength, Le Guermand sat down next to one of the crates. He picked up the assault rifle next to the body and started hacking at the top.

His vision was blurry. His brain wasn't getting enough blood. In a burst of rage, he gave the crate a final blow, which broke the oak planks apart.

Wood shards and a bundle of old papers landed on his lap.

Papers. Nothing but stupid pieces of paper.

His mouth went dry, and his hand stiffened. He stared at the yellowed sheets full of symbols. He didn't recognize much, but the black skull was unmistakable. He focused on it. No, it wasn't the familiar skull on his SS helmet. It was misshapen—and it was wearing a grotesque smile.

François Le Guermand started laughing uncontrollably, like a madman, as he slipped into the shadows.

BOAZ

One of two pillars guarding the temple entrance,
derived from Hebrew, meaning "in strength"

1

The speaker, a Generation Xer with jet-black hair, stood in front of a stylized sun painting. He scanned the room. It was silent.

This space in Rome's Alessandro di Cagliostro Freemason Lodge resembled a large dark-blue cavern. Thin rays of light shone down from the ceiling, which was adorned with stars to make it look like the night sky.

To his left and right were forty or so men in black suits, white aprons, and gloves. They were impassive, motionless, like statues made of flesh. There were also a few women in long robes.

He turned to the east, toward the man presiding over the meeting. "I have spoken, Worshipful Master," he said.

The master waited a few seconds and then pounded a wooden mallet on his small desk. Behind him hung a huge all-seeing Egyptian eye.

"Brothers and sisters, I would like to thank our brother Antoine Marcas for coming from France to speak to us. His lecture on the origins of ancient Masonic rites was quite instructive. He claims to just be a little curious, but it's clear that he has taken great pains to educate himself in our mysteries. I am sure you have many questions. Sisters and brothers, you may speak."

A brother clapped, asking to be acknowledged. The senior steward spoke the ritual words and invited him to speak.

"Worshipful Master in person, Worshipful Masters from the Orient, and my brothers and sisters, as we all know, our lodge was named after Alessandro di Cagliostro, and

I would like to ask our distinguished brother Marcas to clarify, if possible, the origin of the Cagliostro ritual."

The speaker looked over the notes he had jotted down on three-by-five cards. "In 1784, in Lyon, France, Cagliostro inaugurated his High Egyptian Masonic Rite in the Triumphant Wisdom Lodge. According to current biographers, Cagliostro was initiated in Malta at the Saint John of Scotland Lodge of Secrecy and Harmony, which is where he founded the ritual that now bears his name."

Another man clapped.

Antoine Marcas took a closer look at the audience. Both Italian and French lodges were represented. He recognized the Grande Lodge brothers with their red-trimmed Scottish rite aprons and the Memphis Misraïm sisters dressed in white.

The worshipful master gave the floor to a brother with a strong Milanese accent, which made him sound very serious. "Italy's declining institutions and political corruption continue to make headlines. And the country's troubles appear to be affecting the rest of Europe, especially France. Some are accusing the Freemasons of being at least partly responsible for this situation. What do you have to say about this?"

Marcas nodded. He didn't like political questions.

Fifteen years earlier, his idealistic trust in the secular values of the republic had motivated him to become a Freemason. He was also excited by the promise of personal development. Since then, he had watched the image of freemasonry decline in France. Before, the media had praised Freemason contributions to education and conflict resolution. Now they were focused on scandal and mysterious networks of shadowy figures.

Marcas took time to choose his words. He wouldn't fully disclose his thoughts about anti-Freemason media campaigns or about the brothers who didn't deserve their aprons. For a while, Marcas had attended a lodge that was full of money launderers and others in cahoots with politicians skilled at rigging public contracts. The lodge was nestled in a suburban Paris townhouse and was rotten to the core. When he'd found out what was going on—a full year before the media went wild over it—he had changed lodges, refusing to condemn all of freemasonry with a handful of corrupt individuals. But doubt had taken seed. And so he dived into the history and symbolism of free-masonry, as if the past could wipe the present clean. Still, every time he read about a scandal involving a Freemason, he took it as a personal affront.

"France has not escaped the evils affecting all Western democracies. There's a rise in extremism, along with wide-spread distrust of elitism and power. Whether we deserve it or not, many people who don't know us consider us both powerful and manipulative. It's hard to shake that 'hood-winker' slur. Let's not forget, too, that a good scandal—whether it's real or not—sells newspapers."

Marcas answered a few more questions, mixing his expertise with humor.

Then there was silence. The worshipful master took the floor and began the closing ritual, finally calling for the chain of unity.

One by one, the men and women rose, removed their gloves, and crossed their arms, taking their neighbors' hands to form a human chain around the center of the lodge.

The worshipful master repeated the words of the ritual. "This chain binds us in time and space. It comes to us from the past and stretches toward the future. It connects us to those who came before us."

Each phase of this ritual and many others had been refined over the centuries, and every participant knew his role perfectly, as though it were a play.

The stewards held mallets across their chests. The mas-ter of ceremonies struck the floor with a metal-tipped cane while a mason called a tyler continued to guard the door, a sword in his right hand.

Marcas proclaimed the final pledge. "Liberty, equality, fraternity."

The meeting was over, and the temple calmly emptied.

In the anteroom, the worshipful master—an aristocratic-looking banker—called out to Marcas in perfect French, "Will you stay and have something to eat?"

Marcas smiled. In every lodge around the world, eating and drinking followed these meetings.

"Alas, no, brother. I'm expected at the French embassy. There's a Victory in Europe Day shindig. But I plan to come back tomorrow to consult some rare books in your library."

Marcas said good-bye to his host and walked down the black marble staircase to the ground floor. He left the building, pulled up his coat collar against the wind, and hailed a cab.

"Palazzo Farnese, please."

As the cab made its way through the Eternal City, Marcas's thoughts wandered. He gazed at the Piazza Campo de Fiori, where more than five hundred years earlier, the papacy had burned philosopher Giordano Bruno at the stake. Marcas thought Bruno would have made a good "widow's son," which some Freemasons called themselves. The widow was the wife of Hiram Abiff, the legendary architect of King Solomon's Temple, and the son was a reference to Hiram's descendants, Freemasons around the world.

Things had changed a bit since Giordano was burned at the stake, although the Catholic Church still frowned on freemasonry. The Church held that freemasonry espoused a naturalistic religion—a parallel religion that rivaled the Gospel.

This didn't bother Marcas. He hadn't attended church in a long time, although he was still very much a seeker. He had been drawn to the Freemasons' ethics and body of knowledge, which were based on the idea that one needed to strive continually toward self-improvement and enlightenment. He liked freemasonry's opportunities for fellowship and education. And the Freemason rituals more than satisfied any yearnings he might have had for the church liturgies that he had left behind.

The sight of the Farnese Palace at the end of the street drew Marcas out of his thoughts. The elegant edifice was glowing, and in the courtyard, expensive cars were performing an intricate ballet as they let out well-dressed partygoers.

Marcas felt for the invitation in the inside pocket of his jacket.

A tingle of enjoyment ran up his spine. He liked the contrasts of his life. Less than a half hour earlier, he had been giving a serious speech in a solemn setting. In a few minutes, he would be mingling with the moneyed set in a luxurious palace that was now the French embassy. And in two days, he would be back at his seedy police station in Paris.

The taxi stopped behind an impressive line of limousines a few hundred feet from the palace. Marcas paid the fare.

He felt a gentle breeze from the south and looked up. The leaves in the nearby trees were quivering. Evenings were cool at this time of year, and Marcas took a moment to enjoy the fleeting springtime air before the brutal summer heat took hold.

Marcas walked up to the doorman, who was wearing a black suit, a white shirt, a black tie, and an earpiece. The guy could have a future as a bodyguard in Hollywood, Marcas thought. The man looked him up and down and let him in without saying a word.

He had barely stepped in when he spotted a hostess in a blue suit walking toward him. With her were two beautiful women who looked to be in their thirties. They offered to show him in.

The night was off to a good start.

2

When it was early May, and the wisteria plants were blossoming, Marek would work late into the night and keep the windows in the lab open to better enjoy the scent of the flowers.

Jerusalem's Archeological Research Institute was headquartered in a sprawling brick building that the English had built. Its high ceilings were reminiscent of the lost grandeur of an empire. Marek loved its antiquated, nearly abandoned look.

He heard the sprinklers click on outside and gazed once again at two of the mementos on his large worktable: his yellowing dissertation and a hockey stick with flaking paint that he had brought back as a souvenir from the United States, where he had lived for a time.

Marek observed two birthdays every year. The first was the day he was born. The second was the day he was reborn. A walking skeleton, he had been liberated in the spring of 1945 from Dachau. He had made two oaths on that day. The first was to flee the cursed continent of Europe and start over again. He had gone to America. Then, in the nineteen fifties, he had immigrated to Israel, becoming one of the country's top specialists in Biblical times—a kind of wiseman, he thought: old, mischievous, erudite.

Marek let his mind drift for a moment before he returned to the file on his desk. Two hundred and forty pages, single-spaced. Five test reports from distinguished geology, chemistry, and micro-archeology laboratories, with diagram after diagram and long lists of references.

When the shifty Armenian dealer Alex Perillian had brought the stone in to be authenticated, he knew right away that it was genuine. Artifacts were a big—and clandestine—business, and Marek had seen his fair share of shady characters seeking certificates of authenticity for worthless relics. But this stone was different. The Tebah Stone, Perillian had called it, bought from a family of goatherds for a hundred dollars. But worth infinitely more.

Marek set down the file and opened the linen cloth. A fragment of a stone tablet lay there. It measured sixty-two by twenty-seven centimeters, and it vibrated with history. The bottom-left corner was chipped, and the end of the inscription was missing, but the remaining words had resisted the assault of time. Was it from pure luck? Or had someone kept it safe? This piece of stone bore a truth passed down through the centuries, a message, written by a hand whose bones had long since returned to dust.

Marek's palms were sweaty. Original texts were extremely rare, and ever since the discovery of the Dead Sea manuscripts, the state of Israel and the major monotheistic religions had kept a close watch over all finds that could shake their foundations.

His conclusions were concise. "Based on mineralogical analyses, the Cambrian-era stone could have originated in one of three geological regions: southern Israel, the Sinai and Jordan, or south of the Dead Sea. Analysis of the surface alterations reveals the presence of silica, aluminum, calcium, magnesium, and iron, along with traces of wood, which date to 500 BCE, plus or minus forty years with carbon-14. It could very well date to the rebuilding of the Temple of Solomon."

Marek stopped. King Salomon's temple was a mythic spot for Jews, said to hold the Arc of the Covenant and the stone tablets on which the Ten Commandments were inscribed. It had been plundered and destroyed by the Babylonian king Nebuchadnezzar. Cyrus the Great of Persia ordered the Second Temple to be built on the same site. Herod the Great embellished it under Roman occupation.

Cyrus's temple reconstruction in 520 BCE was a key moment in Jewish history, and every artifact related to it was priceless. Marek weighed the stone in his hand. The money meant nothing to Marek. This stone was the missing link, the final element in his quest to honor Henri's memory, to fulfill his second oath.

All he needed now were the documents from Paris. He stared at the relic and started to tremble. Was it really such a good idea to be waking the dead?

3

A flute of vintage Tattinger Champagne in hand, Antoine Marcas scanned the vast reception hall. He couldn't help thinking of all the pomp surrounding ambassadors. Yes, France did like to strut. It was hard to get more sumptuous than the Palazzo Farnese. Even the name evoked the splendors of near-absolute magnificence: the Italian Renaissance, an era of princes, freewheeling cardinals, and courtesans skilled at damning the lords of the Church. The wealthy Farnese family had built this residence in the middle of the sixteenth century. They were nobles from Latium who boasted a pope—Paul III—in their lineage. The pontiff's own son, however, had been excommunicated because of his taste for plundering and rape.

Laughter and voices were bouncing off the walls.

"Antoine, I hope you're enjoying yourself. It's quite a change from the police headquarters in Paris, isn't it?"

Startled, Marcas turned around. It was Alexis Jaigu, a former military man who was now an intelligence officer on some assignment in Rome. Jaigu was the friend who had invited him to this affair.

"Alexis! You must save me. Find me a woman in this crowd of beauties."

Jaigu made circles with his fingers and brought them to his eyes. "Tall blonde at two o'clock, flaming redhead at six. Two apparently isolated targets without patrol escorts. Intelligence report: the blonde heads up marketing for a San Paolo bank. The redhead is second-in-command at an Israeli company that dabbles in arms sales to emerging countries."

"Too high-powered for me. You wouldn't have a more classic model—a painter or dancer, someone a little more artistic?"

"So I take it you're finally over your ex-wife. It's about time. How's your son?"

"He's living with his mother," Marcas said, looking away. He didn't like to talk about his divorce. Cops never stayed married long, and Marcas was no exception to that rule. He had spent many sleepless nights after his wife left him, along with difficult weekends with his son who blamed him for the separation. Some men in his shoes found solace in drink, others in one-night stands. Marcas had buried himself at the Freemason lodge, focused on his symbolism studies. It had taken a full year before he started dating again. But he was still single. One of his occasional dates had told him to let go of his ex before bidding him good night. Marcas had laughed. The only time he thought of his ex-wife was when he wrote the alimony check at the end of the month or when he received one of her hateful letters full of accusations.

Jaigu grabbed a toast with Périgord foie gras from a platter. "Hey, do you know the ambassador?"

"I can't say I do."

"So he's not a Freemason, like you?"

Marcas stiffened. "I'm no snitch. Ask him yourself."

"You're joking, right? I don't want to get sent to some faraway consulate in Africa. It's a favor I'm asking. Don't you have some sort of secret code of recognition? A special handshake or something?"

Marcas sighed. It was always the same stupidities: occult influence, signs of recognition—the folklore. How many times had his hand been kneaded by overly familiar non-Masons who had read a few things about freemasonry?

"Sorry, I can't."

"At least say you don't want to, Antoine. How long have we known each other? And you still cover for the ambassador? A man you've never even met? You brothers really do stick together."

Marcas didn't want to get into a long explanation with his now-tipsy friend. He knew Jaigu well, and tomorrow the man would be full of apologies.

"Drop it, Alexis."

"I won't press. And I won't hold it against you. Let me introduce you to two superb actresses who are waiting for nobody but us," Jaigu said, throwing his arm around Marcas's shoulder and leading him to the terrace.

4

Bashir Al Khansa, aka the Emir, rarely went anywhere alone and usually traveled under the cover of night. It was his way of playing Israeli security, which was polluting East Jerusalem. When he had time to sleep, it was in homes carefully chosen by logistics specialists in his movement, which Israeli spies had been trying to infiltrate for a long time.

On this night, Bashir was wearing a thin moustache and a white suit like those favored by rich Lebanese businessmen. A perfect disguise for his meeting with Alex Perillian.

The two men were now sitting in the courtyard, heat reflecting off the old stones. Bashir's two bodyguards watched over the entrance.

Bashir was seething. "Allah is great, showing us to this stone, and you hand it over to those Jewish pigs? They will sully it with their blasphemous hands."

Perillian sighed. "Since when have the respectful servants of the Prophet been interested in a stone engraved by the sons of Zion?"

"Everything found in the land of Allah belongs to Allah. Where is the stone now?"

"At the archeological institute. The scientists are analyzing it, and if it is authentic, the price will be high, and your share will be great."

"The servants of Allah don't care about money from unbelievers! I want the stone."

Perillion was sweating now. "Be patient. I'll get the stone back as soon as the tests are done. Then you can—"

"May Allah curse the infidels who don't acclaim his light. Nobody must know the significance of the stone—especially those Israeli dogs. Do you understand?"

"But there's nothing I can do."

Bashir smiled. "Yes there is."

~~~

Marek was leaning over his worktable, examining his translation of the inscription. On his computer, a software program was matching the concordances with ancient Hebrew texts.

His heart had raced at the idea of being the first to proclaim a fragment linking the chosen people with their destiny. But he had just discovered that he was not the first. In the lower right corner of the stone, an anonymous hand had engraved a Latin cross with branches that widened like the sails of a boat. It was the cross of the Order of the Temple—or the Knights Templar, the order founded by nine Frenchmen in the second decade of the twelfth century on Jerusalem's Temple Mount, just above the Temple of Solomon.

Marek, the venerable master of his Freemason lodge, recognized it immediately. Didn't some people claim that the higher orders of freemasonry were direct descendants of the Templars? Marek thought those stories were nothing but legend, but he knew them well.

Now the cross danced in front of his eyes. What had the Templars been doing with this stone?

The computer screen lit up. Marek examined the word frequencies one after the other. They supported the dating. Except for a single word—a word that didn't exist in the database.

First the cross, then the unknown term.

The phone rang, pulling Marek back to the here and now. As he reached for the receiver, he looked at his watch. It was ten thirty.

"Oh, professor." The caller's accent was melodious. "What luck. I tried to reach you at home first. Happiness to the man who works late!"

"Perillian, if you're calling in the middle of the night for my conclusions—"

"Oh no, professor, that's not it. There's been a miracle. A real miracle. Someone has just brought me another fragment of the same stone."

"You must be joking."

"No, professor. It is from the same source. The family brought it over this very evening."

"Perillian, you realize that such a discovery could have a significant bearing on my current analysis."

"I'm all too aware of that, professor. I don't want to keep such a treasure from you."

"When will you bring it over?"

"Right away. I'll send over a servant. I can't just leave the family who brought it like that, etiquette and all. You can trust the man I'm sending. His name is Bashir. Can you make sure he doesn't get caught up at the roadblocks?"

"Don't worry about that. Fax me his papers, and I'll inform the ministry right away."

"Thank you, professor. You'll see. It's one of a kind, really."

Marek ended the call and turned to the computer screen.

~~~

Perillian smiled at Bashir. "You see—"

He didn't have time to finish his sentence. Bashir, a gun with a silencer in hand, stood over the businessman as he crumpled to the floor. He had aimed for the spleen, granting the man a merciful death—painful, yes, but quick. He had surprised himself with this act of kindness. He usually preferred to watch the life drain from his victims slowly, not so much out of sadism as from curiosity. The life force was there, and then it wasn't. Every time, death was unique, but in many ways it was the same, whether the man was a Jew, a Muslim, or a Christian.

Bashir slipped out of the Armenian's room. His two bodyguards followed without a word, and they got into a car with fake plates. He gave the address of the institute and exchanged his suit for a djellaba. A Jew awaited him tonight. Bashir would see a life extinguish again. And the man would not get the favor he had extended to Perillian. This time he would adhere to a precise ritual.

5

Sophie Dawes scurried across the large room, stumbling more than once because only the outside lights illuminated the space. She gasped each time she hit something. Fear constricted her blood vessels.

The library entrance was just over there. Maybe, just maybe she could escape. She turned the handle, using all her strength. In vain. The elaborately carved wooden door remained shut. Exhausted from her sprint, Sophie collapsed on the floor.

She heard soft footsteps coming toward her. The person was moving along the fresco-covered wall. Sophie could hear the din of the party in the ground-floor reception room. She took a deep breath and crept toward a window.

"It's no use." The voice was firm, definitive.

Paralyzed by fear, Sophie looked up slowly. In front of her stood a young blonde woman wearing a strange smile. She was holding a telescopic baton with a metal tip.

The voice rang out again. "Where are the documents?"

"What documents? I don't know what you're talking about. Please, let me go," Sophie pleaded.

"Don't act stupid," the woman said, using her baton to slowly lift Sophie's skirt. "What you found is none of your business. You are just an archivist. I only need to know where the papers are."

A wave of panic ran through Sophie. She felt stripped naked.

"You were hired as an archivist a year ago, right after your thesis at the Sorbonne. That was quite a presentation you made. The jury really liked it, although you looked a little stiff in your brand-new suit. Let's see, what else can I tell you? Oh yes, you were supposed to go to Jerusalem tomorrow."

"That can't be," Sophie moaned. You can't…"

"But it is. Are you sure you don't want to tell me anything? I can go on. Your thesis director found you that job. He has many friends, or should I say *brothers*?"

Sophie tried to get up, but the baton came down on her. She cried out in pain and clutched her shoulder.

"Quiet, or I'll break your other shoulder blade."

"Please."

"Where are they?"

"I don't know," Sophie cried out. "I don't know anything."

The woman's voice became more sinister. "You shouldn't lie," she whispered. "Perhaps I have not made myself entirely clear."

She swung the black ebony instrument in the air and brought it down on Sophie's neck. Sophie lost all the feeling in her legs.

The voice was singsong now. "You cannot move anymore, but you can still talk. This is your last chance."

Sophie Dawes knew that the final blow would be fatal if she kept silent. She would die right here. Although she was just above a room filled with more than a hundred guests, no one would take notice, and no one would help.

"At the Hilton. My room, number 326. Please don't hurt me," she said, staring into her torturer's almond-shaped eyes. They were keen and distant. Sophie had fallen for this woman at the party. She had introduced herself as Helen and told Sophie that she was studying for an advanced degree in art history. They had talked with passion about Renaissance painters. Sophie thought she was graceful and exciting. She couldn't resist when the beautiful blonde suggested that they go someplace quiet, far from the crowd, to explore the frescos.

The two women had slipped upstairs as the uninterested security guards looked on. The nightmare had begun as soon as Helen closed the door behind them. The blonde had pulled her close as if to kiss her. Then Sophie saw the small black instrument, felt the electric shock, and fell to the floor. The woman then lifted her onto a sofa.

Sophie had come to quickly. She kicked her attacker in the ribs and ran toward the library.

Now Sophie had lost. She prayed that her attacker would just leave. It wasn't fair. She was only twenty-eight. Helen smiled. Her expression looked affectionate, and Sophie felt relief.

"Thank you. Your death will be quicker."

The angel of death kissed Sophie gently on the forehead and swung the baton.

Sophie heard it coming and lifted a hand to shield her face. Her fingers broke under the blow. She collapsed, her eyebrow split open. Her blood flowing onto the polished floor.

Below her, a quartet was playing selections from an opera. The sounds of the party rose through the floorboards and slipped along the ancient walls, filling the private chambers and gilded sitting rooms.

Sophie recognized the Donizetti aria, "Una furtive lagrima," just as she understood the full significance of the three blows: one to the shoulder, one to the neck, and one to the forehead.

6

The first pages of Descartes's *Discourse on Method* had always fascinated Marek: a philosopher holed up in his room with his stove, who, by the sole power of reasoning, had found a solution to every problem. For Marek, this was a key life lesson, a personal approach. Now, in his deserted lab, Marek talked to himself. He bounced ideas off the walls, waiting for order to rise from chaos.

He typed out his thoughts regarding the stone as they took form. "Based on similar ritual formulas found in texts from the same period, this would appear to be written by a temple intendant. It contains a list of materials, including two types of wood—cedar and juniper."

Marek reached for a Bible. The construction of Solomon's Temple was described in the first *Book of Kings*. It was all there: the dimensions, the interior architecture, and the materials. The interior walls were lined with cedar and juniper. The inner sanctuary for the Ark of the Covenant was lined with cedar and gold. And in this sanctuary, Solomon placed a pair of cherubs made of olive wood.

"Undoubtedly, the intendant was addressing the leader of an outgoing caravan."

Marek put the Bible down. Many of the ancient writings focused on administration: accounting, bills, laws, decrees, orders, counterorders. Clearly, humans had always fallen prey to two major demons: organization and hierarchy. The Tebah Stone would have been no exception, were it not for that one sentence.

Three lines before the traditional closing lines, the intendant added a final instruction: "Watch over your men. Make sure that they do not buy or bring back that demon *bvitti* that seeds the mind with prophesies."

He hadn't been able to find the word in any of his reference works on Semitic language and scripture. It was as if the word had not survived the torrents of time and the tribulations of the Jewish people. Now Marek was seeing it long after some obscure functionary had struck it with an official curse.

The phone rang.

"Professor, you have a visitor. The man says you're waiting for a package. I've searched him."

"It's fine, Isaac. Let him up. I'm expecting him."

"As you wish."

The professor hung up and headed into the hallway to wait for the messenger. The elevator doors opened with a whish. A man in a djellaba stepped out. He had a thin face and piercing eyes, and he was carrying a beige canvas bag. He smiled at Marek.

"Professor, I give you respects from my master."

"Thank you. I'll take the package. Then you can go home. It's late."

The man's smile broadened.

"Thank you, professor. Would you be kind enough to offer me some water? I am thirsty."

Marek wanted to yank the bag from the man's hand, but he took a deep breath instead. "Of course. Follow me. There's a water fountain near my office."

The two men walked down the hallway, past classrooms and research labs, until they reached Marek's office.

"Help yourself," Marek said, motioning to the fountain in the hallway.

He didn't wait a second longer to take the bag. Marek stepped into his office and opened it. He removed a dark stone, set it on his desk, and examined its shape, hoping it would contain some clues about that unknown word. After a few seconds, he shook his head. He took off his glasses, and rubbed his eyes.

"Is this some kind of joke?" he asked the man, who had come into his office. "This is a fake, and a bad one at that.

It wouldn't even fool tourists. Has Perillian lost his mind? I'm warning you—"

Before Marek could finish his sentence a sharp blow broke his shoulder blade. He fell to the floor, gasping in pain.

"You don't have to warn me, Jew," the messenger said in a silken voice. "The problem with all you sons of Israel is that you still think you're the masters of my land. Now I'm the one warning you. Your death is imminent. I was asked to kill you with a stick."

The man struck Marek again, this time on the neck. He was barely conscious now, but he remembered every detail of Henri's execution sixty years earlier in Dachau.

He knew the third blow would kill him.

Marek stared his killer in the eye and managed to say the one sentence from the Masonic ritual. "The flesh falls from the bones."

~~~

Bashir brought the stick down on Marek's head. "Another damned Jewish ritual," he muttered.

Blood flowed down the researcher's face.

Bashir put the walking stick in the stand where he had found it and looked around the man's office.

There it was, on the cluttered desk—the Tebah Stone. He slipped it into his bag, along with the papers next to it. He looked at the computer screen, printed the page with the professor's comments, and erased the file. He removed his djellaba, stuffed it into the bag, and stepped over Marek's body, carefully avoiding the blood pooled around the man's head.

In the elevator, he wondered why his client had required that ritual. It was too complicated, as far as he was concerned. Strangling was quicker and cleaner. When he was younger, Bashir had been partial to throat slitting. Then one September night in Beirut, when he was executing a contract at a private party, a spurt of blood had stained his

Armani suit—a superb three piece he had bought in Rome. A suit that had put him back a thousand euros—ruined. He had used guns and rope ever since.

Bashir headed to the front entrance, where the guard, hypnotized by a parade of blondes, was watching television. The man died instantly.

Bashir checked his watch. He had just enough time to get to a hiding place. He removed the video recording from the security camera. This job was almost too easy. He wasn't even getting his usual adrenaline rush.

He paused a few seconds and hit the yellow alarm button. A siren ripped through the silence. Police cars would arrive in a matter of minutes, their lights flashing.

He felt his blood flowing to his brain and heart. Now he was getting that rush. He ran toward his car, where his two bodyguards waited.

The plan had worked perfectly. The safe house was five minutes away. Bashir felt for the stone in the bag as he watched the street fly by. Another fine night in Jerusalem.

7

This time, his charm was working. The French movie producer laughed every time Marcas made a joke. Perhaps he'd suggest that they go downtown for a drink and more conversation. Just as Marcas was about to do that, he felt a hand on his shoulder. He turned to find Alexis Jaigu leaning toward his ear. "Come quick. I need you. Now."

Marcas shook his head. No, not now. He wasn't going to miss out on his chance for a little Roman love.

Before he could protest, his friend pulled him aside and whispered, "It's urgent, Antoine."

"What's going on?"

"Come and see for yourself."

Marcas turned to the producer and excused himself. "I won't be long," he said with a smile.

The party was in full swing. A DJ had replaced the quartet, and guests were dancing to the latest hits.

Marcas followed Jaigu, who took the stairs two at a time, nearly in rhythm with the Benny Benassi selection coming out of the speakers. Marcas's ten-year-old son had introduced him to the group.

Two men were guarding a large wooden door. They stepped aside for the intelligence officer. Inside, Marcas saw two other gorillas bending over a mass. He walked closer, finally making out the body of a woman in a pool of blood.

Jaigu squatted next to the body.

"This can't get out to the media," Jaigu said. "It would be a disaster for the embassy's image. Our relations with the Italian administration are already tense. The press would have a heyday."

Marcas glowered. "Alexis, what am I doing here? You know I have no authority. This is a job for the head of security."

Jaigu didn't take his eyes off the lifeless body. "I know, but you're a homicide detective. And the victim is a personal friend of the head of security. We have to be spot-on with this. Please. As a favor to me. Just take a look. Our chief security officer will be here shortly."

Marcas sighed. "We need to lift fingerprints, examine the body, and—"

Jaigu interrupted him. "I just want your first impressions. Security has orders to cordon off the embassy. We have a witness."

Marcas leaned over the body. The metallic odor of the woman's blood and the sweet smell of beeswax floor polish mingled with her scent. Probably Shalimar, Marcas thought. "What do you know so far?"

"The victim went upstairs with another woman around forty-five minutes ago. One of the guards saw them. Ten minutes later, the other woman came down and disappeared. The guard figured he should check on this one. He alerted us as soon as he discovered the body."

"I still don't get what you want from me. I can't do anything here, and your security chief will be furious. I would be. Why isn't he here, anyway?"

Jaigu gave a sheepish smile. "Okay, okay. You caught me. I've been at war with her."

"Her?"

"Special Agent Jade Zewinski. Fearsome—ask anyone who knows her. Some people don't even bother calling her by her last name. They just call her Jade because she's hard as stone. Joined the army young, rose quickly, intelligence, commandos, tours in the Middle East and Afghanistan. Lots of rage and lots of connections. Luckily, the guard who found this woman is a friend of mine, and he contacted me first. I just want your thoughts so I can tell the ambassador before she gets to him."

"You're out for a promotion on this?"

"Listen, anything you find could help us solve this case. First impressions are important in a murder investigation, right? And on top of that, if I could stick it to that pain in the ass Jade, well, why not? It's the first murder in this palace since the Farneses lived here, and the victim happens to be a friend of hers. That should put a dent in her career. If it doesn't get her transferred to a French embassy in Latvia or Angola, I'll apply for Freemason initiation just to learn your handshake."

Marcas didn't want to get involved in a power struggle that had nothing to do with him. Still, the murder was intriguing, and he started to go over the body, paying special attention to the forehead and shoulder. What a strange way to die. It reminded him of something, but he couldn't put his finger on it.

8

Special Agent Jade Zewinski pushed her way through the guests. The call to her cell phone had interrupted a tête-à-tête with a handsome Italian actor. He was insufferable and pretentious but attractive enough for a romp in the sack. Jade had left the buck standing there with his Champagne. She didn't even excuse herself.

Her second-in-command didn't waste any time when she got to him. "It's your friend," he spit out. "She's dead. They found her upstairs. I'm so sorry."

The blood drained from her face. She felt a lump in her throat. She and Sophie had known each other since high school in Paris. Back then, they were like sisters. They hadn't seen each other in more than a year, though—until two days ago, when Sophie had shown up in Rome. She'd changed. She was more mature and had lost nearly all of her youthful spontaneity.

Jade's second-in-command cleared his throat. "Ma'am, Jaigu is already up there."

Jade stiffened. "What the hell?"

"He got the news before we did. I don't know how."

"That shit's got no business being at our crime scene. He's just an intelligence officer. Have the men toss him out."

"That's hard to do, Chief. He's got the ambassador's ear."

Jade picked up her pace, bumping into an Italian minister and nearly knocking over the German ambassador. She was thinking about Sophie. At breakfast in a small café on the Piazza Navone, Sophie had filled in the gaps. She had finished her degree in comparative history and taken over her parents' Paris bookstore on the Rue de Seine. It specialized in old esoteric manuscripts. Demand was exploding for alchemy treatises, Masonic documents, and occult breviaries from the eighteenth century. She had customers from all over the world.

On the side, she had become a Freemason, mostly out of curiosity. Her thesis director had sponsored her. The path fascinated her, and she volunteered as an archivist at the Grand Orient Freemason headquarters in Paris. With her knowledge of ancient manuscripts, she had quickly organized and documented the tons of archives hidden away there.

Jade had made a face when Sophie mentioned the Freemasons. There was no love lost with these people. She'd rubbed shoulders with brothers twice in her life and had bitter memories of both occasions. The last time, she'd missed out on a position in Washington because an initiate had skillfully worked his connections. She hated this kind of old-boys network, although Masons were not the only ones with power in French diplomatic circles. In fact, they weren't as powerful as Catholics and aristocrats, but still...

Sophie had stopped in Rome while en route to Jerusalem. She had seemed tense, saying she was on an assignment for the Grand Orient. She was supposed to be giving some documents to an Israeli researcher. She kept glancing around during their breakfast together, as if she suspected someone was watching her. She had asked Jade to keep a briefcase with the documents in the embassy safe. Jade joked about her paranoia, but agreed to keep them anyway. Then they talked about their relationships, an endless topic. Sophie mentioned an older man—a rich American customer who came through Paris occasionally—and some special women friends.

Sophie had laughed and flirted with her friend. But Jade had always made it clear that she only had eyes for men.

Now Sophie would never laugh again.

On the way up the stairs, Jade decided to keep quiet about Sophie's documents. She had a hunch that they had something to do with her friend's death. She pushed the thought out of her head when she spotted the two men bent over the body.

"You've got no fucking business being here," she yelled. "Get away. Now, damn it!"

~~~

Marcas started. Her voice carried authority, and she was obviously used to giving orders. He looked up and saw an athletically built woman with short blonde hair. She was wearing loose dark-colored pants and a suit jacket—fitted to give her access to her service weapon.

When he stood up, she was right in his face, staring at him with a clear look of disdain.

"Hold up," Jaigu intervened. "I asked him to come. He's a homicide detective with the Criminal Investigation Division in Paris. I thought he could help us."

Jade shot Jaigu a look. "Since when does a man like you think? If you really wanted to use your brains, you would have kept him away from the crime scene. Until further notice, I'm head of security for the embassy. So at the risk of repeating myself, I'll try to appeal to your inherent intelligence: get the fuck out of here, and take this dude with you!"

Before Jaigu could respond, Marcas spoke up. "You owe him more respect than you've shown. But I understand your point of view. I'll leave you to your investigation. Everyone has a job to do. Alexis, come on. I've seen enough."

What a harpy, Marcas thought as he walked away with Jaigu. She would have ripped him a new one if she'd gotten the chance. Whatever. With any luck, he'd find his movie producer and cap the evening with a little seduction.

Jaigu interrupted his fantasy. "So what are your impressions?"

"About what, that shrew of yours?"

"No, the body."

"I don't know. There's no clear logic in the blows she received. She probably died from blunt-force trauma to the forehead, but I don't understand why she was hit on the shoulder, unless it was to make her suffer. A broken clavicle can be quite painful. For the rest, you'll have to trust your Amazon and the Italian police."

"I doubt that. There's no way any Romans cops will set foot in the embassy. Officially, the woman's death will be listed as accidental."

Marcas looked at his friend for a long time. "You're not really going to cover up a murder, are you? That's illegal."

"Don't worry. We won't keep anything from the French authorities. But the Italians have way too many mob-related murders to worry about. A French woman suffering a fatal head injury from a fall will go by the boards. So put all this behind you and have some Champagne on the republic's dime. I have to go see our friend the ambassador."

9

Jade Zewinski stared at her friend's bloody body. Two hours earlier, they had been joking at the reception, challenging each other to come on to this person or that. Jade remembered Sophie's oval face, the rebellious lock of hair, her childlike smile. Now Sophie's lifeless body lay in front of her, a mass of dead flesh that would end up in a coffin, her face smashed by the baton on the floor next to her.

Jade shook herself out of her trance. She needed to act quickly. A guard had seen the woman who had come up with Sophie, and a description had been sent to all the security agents.

She shouted out her orders. "Get the on-call doctor here. Have him fix her up a little. Make sure there's respiratory assistance for the transfer. The oxygen mask will cover up the wounds."

The doors slammed shut. Only two men remained. They were gendarmes, men who were quick and could be trusted.

Her phone vibrated in her pocket. She recognized the ambassador's voice.

"Special Agent Zewinski, what's going on?" the ambassador asked. "How serious is it?"

They used a code for the level of emergency. It was based on the Richter scale. Nine meant the ambassador's life was in danger.

For Jade, Sophie's death was an eight. But she gave the ambassador a detached, professional assessment. "I'd say a five." The event was worrisome, but controllable.

"Okay, give me a quick rundown. Then I've got to take care of our guests."

"Yes, sir."

She gave the ambassador a synopsis. He wanted to know if the death could have any political implications. Jade reassured him that the victim was not on the embassy's staff. Neither was she one of the evening's VIPs. The ambassador was polite enough not to sigh in relief.

Jade knew the protocol. The body would be flown to Paris the next day with a falsified certificate indicating an accidental death. This would allow them to get the body through customs.

She would make the arrangements herself first thing in the morning. She would order the coffin, and with any luck, the body would reach Paris by evening.

Jade had no illusions that the killer was still on the premises. Jade was sure. She'd have to pull the security footage.

Jade bent down and touched Sophie's hand one last time before turning to leave. She would find the son of a bitch who murdered her friend.

She pulled the heavy door open and almost slammed into Jaigu's detective buddy, who was out of breath.

"I need to check something on the body," he said.

"That's out of the question. Get out of here before I have you removed."

"Don't be idiotic. Listen, even if you won't let me see her, go in and check the body. Look at her neck. Please. It's important."

Jade glared at the cop and then shrugged. "Okay, but if you're wasting my time, you'll regret it."

She went back to the body and then returned to the detective. Now she was even more troubled. "There was a blow to her neck. It probably broke her cervical bones. How did you know?"

The detective reached for her arm. "We should talk about this somewhere else," he said.

Jade pulled away. "That's enough. Talk! Right now, right here!"

"Sophie was your friend, wasn't she?" he said after a few seconds. "Did she have some connection to the Freemasons? Was she a Mason?"

"What does that have to do with her murder?"

"Answer me, please. It's not a trick question."

Jade pursed her lips. "Yes, she was a Freemason. Now explain yourself."

The detective scanned the paintings of Florentine masters. "The flesh falls from the bones," he said.

10

Helen struggled to contain her rage. She had searched the hotel room twice and had found no trace of the documents. Her boss would by very displeased with this turn of events. That bitch had played her.

She sat on the soft bed and tried to regain her composure. She had been trained to think calmly. She took deep breaths and chanted, something she had seen a Serbian priest do during the Bosnian War. She would never forget the serene look on his face amid all the chaos. He even wore that look in death, after he had been shot in the gut. Helen didn't know anything about liturgical chanting—she had no interest in religion—so she made up her own phrases and pulled them out in moments like this one.

She had to think.

Dawes had seen only one person in Rome, her school friend who worked at the embassy. Nobody else could have the documents. They had to be in the embassy, but she couldn't go back there. She had failed in her mission.

Helen left the room, slipping her passkey into her pocket. Ever since hotels had abandoned keys for magnetic-strip keycards, it was a child's play to break into rooms. She had bought a little electronic encoding machine at a Chinese shop for a mere ten thousand euros. Now she could go wherever she wanted in any hotel in the world that hadn't started using radio-frequency identification or another more secure system.

She took the elevator down and slipped out unnoticed. She would wait until morning to report in.

11

Jade had Marcas repeat himself.

"The flesh falls from the bones," he said. "It's a sentence from a Freemason ritual referring to the murder of Hiram, the founder of the order."

"What does that have to do with this murder? Bring it down a notch so a simple layperson like me can understand. I gather you are a member of that group."

Marcas rubbed his cheek. He could already feel the stubble.

"Three blows: to the shoulder, to the neck, and to the forehead, as in the legend of Hiram. You see, according to Masonic tradition, the architect who built King Solomon's temple held powerful secrets. Three workers grew jealous of him. They conspired against him, and one night they set a trap."

Marcas could see the tension in Jade's arms.

"This is ridiculous!" she spit out. "Sophie just got murdered, and you're reciting the Bible. I must be hallucinating."

"Let me finish. The first worker struck him on the shoulder. Hiram refused to talk and fled. The second worker hit the architect on the neck. He managed to escape again. But the third worker finished him off with a blow to the forehead."

Now she was listening.

"This story is very important to us. It is highly symbolic. But there's something else."

"What?"

"These murders generally accompany a period of anti-Masonic persecution."

"There you have it—a conspiracy! You're out of your mind."

"And you're close-minded! For more than a century now, there have been murders such as this one. It's always the same: a blow to the shoulder, a blow to the neck, and a blow to the forehead. It's almost like marking the victims as martyrs."

"How do you know about these murders?"

"I've heard about them at various lodges."

"And?"

"This is undoubtedly a message."

"So do you have any idea who it's from? You've got so many enemies."

"Most people who don't like us aren't enemies. They're just ignorant."

Jade shook her head.

"Go back to your stories and legends. I have a murder to solve, the murder of someone very dear to me. If she hadn't joined your sect, she'd be alive."

"Don't insult me," Marcas said. "I don't belong to a sect, and I don't think your friend would have shared your point of view. Since you're not interested in what I have to say, I'll leave. I have my own cases to tend to."

His voice bounced off the palace walls, which had echoed so many other arguments and conspiracies since the time of the Farnese family.

This time, Jade grabbed his arm, and it was Marcas who was glaring. He didn't like this woman and wanted her to know it. "Special Agent Zewinski, your ignorance matches your incompetence. Remove your hand. It's in your best interest."

She shot him a challenging smile. "What are you going to do?" she said. "Call your boyfriends to come over and put a spell on me?"

Marcas's anger rose two notches, but he didn't show it. "Oh no, just the media. Your bosses at the foreign office will love it. It's not every day that a French national gets bumped off at the Farnese Palace."

"You won't have time to do that."

"You forget my *boyfriends*. Some of them are reporters and editors," he said, taking out his cell phone. "Would you like me to make a call? I'm all for transparency."

Jade balled her hands into fists. "That's blackmail. Transparency my ass. How ironic from a Mason. You and your buddies love conspiring in the lodge."

"Don't be stupid."

"You've got to understand how we outsiders—the common mortals—see it. Meetings that ordinary people can't attend, aprons, hand tools that never get dirty, and all that playacting. And oh, if you need a job, just call your Mason buddy. He'll take care of everything. But silly me, I'm just making all of that up, aren't I."

"I won't do you the honor of making a response."

"A thousand apologies. After all, I'm just a layperson—what do you call us? Profanes?—deprived of the light of the Great Architect of the Universe?"

"We have nothing to hide."

"You could have fooled me. But then, everyone has secrets."

Marcas narrowed his eyes. "So what are yours?" he asked.

"My secrets? Let's just say I'm an exception. I don't have secrets. I don't lead a double life as a cop and a hoodwinked brother. But I do have to admit that it would have given me a leg up in my career."

"And just maybe it would have knocked that chip off your shoulder. In the meantime, though, you'll just be pulling off some secret agent body-vanishing cover-up of your friend's murder."

Marcas and Jade stared at each other a good ten seconds, and then the cop turned on his heels and walked away.

12

"So what is this stone?" Bashir said to himself when he got to his hideout, a small apartment not far from the archeology institute. Unwrapping the item, he wondered if it was worth more than what he was charging his client. The frenzy for artifacts from Palestine hadn't slackened since the 1946 find in Qumran—the Dead Sea Scrolls, an ideological bombshell. For conservative Jews the scrolls proved that Christians were nothing more than the descendants of a very minor Jewish sect, the Essenes, who predicted the Apocalypse and ran off to the desert. Jesus was just a bottom-tier prophet. Later, of course, other studies brought into question the Essenien origin of the scrolls, and the famous purification pools that attracted tourists were now thought to be ordinary sedimentation pits.

In any case, ideology didn't interest Bashir. Money did. Some decadent Westerners were willing to pay a small fortune to get this find to Paris. He pulled out the documents he'd retrieved along with the stone and looked them over. Then he opened a map on his laptop and studied the coastal road that ran along the Sinai Desert from Eilat—a real furnace this time of year. And he'd encounter a number of Egyptian Army roadblocks. Too risky. Egypt was a bad idea.

He clicked again and tried flights from Jordan. He could cross the border when it opened in the morning, although it would be no picnic. Searches were systematic. But he had an idea. He could get to Amman by midmorning.

He reserved the flight from Amman to Paris, via Amsterdam.

13

Marcas rolled the toothpick from the salmon hors d'oeuvre between his fingers. What a ridiculous confrontation he'd just had with the head of security. He was annoyed with himself for backing off, but what good would it have done to argue? She had attacked him for being a Freemason, and nothing would have changed her mind. She would never understand his real commitment and the beauty of the rituals. She saw only the dark side.

He looked around, searching for the movie producer, but she was nowhere to be seen. Half the guests had left, and Jaigu had also disappeared. He was probably writing his report for the ambassador and busy undermining his colleague.

Marcas had turned toward the cloakroom when he heard Pink Martini's "U Plavu Zoru," a heady mix of violins, congas, and chanting. He recognized the warm, sensual voice of China Forbes, the group's vocalist. Marcas closed his eyes to savor the moment.

His reverie didn't last long. He opened his eyes to the sight of Zewinski standing in front of him, hands on her hips. She was blocking his way.

"We're needed."

"We?"

Zewinski held out a crumpled paper. "Yes, we. You and me. The cursed couple. The spook and the hoodwinker, if you prefer. Here. You do know how to read, don't you?"

Marcas began scanning the fax, bristling at her repeated use of the word "hoodwinker." The term was a reference to the blindfold a Freemason wore during his initiation, when he acquired knowledge and moved from darkness to light. Marcas put the insult out of his mind and read the missive. "The above-mentioned police officer will make himself immediately available to the consular authorities. He will fully cooperate with the head of security."

Great. Marcas thrust the paper back at her. "I presume you aren't responsible for this."

"You are clever, aren't you? If it were up to me, I would have my men toss you out of the embassy. It seems that your friend Jaigu told the brass that you were here."

"Listen, let's not play games," Marcas responded. "Neither you nor I want to spend any more time together than necessary. I'll send you a report tomorrow certifying that I didn't see anything upstairs. You'll keep your investigation, and I'll be left alone. I'll go back to Paris and that will be that."

"Deal," she said, smiling for the first time. "And of course, not a word to your friends at the lodge."

"That goes without saying. Besides, if I described you to them, they wouldn't believe me. So much kindness and grace in a single person is the stuff of dreams."

"It will be a pleasure not to see you again, Inspector."

"Same to you."

She shot him a biting look and headed toward a group of guards near the kitchen doors.

Marcas started to leave but changed his mind. Instead, he moved closer to the group. Jade's voice was raised. She looked furious. One of the men pointed at Marcas. She rolled her eyes.

"What now?" she said.

"Here's my card. I'm staying at the Zuliani in case you need me," he said, flashing her a smile.

She looked him up and down. "You're too kind, but I don't think I'll need you or your card. Just drop your letter off at the embassy."

He surveyed the kitchen. "What's going on?"

"Nothing. The butler is coming to. He was knocked out, apparently by one of the waitstaff hired for the evening.

With any luck, he'll be able to describe her. Good night," she said, turning her back on him.

Marcas shrugged and took off for the cloakroom. The spook and the hoodwinker—he liked it. It was just possible that she had a sense of humor.

The vision of the young woman's body came back to him. Who was twisting the Hiram ritual, a key Freemason observance? Who would push provocation so far as to execute another person in that way? The reenactment of Hiram's death in Freemason rites was a parable full of philosophical meaning. So what was the message the killer or killers were trying to send?

The murderer had to have inside knowledge. The witness mentioned a woman—a Mason-killing woman. It was grotesque and worrisome. His head spinning, Marcas left the embassy and hailed a cab at the end of the street.

He was fatigued and confused. But in the backseat of the cab, his brain rebooted. He analyzed, compared, and reconstructed the scene. Inside the embassy, a young woman's life had come to a tragic end. Whether he liked it or not, she was a Freemason sister, and her homicide was now his problem.

The taxi stopped at his hotel, which was in one of the few quiet neighborhoods in the Eternal City. It had long, narrow streets that cars avoided, sidewalks lined with lemon trees, and vast villas built during the fascist era.

Once in his room, he pulled out a leather-bound notebook and leafed through it to an empty page. He carefully opened the red-lacquer pen his son had given him for Father's Day and set to work.

He jotted down the ritual used by the killer and reviewed his recollections of similar slayings he had heard about in his research of Freemason history. The scholar who had related these stories—the worshipful master at the Trois Lumières Lodge and a specialist in Spanish history—had died ten years earlier. He had recounted two series of attacks against Freemasons one hundred years apart. Marcas had no idea how much truth there was to the stories or if they were just amplifications of the various persecutions brothers had been subjected to over the centuries.

The first had occurred right after Napoleon's troops had left Spain. A hundred Spanish brothers were decapitated for their support of the Frenchman's ideas and their hostility to the monarchy. The second was during the Spanish Civil War, which pitted supporters of the republic against rebels led by General Francisco Franco, a sworn enemy of freemasonry.

Marcas would have to find his notes. He remembered something about executions in Seville, a pillaged lodge, and Freemasons discovered with their skulls cracked open. "Hiram" was written in blood on their foreheads.

JAKIN

*The other pillar guarding the temple entrance,
a symbol of righteousness*

14

Marcas awoke with a start, the image of Sophie Dawes's body sprawled on the embassy floor in his mind. He got up and stretched, trying to shake the sadness he felt for his sister Freemason. The chain that united them had lost a link.

Marcas skipped breakfast and headed straight to the temple on the Via Condotti. A white-haired man who had to be at least ninety held the job of overseeing the archives at the Alessandro di Cagliostro Lodge. When Marcas asked for the records of violence against Roman Freemasons, the man brought out a faded green box filled with papers that had seen better days.

Marcas sat down in a deep leather chair and delved into the contents. The three blows to the body were too close to the legend of Hiram's death to be a coincidence. He made his way through open-meeting reports and press clippings about fascist groups ransacking lodges during Mussolini's reign. Then nothing at all until the Allies liberated Italy.

Frustrated, Marcas asked the old librarian about unexplained Freemason murders.

"My memory is not so good anymore," the librarian said, scratching his head. He shuffled over to a chair and settled in. "I do recall that right before the Allies arrived, three lodge officers from Rome and Milan were found murdered in a mansion not far from the Coliseum. Their faces were smashed in."

"Do you think it might have been the Blackshirts or the SS?" Marcas asked.

"A brother who was in the police told me he didn't think either of them was responsible. The Blackshirts used other methods, and Hitler's strongmen tortured their victims before executing them or just shot them and threw them in common graves."

The old man was choosing his words carefully. He seemed to recover some deeply held energy as he talked about that dark time in history. No doubt it was a remnant of the courage and daring he had needed to survive.

The librarian handed Marcas another file that was even dustier. It was filled with press clippings from the nineteen thirties. One of the articles gave an account of the 1934 murder of a researcher, a Freemason who had been beaten to death. His skull was crushed. Next to the story, someone had written "Hiram?" in purple ink. Marcas made photocopies and opened his red notebook to jot down a list of similar murders.

1934. Florence, a brother.

1944. Rome, three brothers.

2005. Rome, a sister.

He thanked the old man and left the Roman lodge.

15

Bashir was driving a pickup he had borrowed from someone who owed him a favor. He had chosen his cover with care: Jordanian excavation-equipment sales rep. The bed of the truck was filled with rubble from a construction site. Among the rocks was the stone he had stolen from the institute.

When he reached the Allanby Bridge border crossing, a zealous Jewish border guard wanted him to unload the truck.

He'd expected this. At that moment, an associate who was following him in a car pulled out of the line of traffic and started honking. A swarm of Israeli army officers descended on the man, fingers on their triggers.

The border guard turned to see the commotion and then yelled at Bashir. "Get out of here. Go back to your country of dirty nomads."

One obstacle down. When he arrived in Amman, he'd ditch the truck, change his clothes, and pick up his new identity: Vittorio Cavalcanti, a Milanese tourist going home after seeing the marvels of Jordan. He would have a large suitcase full of souvenirs, including the Tebah Stone.

16

"So, do we agree? Ms. Dawes experienced an unfortunate fall at the embassy in Rome. The administration will not comment on the incident."

The French diplomatic system was working at full tilt the day after Sophie Dawes's murder. Zewinski had brought the body back to France. The coroner's office had contacted the family to come and identify her.

Three witnesses—all members of the embassy security team—had provided signed affidavits stating that Sophie seemed to have had too much to drink. She had lost her balance while going down the marble steps and had hit her head. None of the guests had seen anything, and no reporters had gotten wind of the accident. A life had been erased, a death touched up.

Sophie's father was an elderly man with Alzheimer's disease. He did not come to identify the body. A distant cousin was brought in at the last minute to sign the papers and then disappeared as just as quickly.

The body would be buried in two days without any ceremony in a cemetery in the suburbs of Paris.

Meanwhile, intelligence services were piecing together the victim's short life. At the same time, agents were contacting the Grand Orient de France Freemason Lodge to let them know that one of their archivists had died in an unfortunate accident. The minister of the interior had already scheduled a meeting with a Grand Orient advisor, who was also a high-level civil servant.

The foreign office representative shot Pierre Darsan of the interior ministry a questioning look.

Darsan continued. "We need to make sure everyone keeps this under wraps. The gendarmes who witnessed the *accident* will be transferred to other embassies tomorrow."

"What about Zewinski?"

"She did an expert job of handling things. We'll debrief her and keep her on to investigate what really happened."

"And the police inspector, Antoine Marcas? What was he doing there?"

"A coincidence," Darsan said. "Apparently he was taking a few days off in Rome. He and our man Jaigu are friends. Since Marcas was at the reception, Jaigu pulled him in on the preliminary investigation. He could be useful. He's a Freemason. Marcas should be boarding a plane back to Paris as we speak."

"Can we count on him staying quiet?"

"I can make that happen."

"Fine," the foreign office representative said as he stood up. "Darsan, it's your investigation now—unofficially, that is."

As soon as the door closed behind him, Darsan went to the window. The room was silent, except for the muffled sound of traffic outside. He smoothed his mustache, a habit he had picked up in Algeria forty years earlier, and returned to his desk.

He lit a cigarette and opened Antoine Marcas's file: forty years old, a homicide detective, a short stint in the anti-gang unit, commendations from his superiors, on the fast track toward becoming chief, then an unexpected spell in police intelligence services before suddenly requesting a transfer to a simple Parisian precinct. An additional page specified that during his stint in intelligence, he attended a certain Freemason lodge that also had several members who were involved in a money-laundering scheme. He was divorced, had a ten-year-old son, paid his child support every month, and spent his spare time writing articles about Freemason history.

Darsan closed that file and opened Jade Zewinski's. She boasted a remarkable career for someone her age with no family connections. She ranked in the top ten of her class at the military academy and did commando training, foreign intelligence, and two operations in the Middle East, followed by security in Afghanistan for visiting media and politicians. After that, she had been sent to Rome.

He went through another ten or so pages before a press clipping caught his attention. Her father had committed suicide after his business failed. Smiling, Darsan read the article twice. Apparently Jade Zewinski had at least one good reason to dislike the Freemasons. He closed the file and called his secretary.

17

A breeze carried the scent of the sea, which mingled with the fragrance of the pine trees. Five men and two women walked slowly, taking time to contemplate the beauty of the Croatian landscape just below the Hvar fortress. The tallest of them, a gray-haired man with a buzz cut, pointed to a small headland jutting out toward the sea, flanked by two crumbling stone walls rising from the rocky soil. To the left, near the cliff, a small chapel surrounded by three majestic yew trees bore a pale mineral sheen in the bright sunlight.

The group headed in the indicated direction, following an uphill path lined with aromatic herbs. It ended at a natural belvedere.

They sat down on a wooden bench facing the Adriatic Sea, which shimmered in the bright morning light.

One of them, a short sweaty man with a red face, turned to his neighbor and nodded toward the chapel, which was padlocked. "What a fabulous view. I'd love to live here. It's perfect, an ode to the glory of nature. Why, then, did you leave that Christian building? We've owned this land forever and can do what we want with it."

The gray-haired man sitting next to him smiled and patted his shoulder. His steely eyes were bright. "Patience. I assure you it is no longer in use, and I have set it aside for a rather special purpose. You will see, but first, let's talk about what has brought us together. We now have the Tebah Stone, or at least it is in good hands. Sol should pick it up in Paris shortly. Unfortunately, the Rome operation was a failure. We don't have the documents."

Nobody reacted. Finally, a thin balding man with light brown eyes spoke up. "That's regrettable. I remind you that we need three things to solve this mystery. The first has always been in our possession. The second is engraved on that Jewish stone, and the third, which you failed to get, remains in enemy hands. And now they will be on guard. The murders in Jerusalem and Rome bear our signature. That was your idea."

"We will get them. I've already given the orders."

"He's right," the short man chimed in. "I told you this operation could be dangerous and draw attention to us. What for? You and Sol have been leading us on a ghost hunt. Don't forget that our enemies are powerful and have a sprawling network."

"Enough. Let me remind you that the ritual surrounding their deaths fulfills a promise made by our ancestors."

"I still think we are losing our focus with this folklore. We have more important goals. This is a minor operation."

The man with the buzz cut glanced at the chapel, stood up, and softened his tone. "You're right. I don't know what came over me. The weather is excellent. Let's not argue. I suggest we go commune in the chapel."

The others stared at him, as if he had gone mad. He burst out laughing.

"Come with me. Let's enter the house of Christ and his mother. It was once called the Chapel of Our Mother of the Passion."

The group walked over to the chapel. The man with the buzz cut unlocked the door and opened it. The smell of wet stone and something indefinable struck them. The gray-haired man flipped a small switch, and three lights went on.

The inside of the church was simple, with whitewashed walls and restored stained-glass windows. A large wooden crucifix with Jesus wearing a crown of thorns reigned over the altar. It would have been a classic religious setting, were it not for the metal structure planted in front of the altar, a sarcophagus over six feet tall and shaped like a woman. Her body had generous breasts and hips, and flowing hair graced her serene face. The group immediately recognized what it was.

"The Iron Maiden!" they exclaimed, almost in unison.

Their guide led them to the strange object.

"Yes, my friends. One of our companions found this in the cellar of a castle near Munich. It was built in the fifteenth century and has been fully restored."

A man with a British accent interrupted. "I saw something like that in a horror movie. I thought the filmmaker made it up."

"Not at all. The maiden dates from medieval times in Germany, when Sainte Vehme's courts were responsible for executing bad Christians and criminals. The jurisdiction behaved like a secret society with strange rites, a remnant of which stands before you."

He pressed a hidden button on the side of the sarcophagus. With a click, the front, with the woman's face and body, opened slowly, revealing rows of iron spikes.

"Amazing, isn't it? The judges would place the sentenced soul in the sarcophagus and shut it, and the spikes would pierce the victim in precise places, including his vital organs. As you can see, two of the spikes are positioned to penetrate the eyes. The name 'Iron Maiden' pays homage to the Virgin Mother. These were very religious people."

"Ingenious."

"Does someone want to try it, just to see?"

They tittered. As hardened as they were to other people's pain, they were sensitive when it came to their own.

The leader turned to the red-faced man. "You, perhaps?"

"No, thank you. I think I'll pass. Let's get out of this dreary place."

"I don't think we will. At least you won't."

There was the sound of footsteps in the entryway. Two strongmen appeared. In a matter of seconds, they swooped down on the small man, immobilizing his arms. He seemed tiny next to the square-jawed giants.

"Are you out of your mind? Let me go!"

"Shut up."

The leader's voice rang out. "Sol checked the accounts for our activities in northern Europe. You cooked Orden's books, and you've been stealing from us."

"That's not true."

"Quiet. You embezzled more than a million euros. What for? To build a villa in Andalusia! That was a big mistake!"

The accused tried to fight back but was helpless.

"Put him in the maiden."

"No!" the man shouted, still trying to free himself from the clutches of the giants. One of the strongmen struck him in the head with a club and shoved him into the metallic structure, partially closing the front. The spikes were just inches from him.

"Please, have pity on me. I'll give it all back. I have a family. Children."

"Now, now. You know full well that to enter our order you abjure pity and compassion. At least try to die like a man of the Thule. Fear is foreign to us."

The man's sobs bounced off the wooden crucifix—Christ suffering for humanity—and filled the chapel.

The man with the buzz cut and steel-colored eyes pressed another button camouflaged in the maiden's eye. The whirr of a small motor resonated.

"I added a motorized system with a timer to control the speed. If I set it at ten, your agony will last ten minutes. It can go as long as two hours."

"I'll give the money back."

"You'll have to forgive me, but I've only tested this contraption on a few guinea pigs. Weight and height also play a role. Perfection is not of this world."

The front closed a bit more, and the iron stakes tickled the victim's eyes, stomach, knees, and genitals.

"I am too kind. I set it for a mere fifteen minutes. Adieu, my friend," the man said, turning to the others and adding, "How about lunch? An excellent meal awaits us."

18

Marcas's phone rang as soon as he entered the terminal at Charles de Gaulle Airport in Paris.

"Zewinski here. I need to see you right away."

"I'm not your subordinate," Marcas said, ready to hang up. "I don't take orders from you."

"These don't come from me. They come from the ministry, so you're out of luck."

"Then meet me at the Bibliothèque François Mitterand in an hour," Marcas said. As much as that woman irritated him, he couldn't shake Sophie Dawes's murder.

"Why there? Is that one of your Freemason haunts?"

"I just like the place. The cafeteria is good for private conversations."

"Hey, didn't President Mitterand get himself elected with the help of his Freemason connections and appoint some of your brothers to his cabinet?"

"So they say, but he distanced himself later. You know how good he was at calculated ambiguity." Why was he even discussing this with her? "In an hour," he concluded, ending the call.

If only she knew how much he hated influence peddling, even though he'd applied to be a Freemason in 1990 as much out of opportunism as curiosity. He was still a rookie cop when Freemasons in high places singled him out. After a dinner with quite a bit of drinking, a superior officer asked him if he wanted to be a Freemason, as if it were like joining a tennis club. Marcas didn't know how to answer at first but quickly realized that it was idiotic to refuse the invitation.

Freemasons had been numerous in the French police system since World War II, and as one climbed the ranks, the number of brothers rose.

A month after the invitation was extended, three people he didn't know came to see him—at his apartment—to discuss his commitment. They asked questions about his lifestyle and tastes and tried to dissuade him from joining the Masons.

A month after that, Marcas was summoned to a Freemason temple in the fifteenth arrondissement. He waited in a small black room full of alchemical symbols, where he meditated and wrote a philosophical testament. Then, blindfolded and stripped of some of his clothing, he underwent tests symbolizing a perilous journey across water, air, and fire to finally reach the light, the crucial moment of rebirth.

There was nothing really secret about the rite, and anyone could read about it in one of the thousands of books about freemasonry. But Marcas understood on this night that going through the ritual had added a new dimension to his being and had changed him. He had felt something indescribable, as though he were frozen in a moment of eternity. It was hard to articulate. This wasn't magic. It was an alternative awareness that he had never before experienced.

After his initiation, Marcas met the other brothers in the lodge, none of whom held influential positions. He was almost disappointed: no well-known politicians, no emblematic judges, no celebrities. Just ordinary people: cops like him, teachers, some business owners, a handful of craftsmen, a few retired academics, and a cook who had received some attention for getting a Michelin star.

But Marcas applied himself and rose from apprentice to fellow craft and master mason.

When he was preparing for the police chief's exam, he was invited to join a group of a hundred or so police officials from different lodges. Marcas never knew if being one of them had earned him points, but he did build a solid network of connections.

That was history. He didn't need to explain any of it to the snide Embassy Security Chief Jade Zewinski.

A chilly rain had started falling, and precipitation always threatened to transform the Bibliothèque Nationale de France's outdoor plaza into an ersatz skating rink. It was because of the hardwood decking the building's architect had insisted on. The unintended consequence was a high incidence of slips, falls, sprains, and breaks. Shortly after the library opened, some anti-slip decking strips were added to partially mitigate the problem. Still, Marcas almost lost his footing on an unprotected set of steps. He grabbed the railing. Righting himself, he continued toward the library. The wind had picked up, and the towers—shaped like books for those with an active imagination—were standing like fortresses against the sheets of rain.

He pulled his raincoat tighter. The large yet frail tropical trees that adorned the immense central patio were whipping back and forth in the wind, tugging the lines that moored them. Finally reaching the entryway, he saw that the escalator, as usual, wasn't working.

A small group of people was waiting patiently as two bored-looking guards inspected their bags. A dozen or so umbrellas were the only bright spots of colors in this metal and dark-wood interior.

Marcas made his way up a floor, crossing the metal footbridge that led to the library cafeteria. He pushed open a heavy door and scanned the large room. Four students were huddled around their notebooks and whispering. A Japanese couple who looked like tourists were people-watching, and an elderly woman was reading an antiques magazine. No Zewinski yet. Marcas ordered a coffee and sat down.

He was fiddling with a brochure advertising vacations in Cuba and Santo Domingo with seductive photos of palm trees and white sand beaches when he heard a coat rustling. He looked up and saw Special Agent Zewinski walking purposefully toward him—tall, blonde, chiseled features, determined eyes. She was a shrew, he thought, but a damned good-looking shrew.

She sat down across from him without taking off her coat. "Hey, *brother.*"

Marcas tightened his jaw. Her tone pissed him off, just as it had in Rome. He started to get up to leave, but she reached for his arm.

"Wait, I was just joking. You Freemasons have no sense of humor. I won't do it again."

She brought her hands together to give him the *namaste* sign. Marcas settled into his chair again.

"It might surprise you that I do have a sense of humor. But I don't think it's necessary to make a joke at someone else's expense. That said, maybe you can tell me why I'm here."

Her face became serious, and the look in her eyes darkened. For the first time, he noted their color: light brown speckled with green.

"I know why Sophie was killed."

19

Marcas ordered another coffee and folded his hands on the table. Some more students had sat down at a nearby table and were staring at Jade.

She lowered her voice. "Someone's after a bunch of damned papers that belong to your Freemason buddies. Sophie told me she was on an assignment for the Grand Orient. She was taking the documents to Jerusalem. She didn't tell me what they were—some big historical deal apparently. She asked me to put them in the embassy safe."

"So she was being careful with some historical documents. How do you know her killer wanted them?"

"She was all paranoid about them, making sure that I put them under lock and key, and then, after she was murdered, I went to her hotel room to pick up her personal effects, and someone had sacked the place."

"Do you have the papers?"

"Of course. I brought them back to Paris with me."

So that was why Zewinski wanted to see him. She had his attention now. Historical masonic documents in the hands of the profane could be dangerous.

"Have you read them?"

"I didn't understand a thing. You'd have to be a historian or a member of your cult to understand that crap. It's something about rituals, geometric constructions, and Bible references. I'd say the papers date back to the eighteenth or nineteenth century."

"You should return them to their rightful owners. They are the only ones who can explain why someone would kill for them."

Jade glared at him. "I know what I have to do, but for now, they are evidence in a murder investigation that doesn't exist. They'll get back to your friends in due time."

"So, why are you telling me this?"

Zewinski ran her hands through her hair and waited a minute. "You don't know it yet, but we'll be working together after all. There was a meeting at the Interior Ministry earlier today, and we've been officially assigned to this entirely unofficial case."

Marcas took a slow sip of his coffee to give himself some time to think.

"In case you don't know it, I'm on vacation. I'm supposed to be off for another two weeks, and I have lots of fun activities planned, none of which include you. I'm really very sorry about your friend's death, but I will not, under any circumstances, be involved in this case."

Zewinski smiled. "But you don't have a choice. Apparently one of the higher-ups is a fellow of the light—that's what you call it, don't you? And he wants you to illuminate this case. I'm no psychic, but I predict you'll be getting a call from your superiors in no time at all."

"Well, in that case, thanks for the heads up."

"Look, I came to get things straight between us. If we're going to work together, we need to be clear. I'm going to have to stick my nose into your apron-wearing clown act, and I'm not happy about it."

Marcas set down his coffee.

"I'll wait until I get my orders. In the meantime, I just have one question."

"Shoot."

"Why do you hate Freemasons so much?"

Her eyes hardened. She stood up abruptly and adjusted her coat.

"You're right. I don't like what you represent, and I know that Sophie died because of some scheming done by your devious little brothers, adepts of the Great Architect of the

Universe. This meeting is over. We'll see each other in a setting that's more official before the day is out."

Marcas stared at her as she turned her back and stomped out, slamming the cafeteria door. There was no way he would team up with that Valkyrie. He paid for the coffees and left, swearing under his breath. Why had he accepted that invitation to the embassy? Besides, he was supposed to fly to Washington next week to meet with American Freemasons at Georgetown University. They'd been planning the meeting for months to share information on alchemical iconography in eighteenth-century rituals.

As he left the library, though, he admitted that his plans were already ruined—a sister had died, after all.

20

His client was not going to be happy. His connection to Paris had been canceled—some anomalies in the plane's hydraulic system. All the passengers en route to Paris had been asked to disembark at Schiphol Airport in Amsterdam.

Bashir picked up his luggage—which held the precious Tebah Stone—without any grousing. He left that to the other travelers, most of them French, who were having a go at the airline employee trying to get them on other flights. He opted to take the train to Paris after spending a night in Amsterdam for the pleasure of it. After all, he wasn't Bashir the feared Palestinian hit man now. He was Vittorio, a fun-loving Milanese Italian who liked wine and pretty women.

A little delay wouldn't make any difference. What was so urgent about some archeological artifact? He knew practically nothing about his client, a certain Sol. Their contact was limited to e-mails sent through a series of addresses. "Meeting in Paris ASAP," the most recent one read. "Contact Tuzet at the Plaza Athénée. Ask for the keys to his Daimler."

He didn't know who Tuzet was, but as long as he got paid, he couldn't care less. Before leaving the airport, he swapped his suitcase full of travel souvenirs for a small carry-on for the stone and the accompanying documents. He also sent an encrypted e-mail to Sol, advising him of the delay and saying he would take a bullet train in the morning. He would arrive in the early afternoon.

Now he had some time to kill. He headed downtown. Perhaps he would visit the red-light district. He had heard of some fine restaurants, too. So maybe he would satisfy both appetites tonight: first a little food, then a little sex. Maybe more than a little of each. Strolling the streets and considering his options, he passed a Muslim mother in a niqab. The contrast between the exposed prostitutes in the windows of the red-light district and this mother, entirely covered to protect her from the eyes of men, was striking. Yet weren't they the same? The prostitute exposed herself to please her male customers. The religious woman might say that she was covering to please God, but wasn't she also doing it to please her husband—the man in her life who desired her? Bashir couldn't help thinking how odd it was that Europeans were more shocked by a veil than a thong.

Secular and Islamic tensions had risen in this country since the slaying of a controversial movie producer, Theo Van Gogh. He had made a film focusing on the oppression of women in Islam, and in retaliation, a Dutch-Moroccan Muslim had shot him to death. The slaying had fed the flames of anti-Islamic sentiment, and the people of the Netherlands, who liked to think of themselves as so open and tolerant, were witnessing the same growth of sectarianism that was affecting the rest of Europe. The extreme-right presence of the Vlaams Blok, along with its hateful nostalgia for the supremacy of the white race, was evidence of that.

Bashir didn't like Jews, but he had no affection for contemporary fascists either. He had gone into a rage when he found a portrait of Adolph Hitler in the room of one of his young cousins who overflowed with admiration for the Führer.

This wasn't an isolated incident. A certain portion of the Arab world saw Hitler as a dictator, yes, but also as a standard bearer for the fight against the Jewish peril. *The Protocols of the Elders of Zion*, a fabricated text first published in 1903 in Russia, could still be bought in souks all over the Middle East. In the nineteen twenties, Henry Ford had underwritten a half million copies of the publication, which described a Jewish plot to dominate the world.

Bashir found this grotesque admiration to be pitiful. The Germans had recruited the Arabs as partners during World War II to fight the British. Egypt's Anwar el Sadat, who signed a peace treaty with Israel in 1979, had spied for German Field Marshal Edwin Rommel during the war. The grand mufti of Jerusalem, whom Hitler hosted with full honors in 1941, had blessed three Muslim SS divisions: Handschar, Kama, and Skandenberg. "The crescent and the swastika have the same enemy: the Star of David," the mufti had said.

But Bashir knew that Nazi ideology classified Muslims as inferiors, not much better than Slavs or Latins.

He had met European neo-Nazis in training camps in Syria, Lebanon, and Libya. He knew these skinheads, who gave lip service to the Palestinian cause, would go home and organize racist attacks there.

Bashir had second thoughts about his evening plans. His taste for a tempting nightcap had waned. Instead, he turned toward the city center to find an Indonesian restaurant and order a *rijsttafel*, an assortment of small, tasty dishes the Dutch loved so much.

A bicycle bell rang out behind him, and he barely had time to jump out of the way to avoid being run over. Collecting himself, Bashir saw that he had landed in front of a shop with a window bearing a huge florescent-red mushroom on a dark purple background. The man who had almost hit him parked his bike in front of the same shop, smiled, and walked in. Bashir decided to follow and take a look around. Shelves holding hundreds of small bags containing mushrooms and spores lined the walls. It was like a garden center for potheads.

The young Dutch man at the counter looked as serious as a theology student. He was giving a German couple expert advice on growing magic mushrooms. "It's all about the soil," he said, sounding sententious. The couple had chosen twenty or so bags of spores, enough to fill an entire greenhouse.

Bashir picked a bag containing five specimens of a white-fringed mushroom with a phallic cap: *Psilocybe semilanceata*. He felt their texture and made a face. Not good enough. He waited for the salesman to finish with his customers and asked in English if he didn't have something better. The employee came around the counter and pointed to another display of multicolored bags decorated with laughing elves. Bashir shook his head.

"I want the best quality. Money is not an issue."

The salesman smiled and retreated to the back of the store. Bashir could see him removing a box from a refrigerator. There were no comic gnomes, just sturdy, bright-colored plastic boxes containing mushrooms that might have been collected the day before. The salesman returned, took out four mushrooms, and set them delicately on a brushed-aluminum tray.

"The nectar of the Gods, man. Takeoff guaranteed with no hard landing. But you have to be lying down."

"How much?"

The young man put on a contrite look and said, "I don't have many left, and you can't grow these jewels just anywhere."

"How much?"

"Three hundred euros, and I'm taking a loss, man."

"Fine."

Bashir paid and on his way out held the door for an elderly woman with snow-white hair and a fox terrier.

A strange country, he thought as he headed toward Dam Square, in front of the royal palace, where the queen never went. He thought about Sol and the macabre staging of the murder. He would probably never get an explanation.

21

The supple wooden bar sagged under the weight of her leg as she stretched over her thigh, reaching for her calf and making a final effort to grab her ankle. Sweat trickled down her forehead to her cheek, which was now pressed against the leg.

The pain shot up her leg and through her hips as she pushed her flexibility to the limit.

"Pain gives birth to dreams," the French poet Louis Aragon had written, and for Helen, the more intense it was, the clearer her thoughts became. She had many techniques for emptying her mind, but nothing worked as well as torturing her body with extreme stretches.

Hvar's neo-medieval building had twenty-five rooms, three meeting rooms, relaxation rooms, a Jacuzzi, an Olympic-sized swimming pool, a heliport, and a pier that could host large ships. It was Orden's second-largest estate after the one in Asunción, Paraguay, which had a ranch and a golf course, as well. Orden had similar estates in Munich, Cannes, London, and five other cities in the Americas. Two palaces were under construction in Asia. Members used them for retreats and meetings far from prying eyes.

The castle, entirely renovated by the state in 1942, had served as offices for the German diplomatic delegation and had also housed an outpost of the Ahnenerbe, the Riech's institute for archeological and cultural studies of the Aryan race. When Yugoslavia was liberated, the castle became a people's palace under Josip Tito and was used solely by the aged statesman's bodyguards.

After the fall of communism, a consortium of German and Croatian businessmen quietly bought the building to house the Adriatic Institute of Culture Research, one of Orden's many retreats.

Surviving members of the Ahnenerbe, all with the Thule, chose the name Orden following the demise of Nazi Germany. "Before Hitler, we existed. After his death, we will continue to exist."

Anyone looking for the owners of the castle would find a Zagreb-based real estate company held by a Cyprian trust and managed by three phantom foundations in Liechtenstein. The same setup was used for other properties the organization owned. Only the most astute observer would notice that all these luxury residences were cultural institutes whose focus varied from one location to the next: artistic symbolism in London, for example, or the working-class culture in Munich, or pre-Colombian musical instruments in Paraguay.

Unfolding from her position, Helen felt a rush as her body released the tension. She had the sensation of being weightless. She picked up the wall phone and called the front desk to schedule a massage. Grabbing a towel, Helen gazed at the sea outside the gym's large window. The waves glistened in the moonlight. Three lit-up yachts passed in the distance, and a fishing boat was leaving the shore.

"Tired?"

She turned to see a man in the doorway. She felt his steel-gray eyes giving her a once-over.

"A bit. And you?"

"Same old routine. You must succeed this time. We are counting on you."

"Yes. I won't fail again."

"I should hope not. Will you be joining us for dinner?"

"No. It'll be an early night for me."

"Good night, then," the man said. After a moment, he added, "You bear such a resemblance to your mother. It's like I'm seeing her all over again in you."

"Good night, Father."

He looked thoughtful, then turned and left.

Helen wiped her forehead and looked at herself in the mirror. The mention of her mother catapulted her back to a time when she wasn't called Helen or any of the other names she used for her missions, a time when she was simply Joana, a child lost in a civil war. The last image she had of her mother was a Serbian officer shooting her between the eyes. Her skull had exploded before her body crumpled to the ground. The officer then put a gun to Helen's head. He couldn't have been more than twenty-five years old. He leaned in, and she felt the heat of his breath on her ear. "I'm not going to kill you," he said. "I'm not a pig like your father, who massacred my village and killed my twelve-year-old sister. You'll live to tell him that I'll wring his neck with my own hands. Nod if you understand."

She had nodded.

The man holstered his gun. It was over. Five minutes later, the Serbs were gone. Helen had fallen to her knees next to her mother's body, howling in hatred and pain. But when her father returned, she was done crying. Without emotion, she gave him the message.

A year later, her commando unit captured a small band of Serbians. She recognized her mother's murderer. Her father let him loose in an abandoned village and offered her a manhunt. She took half an hour to kill the man, first lodging bullets in his knees, then taking a knife to each part of his body. His shrieks echoed off the crumbling walls of the houses. "You made me the person I am today," she whispered calmly in his ear. "You gave me a gift, that of granting death." Then she shot him between the eyes. She was sixteen.

It took her only a few years to build her reputation as an efficient and ruthless killer. At the end of the war, she transitioned to working as a contract killer and brokering traffic of all kinds. There were few women in the field.

Croatia gained its independence, and her father became a respectable businessman who specialized in international tourism. But in the background, he stayed close to many former members of Ustaše. He made frequent trips to Germany for business and politics. Croatia maintained strong ties with Germany, and the Germans, in fact, had secretly underwritten the heavy artillery that the Croatians used against the more powerful Serbs.

Joana's father had connections in a number of far-right groups in addition to Ustaše, and he introduced her to powerful people, initiates who had revealed to him both political and sacred secrets. The Orden brotherhood had for centuries guarded the secrets of Thule, the cradle of the pure Aryan race. Joana knew why fate had chosen her. Revenge and violence were nothing, compared with the feelings of potency and control they conveyed.

Joana headed toward the showers. An intense sensation spread over her skin under the burning-hot water, as if she were fusing with some incandescent wave. The heat relaxed her muscles, and a welcome feeling of languor took over.

Just as she was about to succumb to the sensation, she turned the faucet to cold, and icy water chased away the calming heat. Her body began to tremble. Her arteries and veins constricted.

She cut the flow and stepped out of the shower, glowing.

She picked up a rough terry towel to dry herself off, and her mind drifted back to Sophie Dawes's execution. She slipped her hand between her thighs, then stopped. No, she wouldn't allow herself that pleasure until she had gotten the documents.

Her next destination: Paris. Her next prey: Sophie Dawes's friend.

22

Zewinski stood in Darsan's office, feeling encouraged by the meeting. Finally: a ministry official who didn't beat around the bush and took full responsibility. He had perfectly understood her pain and had put her in charge of the investigation, which meant that Marcas would work for her. His role would be limited to shedding light on the Masonic issues—if the murder was at all related to that world—and smoothing relations with the police if it was necessary.

"I'm not a Freemason, if that reassures you," Darsan said, looking her in the eye for a long moment. "There will be no pressure."

Zewinski had carte blanche for a month. She would get an office in the seventeenth arrondissement, along with an assistant from special ops who was used to working off the grid.

"Show Marcas in," Darsan said.

She stepped into the hall and moitioned to Marcas.

~~~

Zewinski had been right. His boss had called, cutting his vacation short and ordering him to lend a hand. He hadn't known how to react. The specific nature of the murder was the only reason he was involved. So here he was, heading into the office of an important ministry official—technically his boss's boss's boss, or something like that. He wasn't entirely sure of the hierarchy.

He didn't find Zewinski's grin at all reassuring—it was more of a threat. He closed the door behind him.

Pierre Darsan was fingering a metal ruler.

"Inspector, I'm going to get straight to the point. We need to solve this case quickly and quietly. This embassy murder raises two important issues. The first, and the most important, is the breach in security in one of our diplomatic posts. We can't have just anybody getting into an embassy and doing what they please. It can't happen again. Because this is an issue of diplomatic security, Special Agent Jade Zewinski, the embassy security chief, will lead the investigation."

Darsan was watching Marcas for a reaction, but the inspector remained impassive.

"And what is the second issue?" he asked.

"It turns out that the victim worked for the Grand Orient, and one theory, as you know, is that her elimination may have been related to your group."

Darsan had carefully articulated each word. "That's where you come in. You'll have a twofold role: cop and Freemason. Being a Freemason is nothing out of the ordinary. There are at least five just like you working in the offices here and as many in every other department. That doesn't bother me, as long as it doesn't interfere with business as usual. Do you follow me, Inspector?"

Marcas knew where the judge was going with this.

"No, sir, I don't."

Darsan pursed his lips until there was almost nothing left of his mouth.

"Don't play the wise guy, Marcas. I'm expecting you to conduct a serious investigation and to tell me everything. Your duty as a police officer comes above and beyond your commitment to freemasonry. I'm sure your group is doing its own investigation. I don't want the lines blurred. Is that clear?"

Darsan was quiet for a long moment. "You will be working under Special Agent Zewinski. That's an order. I expect you to cooperate with her, advise her, and provide anything she needs for the investigation." Darsan gave him a pleasant smile.

The man's expression could change in a flash, Marcas thought. Threatening one second, friendly the next.

"Between us, Inspector, let's forget freemasonry for a moment. We are both members of the national police force. Ms. Zewinski received her training in the army. Sure, she's from the elite forces, but she's still a military officer—disciplined but not particularly adept at subtlety and nuance. You're skilled in those areas. I think you'll be able to smooth the way for her."

Marcas didn't like Darsan's insinuations or his attitude but remained impassive.

Darsan smiled. "Perfect. We understand each other. You will keep me in the loop. Now let's get the others in here for a briefing." He picked up the phone. "Send them in."

Marcas turned to the door. Zewinski and a man he hadn't seen in months walked in—Anselme de Mareuil, special envoy from the Grand Orient Lodge.

Darsan began. "Let me introduce Mr. de Mareuil, the ministry's Freemason liaison. Mr. Mareuil, this is Special Agent Jade Zewinski, who's leading the investigation, and I believe you know Inspector Antoine Marcas, who's with the police."

There were nods all around, and everyone took a seat at Darsan's worktable. Darsan turned to Mareuil.

"So, Mr. Grand Envoy—is that what I'm supposed to call you?—can you explain what your employee was doing in Rome?"

Anselme de Mareuil's face was drawn. He looked at both men at the table before locking eyes with Jade. "Sophie Dawes worked in the Grand Orient's archives. She was on a research assignment and stopped in Rome to see her friend at the embassy, Ms. Zewinski."

"What was the nature of her research?" Darsan asked.

Marcas watched Mareuil size up Darsan. He knew that Darsan wasn't especially receptive to Masonic ideas.

"Just something related to Masonic history," Mareuil said. "Tell me, did anyone find the documents she was carrying? They are the property of the Grand Orient."

Marcas shot a look at Zewinski.

Darsan ignored the question. "Tell me more," he said.

Mareuil rubbed his face and began. "In June 1940, the Nazis pillaged French Freemason temples, particularly in Paris and seized tons of archives. Truckloads were sent to Berlin to be studied in detail. At the end of the war, the Soviets made off with the documents. Two years ago, we recovered the last of our archives, which had been in Moscow since 1945."

"Why were the Germans so interested in Masonic history?" Darsan asked, smoothing his moustache.

"First, they wanted to know the extent of Freemason influence. The Nazis thought Freemason and Jewish schemes were behind every bad turn of events. They wanted names and addresses. And they wanted information on so-called subversive activities."

Mareuil paused and looked at Darsan. "They had the same kind of paranoia about the Masons as you see today."

Darsan scowled. "We're not here to judge."

Mareuil continued. "Their second motivation was more esoteric. It was related to occult influences in Nazi ideology."

Zewinski cleared her throat. "I'm lost here."

"Do you know where Hitler got the idea to use the swastika as a symbol? From a racist secret society called the Thule Gesellschaft, which used it as its emblem," Mareuil said.

"The Thule what?"

"It was a sect that existed before Hitler joined the National Socialist Party, and it grew in power with the rise of the Nazis. The Thule originated in 1918 in Bavaria. It was started by a faux aristocrat named Rudolf von Sebottendorf. After World War I, the organization drew from the ranks of German intellectuals, industrialists, and

the army. Its members went through initiations, met secretly, and used special signs of recognition."

Zewinski sneered. "That sounds just like the Freemasons."

Mareuil ignored her. "The Thule wanted to build a pure
Germanic society devoid of Judaism and Christianity and
heir to the ancient kingdom of Thule. That was the mythical cradle of the Aryan race somewhere in the icy North. It
was said to have disappeared after a natural disaster."

"Something like the legend of Atlantis," Marcas
interjected.

"Yes, an Atlantis composed of fervent anti-Semites with
blond hair and blue eyes."

"That's grotesque," Darsan said.

"Yes. We all know what that led to. Many dignitaries
and influential people in Hitler's circle belonged to the
Thule, including Himmler, the head of the SS; Deputy
Führer Rudolf Hess; and Alfred Rosenberg, who was
the party's theoretician. In fact, Rosenberg was the man
who had our archives pillaged. He was after our esoteric
documents."

"I've heard that name before," Marcas said. "Wasn't he
condemned at the Nuremberg Trials?"

"Yes, sentenced to death and executed. He was a crank
who wanted to wipe out the three major Abrahamic faiths.
He was convinced that the Aryan race had the Tables of
the Law—the commandments given to Moses. This divine
revelation wasn't intended for Christians, Jews, or Muslims,
but instead for the Aryans and was meant to ensure their
supremacy over all other races and religions."

"I don't see the connection with freemasonry," Marcas
said.

"For the Thule, the stakes were high. They wanted to
reestablish Nordic paganism."

"So they were wackos," Zewinski said. "I don't see the
connection either."

"The Thule latched onto a long-standing fantasy about
Freemasons—that they were responsible for the French

Revolution. As far as the Thule was concerned, the Freemasons were the first to hack away at Christianity once it had become dominant in Europe."

Zewinski sat back and crossed her arms. "Still lost here."

"To make a long story short, they thought the Freemasons held some absolute secret."

"A secret?"

"Yes, and those fanatics believed it enough to pillage Masonic temples all over Europe. They took everything back to Germany to be studied."

Darsan stood up and walked to the window. "Okay. So what? The Nazis were dangerous madmen, and the craziest ones belonged to the Thule. What good does that do us? We have a murder to solve."

Marcas leaned forward. "So Dawes was working on the recovered archives?"

"Yes," Mareuil said, looking directly at Marcas.

Marcas knew there was more. He turned to Darsan, who had walked over to his desk.

"We have Sophie Dawes's documents," Darsan said. "If that's what the killer was after, she failed in her mission. To be honest, I read them. They're completely incomprehensible. We'll get them back to you when the investigation is over. You're lucky. Marcas is, well, one of yours."

Mareuil stood up. The others followed suit.

"Before you go," Darsan said, "Inspector Marcas, you noted that Ms. Dawes's murder had some Freemason implications."

"She was struck three times: on the shoulder blade, on the neck, and on the forehead," Marcas said.

"Hiram's death," Mareuil said in barely a whisper.

Darsan opened the door for them. "We got a report from our ambassador in Jerusalem. There was an unusual slaying in an archeological institute. The victim, a scholar, had been beaten. He had taken blows to the shoulder, neck, and forehead."

The blood drained from Mareuil's face.

"Didn't you say that Ms. Dawes was headed abroad?" Darsan asked.

"Israel was not on her itinerary," Mareuil said.

"It's a strange murder. But there's something that makes it even stranger," Darsan said. "The researcher in Jerusalem was killed the same night as Sophie Dawes. I wish you a good day, Mr. Mareuil. Marcas, Zewinski, keep me updated."

23

Once in the hallway, Marcas made plans to meet with Zewinski in the morning. Then he caught up with Mareuil.

"Anselme, it's been a while," he said. "What a surprise to see you here."

"Yes, it comes with my duties as special envoy," Mareuil said. They had known each other for years.

"Do your duties include withholding information?"

"What makes you ask that, Antoine?" Mareuil said as the two of them neared the front entrance. "It looks like you'll have your hands full with that woman partner of yours."

"Don't change the subject."

"I'm just saying. You never know. Maybe you could soften her up. She's a looker, and you need to get over that damned divorce."

Marcas glared at him. "Where was Dawes going? She was headed to Jerusalem, wasn't she?"

Mareuil stopped walking and turned to Marcas. He was silent for a moment and then cleared his throat. "Let's grab a bite to eat," he said. "I'll explain."

"I suggest we go to the Left Bank. I know a place."

They exited the building and started walking toward the Rue de l'Ancienne-Comédie. Marcas liked to frequent a Catalan restaurant there. From the outside, it looked like a bookstore.

"Good choice," Mareuil said shortly after they were seated at their table. Factoids on the history of Catalonia were printed on the paper tablecloth. "I've never been here before."

Marcas dispensed with pleasantries and got straight to the point. "So, Anselme, tell me what you know," he said.

"Do you come here often?" Mareuil asked, apparently in no hurry to answer. He opened the menu.

"Every so often. Excellent tapas. You should try the blood sausage too."

"Was your father Catalan?"

Marcas scowled. "No, but he lived in Barcelona a long time. Let's get down to business."

Mareuil, however, was still ignoring him. He was examining the wine display that filled an entire wall. "What kind of wine do they produce in Catalonia?" Without waiting for an answer, he changed the subject. "See Le Procope across the street?"

"I mostly see the line of tourists waiting to get in."

"Oh yes, Paris and its famous sites. Le Procope has been there since the eighteenth century. It was one of the first places in town where you could get coffee and hot chocolate—but not too much, because it was considered an *inflamer* at the time of Voltaire. That was another way of saying an aphrodisiac."

"Are we really going to spend our time here talking about beverages in the Age of Enlightenment?"

The waitress, a flat-chested woman with an angular face, walked over to their table. Marcas and Mareuil placed their orders, and Mareuil asked for a glass of tempranillo.

"She shouldn't pull her hair back like that," Mareuil said as she headed to the kitchen. "Her face isn't right for it." He sighed and took a blue folder out of his leather briefcase. He opened it to a yellowed typewritten page. "In the nineteen fifties, a historian wrote up a report about the documents that were stolen during the war. Here, take a look."

Marcas took the report and started reading.

Part of our archives, like those of the Grande Loge de France, remained in France in the hands of the Vichy government's Secret Societies Department. The majority of the documents, however, were sent by train to Berlin, where Nazi scholars picked through them. Political documents ended up with the

Gestapo, which used them to identify people who opposed fascism during the period between the two wars.

The documents of a more esoteric nature were shipped to a special institute called the Ahnenerbe, founded in 1935 by Heinrich Himmler to look for traces of Aryan influence around the world. The institute had considerable means and employed up to three hundred specialists—the elite of the Nazi scientific community, including archeologists, physicians, historians, and chemists.

Ahnenerbe's research was under the control of a secret society called the Thule, which had infiltrated the centers of Nazi power, including the upper echelons of the SS.

We have few documents on this dangerous sect, but we know that two members of the Thule were in charge of the Freemason archives. One of them, a certain Wolfram Sievers, general secretary of the Ahnenerbe and a dignitary in the Thule, was sentenced at Nuremberg. During his trial, one of our Freemason brothers, a captain in charge of interrogations, learned that Ahnenerbe researchers were on the verge of making a breakthrough that would be key to the future of the Aryan race, one that would be more important than the V-2 rockets. Our brother took down Sievers's statement but observed that he seemed to have lost his mind.

Marcas stopped reading and looked at Mareuil. "So what if Sievers seemed nuts? The Nazis were a bunch of crazies, as Zewinski would say."

"We know that economic, social, political, and cultural factors all contributed to the rise of Nazism. Hitler was probably not a puppet of the Thule, and he was entirely responsible for the regime's atrocities, but it is clear that there was a time in his life when the Thule influenced him. Read on. The key to Sophie's murder is perhaps connected to those archives."

Marcas shrugged and focused again on the dog-eared pages.

When the Germans sensed that the tide was turning after the defeat of Stalingrad in 1943, they took precautions. The

Masonic archives were split up and sent to several destinations—mostly castles and salt mines—where they could not be easily seized.

In April 1944, with Germany losing the war, SS high command intensified its operation to hide the stolen archives. Whole trains were commissioned to move tons of documents from place to place.

When the Soviets invaded Germany in 1945, Russian intelligence units tracked down everything that the Nazis had stolen. At the end of the war, more than forty train cars full of recovered documents were sent to Moscow. Ultimately, all the Masonic documents stolen from France ended up in the hands of Russian intelligence.

Our grand master has requested the return of those documents. The Soviet Union, however, claims that none of them are in their possession.

The text stopped there. Marcas looked up and gave the papers back to Mareuil. "Someone clearly thought the documents were important. What happened after that?"

"Nothing for forty years, until the fall of communism, when the issue surfaced again. The Russians admitted that they had our archives, and negotiations for the return of the documents got under way. We received the first batch in 1995, with the rest coming in installments through 2002. In theory, they have now gotten everything back to us."

"In theory?"

"That's where Sophie Dawes comes in."

Mareuil sipped his wine before continuing. "The documents were inventoried twice: once by the Germans and once by the Russians. It became clear that the Germans had listed more documents than the Russians. Some were missing."

"Are you saying that Moscow deliberately kept part of the collection?"

"That's what we thought at first, but then Sophie found this."

Mareuil pulled out an envelope. "It's a copy of an interrogation led by the French Army in April 1945 in a small

German village. A man named Le Guermand was arrested when he tried to return to France. He was an SS officer in the Charlemagne Division, a unit composed of French soldiers. They were defending Berlin at the end."

"You're giving me a history lesson here. What's the connection to the lost archives?"

"I'm getting there. A little before the Reich fell, Le Guermand and other SS officers were pulled off the front for a final assignment: to lead a convoy west, no matter what it took. Russian troops took down Le Guermand's truck a few miles from Berlin, but he managed to escape. A French patrol caught him a week later. He was delirious, going on about priceless documents on letterhead with a square and a compass."

"Why did he say all that?"

"He was facing a firing squad for treason. In exchange for his life, he offered to lead the investigators to the last truck, which was somewhere in the forest."

"So what did they find?"

"Nothing. Three French soldiers went off with Le Guermand. The next day, a patrol found four bodies in an abandoned barn."

"No more Le Guermand, no more papers. Is that what you're saying?"

"Not exactly. The Russians actually did find the truck. Sophie had been working on that part of the archives, but key documents were incomplete. She had them with her."

"And you're suggesting someone wants them enough to kill for them?"

"Not someone. The Thule."

Marcas listened as he sliced into his cod with honey sauce.

Mareuil continued, slipping a leather-bound notebook across the table. "They hated us as much as they coveted our knowledge, brother. Here's a diary kept by one of us—Henri Jouhanneau—in 1940 and 1941. He was a neurologist before he was deported. Read it sometime. It's edifying."

"Seriously, I'm having a hard time seeing the relationship between these stories and the murder. As remarkable as the archives are, they're just history, and the Nazis vanished sixty years ago, except for a small minority who are nostalgic for those days. So unless some old SS geezers have decided to leave the nursing home and take up arms again, I don't think this is much of a lead."

Mareuil sighed. "In 1993, the German police discovered an extensive network of extreme-right activists. They were exchanging plans for building bombs. They had the blueprints for Masonic lodges and Jewish synagogues. And some of them were bold enough to share their personal addresses. What were these people calling themselves? The Thule. And if you think they were just a bunch of retired Third Reich lovers and low-life skinheads, you're wrong. They were computer engineers right out of the university, along with highly successful stockbrokers and financial analysts."

"A few extremists. And we're not in Germany. It's a big step from that to a huge conspiracy against the Freemasons."

Mareuil set down his knife and fork and pulled another paper from his briefcase. He read the passage slowly. "What a shame the Führer did not have sufficient time to eradicate your brotherhood from the surface of the earth. Your members deserve to be burned at the stake as a public hygiene measure. Freemasons, the hour of your expiation is near, and this time, we will let none of you escape. Heil Hitler."

Mareuil paused. "That dates from last year. It's from an online message found on a number of anti-Freemason sites. I'm telling you, the three blows are a message."

"In that case, the murder in Jerusalem is connected. But how? What was Sophie going to do there?"

"I don't know," Mareuil said.

They sat in silence.

After a few seconds, Mareuil continued. "Did you know that Freemason scholars met at Le Procope before the French Revolution to discuss philosophy? The place is nothing more than a tourist trap these days, but here we are, you and I, just across the street, talking about similar issues two centuries later. That's what counts. People are dying. Be vigilant—and mindful of the chain that unites us over time and space."

"I find you very philosophical today," Marcas said, getting up.

"No coffee?"

"No, not now."

"I think I'll stay a little. I'd like to become more familiar with Catalonia," Mareuil said, winking at Marcas and giving the waitress a look.

Marcas headed toward the door.

"Antoine?"

"Yes?"

"Jade is a pretty name."

24

Joana groaned as she put down Jade Zewinski's file. Why was it that beauty was always a chief factor in a man's description of a woman? Zewinski's biography was exhaustive, and Orden's quick response was commendable. But the man who had put it together couldn't restrain himself. "An attractive, athletic body and a pleasant face," he had written.

Males could be such cavemen. When a man was describing another man, looks were never considered. A recent target—a Danish arms dealer—was on the verge of obesity, with a face as ugly as they came, and his file never mentioned either of those things. Unimportant details, apparently.

Sol had been very clear on the phone.

"Get the papers. If possible, don't harm the woman. We don't want to ruffle any feathers in the French government. But remember, those documents are the key to a new future for the Orden and for the pure race as a whole. If physical elimination is necessary, so be it. Do you understand?"

"I won't fail you again," she had answered.

Joana gazed at the waters of the bay outside the window. She respected Sol but didn't trust him. He was one of a handful of men behind the renewal of the Thule and a survivor of an earlier day. In a month and a half, the solstice would be celebrated in Hvar, and Sol had promised an unforgettable event. What exactly was he planning? And just how strong was his hold on the organization?

But for now, she needed to sleep. She would leave the castle at six in the morning, taking an Orden helicopter to Zagreb, where she would grab a flight to Paris. Her hotel room was already reserved. She thought about Zewinski and the fun it would be to take her on. Sophie's murder had been a formality, but Zewinski seemed tougher. She fell asleep right away, her mind and body emptied, dreaming of another prey.

HEKEL

The holy place
The middle chamber

~~~

"Why were you made a Mason?"
"For the sake of the Letter G."
"What does it signify?"
"Geometry."
"Why geometry?"
"Because it is the root and foundation of all Arts and Sciences."

—Masonic catechism, circa 1740

25

A soft wind caressed the leaves of the sycamore trees that had escaped Paris's gardeners and their pruning rage. Marcas recalled a childhood image of endless streets shaded by the light green of these familiar trees.

A sense of deep lethargy enveloped the neighborhood around the Marché Saint Pierre as the first rays of sunshine gave the sparse clouds above the capital a mauve tinge. Marcas observed the play of colors on the horizon and remembered a discussion with an American police officer—also a Freemason—whom he had met at an international conference. They had talked about the importance of the Orient, the East, in the Freemason initiation rite, when the worshipful master would say, "As the sun rises in the East to rule and govern the day, so rises the worshipful master in the Orient to rule and govern the lodge."

Marcas liked the allegories that gave precise and even exquisite meaning to events that many people rarely thought about—the sunrise, for example. Every day, light spread from the East, and in the lodge, meetings would begin with the illumination at the east side of the temple.

He experienced a few moments of serenity every time he watched the sun come up. There was nothing magical about the sunrise, but rather a kind of sacred geometry, a mathematical ballet related to the location of the observer, the angle of the sun, and the angle of the darkness. And then the clouds would come into play. It was a phenomenon that involved much more than the sense of sight. Poet Charles Baudelaire had put it this way: "Sound calls to fragrance, color calls to sound."

Alas, fragrances were not in harmony with the beauty of the sky on this morning. Marcas had to sidestep a steaming and smelly pile of dog excrement on the sidewalk. It was seven o'clock, when man's best friends took to the streets to empty their intestines under the watchful eyes of their masters. He had just passed a weasel-faced man dragging a grumpy-looking dog.

He turned onto the Rue André-del-Sarte. At the end of the street was the Rue Foyatier stairway to Montmartre, which was popular with tourists and filmmakers looking for an iconic Parisian venue. The steps ended at Sacré Coeur. A real postcard.

The square was empty, and only the Botak Café was open. The staff had already set out chairs that would be filled with tourists and regulars come eleven. He waved to the waitress and ordered his morning drug: strong hot chocolate—lots of cacao thinned with skim milk. Marcas liked coffee well enough, but he always started the day with hot chocolate.

He pulled out the diary and reread the passages that had caught his attention the previous night.

June 14, 1940
The Germans are parading triumphantly down the Champs-Elysées. Who would have thought it possible? Had lunch with Badcan at the Petit Richet. The atmosphere was dreary. A couple of men had drunk too much and shouted that France deserves this, that Jews and Freemasons will be brought in line. We didn't say anything. What good would it have done? I didn't have the strength to go to the hospital and visit the sick. There were speeches on the radio. We can only hope that Marshal Pétain will shield France from Hitler's hordes and those pulling the strings.

June 15, 1940
Worshipful Master Bertier came early this morning, around seven. He was angry and nearly frantic. The Germans showed up last night on the Rue Cadet and locked the entrance to the Grand Orient Lodge. Nobody can enter. Practically all of our archives are still inside. We didn't have

time to get them out. We've been struck dumb by this defeat. It's an unprecedented disaster for the order. Meanwhile, the Grande Loge de France was raided.

August 20, 1940
A ban on secret societies took effect five days ago, and now Marshal Pétain has closed all Freemason lodges. A long, dark night for Freemasons is beginning. Government officials must declare any Freemason allegiance.

October 30, 1940
My hospital privileges have been revoked. It was suggested that I take time off. A long time off. There's a rumor that some lodges are meeting in secret. The Germans have ordered all Jews to register or risk prosecution. Brothers in the police force are doing their best to alter the records, but most of their colleagues are quite zealous. I fear the subterfuge will soon be detected.

December 21, 1940
Darkness has invaded the world, but light is eternal. We have already put together a dozen meeting places to replace our lodges in and around Paris. What a relief! Had dinner with Michel Dumesnil de Grammont, who is part of the Masonic resistance called Patriam Recuperare. He introduced me to a brother who had a determined look in his eye. His name is Jean Moulin. We embraced before saying good-bye. The fight will be long and hard.

The Pétainists have instituted no fewer than three organizations to keep tabs on us and study what they've plundered. Bernard Fay, who runs the national library, heads up the regime's Secret Societies Department. He's an ardent monarchist, a salon scholar who has hated us for a long time. He even dared to set up his headquarters in our lodge on the Rue Cadet. He's busy working on the few archival documents that the Germans didn't take with them. Next, the Department of Banned Associations is run by a Paris police chief. He and his henchmen can search the offices and homes of brothers whenever they want. Finally, there is the Research Department, which reports directly to

Pétain's inner circle. Its primary focus is political activities. According to a number of well-informed brothers, the first two organizations are under tight German control. The Germans have also set up headquarters in the lodge on the Rue Cadet, but it is on a different floor.

March 21, 1941
Every time I tune the radio to the BBC, the light returns. Several brothers have gone to London to join Charles de Gaulle. They're doing a broadcast called "Les Français Parlent aux Français." The profane don't know that the first notes in Brother Beethoven's Fifth speak directly to us. They also don't know that Radio London is broadcasting the most symbolic passages from Brother Mozart's Masonic opera, *The Enchanted Flute*. The chain of unity is coming together again.

June 28, 1941
Pétain and his reactionary regime have started registering French Jews again, this time in the south. Apparently, they have to declare their assets.

August 11, 1941
The Germans keep gaining ground in Russia. They seem invincible. This morning I saw a poster with caricatures of the good French laboring away, hounded by Jews and Freemasons. The rhetoric is appalling and incredibly stupid from a scientific perspective. We know where their theories comes from. I remember meeting the propagators in Germany ten years ago. The Thule should be cursed forever for what it has done. Now that hardheaded ass Pétain has instituted a law prohibiting former Freemason dignitaries and officers from holding government jobs, just as he did with the Jews. And he has asked for the Aryanization of businesses. Aryanization? Have they actually taken a close look at their führer?

October 23, 1941
It's done. My name was published the day before yesterday in a collaborationist newspaper. "Professor Henri Jouhanneau,

worshipful master, Grand Orient." I feel like everyone has seen it, and now I'm considered a criminal. This morning our concierge said something about it in a very loud voice when she heard me coming down the stairs. She also insulted the Zylberstein couple on the fourth floor. Of course she tells everyone that she's "a full-blooded Aryan." I'm tolerant by nature, but now I'm feeling the poison so dear to our enemies—hatred.

October 25, 1941
Worshipful Master Poulain was found slain in his apartment—killed with three blows: one to the shoulder, one to the neck, and one to the forehead. A parody of Hiram's death. Poulain was one of our most erudite brothers. He was seventy-two years old and a threat to no one. It can only mean one thing. The Thule are here. They've always watched us, always hated us. Now they're killing us.

October 28, 1941
Three French police officers took me in for questioning early this morning. My son was crying, and my wife fainted when they hauled me off. She has to stay strong. They drove me to the Rue Cadet. How ironic. The temple, now a lair of evil operating under the guise of a vast administrative service directed by conscientious bureaucrats. After a three-hour wait, two Germans in civilian clothes questioned me about our order's archives. One of them, an officer who spoke perfect French, asked about my Freemason rank and my interest in esoteric research. He impressed me with his knowledge, and I realized he was a member of the Thule—our worst enemies.

He said he works for a German cultural institute called the Ahnenerbe, which studies ancient civilizations. They're recruiting researchers and scholars—non-Jews, of course— to work on the archives found in the occupied European countries. I told him I would be returning to my job at the hospital soon. He asked me about my research and said that Ahnenerbe has a medical research department. It's conducting experiments that will be very useful to humanity, he said.

My blood ran cold when he said he doesn't put the Jews and Freemasons in the same category. The former are another race. The latter have just made a perverted philosophical choice.

Then, to my great surprise, he let me go, telling me not to leave Paris.

October 30, 1941
I now know they're watching me around the clock. I haven't left the apartment for two days. I can't stay in touch with my brothers in the resistance, and I can no longer keep this diary. I'll drop it off with a trusted friend. I hope to get it back in less uncertain times. I'm afraid. What will become of my wife and son if they kidnap and kill me?

A familiar scraping sound brought Marcas back to the present. He turned to see a street cleaner in his green vest collecting the daily harvest of detritus left the previous night by hordes of tourists who invaded the neighborhood: soda cans, plastic bottles in every color, bright plastic wraps, and shattered liquor bottles. Marcas sighed.

Another ritual slaying—identical to Sophie's and that of the man in Jerusalem. Was it really the Thule's signature? What were they after?

He was finishing his second cup of chocolate when his phone buzzed. Zewinski.

"I'll meet you on the Place Beauvau, in front of the ministry," he said.

26

The Thalys train advanced slowly across the Dutch countryside, which looked dreary under the light drizzle. It could have been Belgium or northern France. The landscape would have been the same. Settled comfortably in a first-class compartment, he stared at the seemingly endless potato fields. How different from the arid Palestinian soil where his brothers struggled daily to extract a meager existence. It was nothing compared with the land the Jews had confiscated and transformed into fertile fields, thanks to American dollars. If only the Arab countries showed such solidarity with Palestine. His land would be an Eden.

Bashir turned his attention to the three men next to him, pale-skinned Hassidic Jews with light-brown side-locks. They were wearing black rekels and hats. If they only knew who he was. He beamed at them and chatted about the weather, using a slight Italian accent. The man sitting closest to him joked that he could pass for one of them if he had a yarmulke. Bashir said it would be a great honor and promised to visit their diamond shop in Anvers the next time he was there.

He had another two hours to kill before the train arrived at the Gare du Nord in Paris. Time for coffee, Bashir thought, getting up to stretch his legs. He grabbed the leather bag containing the Tebah Stone and headed toward the bar car, going down the aisle between the pairs of seats filled with commuting businessmen. A privileged group in dark, well-tailored suits, tablets and laptops on, financial newspapers folded next to them. So conformist, he thought with disgust. Life would be very boring without the adrenaline rushes he was used to.

In the next car over, a shiver ran up his spine. Something was not right. A tiny alarm was going off in his head.

He stepped into the bathroom to think. What fleeting information had triggered his defense mechanism? He ran his hands under cold water and splashed his face. He breathed deeply to empty his mind and bring his unconscious thoughts to the surface. He'd learned the technique from an old Syrian Sufi.

After a minute or so, a connection occurred in the complex circuit of his neurons. The blue-eyed man wearing a dove-gray shirt in the last row to the right. He'd seen him before, drinking a beer in a bar next to his hotel. Both times, the man had been deeply absorbed in a magazine. What was the likelihood of that man taking the same train? Bashir didn't like coincidences. It was a loathing that had saved his life on many occasions.

He didn't want to tip off the operative, so he kept heading in the direction of the bar car. The man was most likely Mossad or Shin Bet. Too blond to be a Jew, but Bashir knew Israeli intelligence recruited many fair-haired agents to track former Nazis in South America. He had probably picked up the tail at the Jordanian border.

Bashir would have to give the man the slip as soon as they reached France. His client wouldn't be happy that he had been followed. He waited a good fifteen minutes in the bar car and started returning to his seat. The man looked like he was sleeping—peaceful, his eyes closed, ear buds in place. Yes, but he did move his foot ever so slightly as Bashir passed, slowing to check his watch.

He settled back into his compartment with the three diamond merchants, who were busy talking in a mix of Dutch and Yiddish.

The Israeli operative wouldn't be working alone. Others would be waiting at the Gare du Nord. From there, it would be nearly impossible to lose them. His only alternative was getting off the train in Brussels and trying to give Blondie the slip. He'd find another way to Paris, but it would make him even later.

When the train entered the suburbs of the Belgian capital, Bashir reached for his briefcase and began to get up. Then the Jew to his right push a piece of paper toward him. On it, a single word was written in large black letters—three of them: SOL.

27

Marcas was standing on the stairs in front of the ministry when Zewinski drove up in a metallic green MG.

"Nice wheels, Zewinski," he said, getting into the car.

"Don't stain the seat leather."

"This is going to be fun," Marcas muttered under his breath.

Zewinski revved the engine. The GPS showed a traffic jam near the Saint Augustin neighborhood, so she headed toward the Champs-Elysées. They hadn't said another word to each other.

Finally, Zewinski spoke. "Let's bury the hatchet, Marcas. I want to find Sophie's murderer. At least talk to me while we drive. It looks like traffic is slow up there."

"What would you like me to talk about?"

"Brief me on freemasonry. Not to convert me, but to give me a general overview. Like what do you do at those meetings?"

Antoine burst out laughing. "That is impossible to explain. It's all in the ritual."

"Likely story."

"You know, it's not all that mysterious. We Masons tend to have inquiring minds. We ask questions and do research. Some of us try to find solutions for pressing problems. I know of lodges that focus on education and immigration. They're like think tanks. In other lodges, the brothers and sisters study symbolism. Just two weeks ago, I listened to a presentation on the color blue. It was fascinating."

Zewinski turned to him, her eyes full of ridicule.

"The color blue? Whatever. So why are you called the Freemasons, and not the free bakers? Or the free butchers?"

She downshifted abruptly, and the engine screeched. Marcas braced himself against the dashboard. Where to start? He couldn't possibly summarize the history of free-masonry in fifteen minutes.

"You need to go back to the year 1717, more specifically to the night of June 24, at an alehouse in the middle of London called the Goose and Gridiron Tavern. A small group of aristocrats, lawmen, and scholars founded the Grand Lodge of England. These men chose to adopt the vocabulary and philosophy of medieval construction guilds, because those artisans built the cathedrals, which symbol-ized the most advanced expression of divine representation found on earth. That's the origin of the analogy: build man as you would build a cathedral. Enlightened minds found the idea attractive at a time when obscurantism reigned in Christianity. And masons were also architects, experts in geometry, which had been a sacred science since the Egyptians."

"And were they already adept at keeping secrets back then?"

"Oh yes. Since the Middle Ages mason guilds had used signs of recognition and passwords, which the Freemasons then adopted. Secrecy protected the Masons from both political and religious powers, who looked at them unfa-vorably. Among the founders were members of the Royal Society, a strange group engaged in esoteric research, alchemy, and the kabbalah—all practices that smelled of brimstone to those in high places."

Zewinski pounded the horn at a German tour bus blocking the Avenue Franklin Roosevelt. "Damned tourist buses should be banned during rush hour."

When she let up on the horn, Marcas told her that FDR was a Freemason. The bus moved, and Zewinski smirked at Marcas. He chose to believe she was gloating over her conquest of the bus and not making fun of him. He continued.

"Four years later, in 1721, a minister named James Anderson wrote the *Constitutions of the Free-Masons*, which explored the roots of freemasonry and standardized the rituals and other practices of Freemasons in London and Westminster."

"Do go on. I get the feeling it just gets better."

"According to Anderson, freemasonry originated in Biblical times, when key figures were said to have perpetuated hidden teachings based on what was called geometry and accepted as a philosophy of enlightenment. The teachings came from Egypt, were used and advanced by Euclid, and were preserved by the Jewish people during the Exodus to the Promised Land led by Moses."

"What a tour!"

"Solomon had initiates to this science build his temple. The chief architect was Hiram Abiff, also known as Adoniram. He was the legendary founder of freemasonry. The Tower of Babel, the Hanging Gardens of Babylonia, and the dazzling genius of great scientists such as Pythagoras, Thales, and Archimedes, along with the Roman architect Marcus Vitruvius Pollio, are said to be linked to these Masonic teachings."

"Is there any historical proof that these great secrets really existed?" Jade asked in a voice that sounded nearly serious.

"No, Anderson's *Constitutions* was based on too much myth to be proved."

"Well, that makes it easy. I can invent my own story too. Look at me. I'm descended from Cleopatra. I'm the Queen of Sheba."

"True enough, and many lodges around the world have worked on finding proof. According to Anderson, the chain of transmission of this knowledge was almost broken twice. The first time was when the Germanic Goths and Vandals invaded the Roman Empire. The second was when the disciples of Mohammed spread across Europe. The Frankish statesman Charles Martel was the one who is said to have saved freemasonry from annihilation."

"Isn't he the dude who stopped the Saracens at Poitiers?"

"Yes. Unfortunately some nationalistic extremists have embraced him as a founding father. Anyway, freemasonry flourished in France, when the cathedrals were being built. And then it made its way to Scotland and England in an even more secretive form, which lasted until 1717, the year freemasonry was officially founded. And there you have it."

"You'll jot down some crib notes for me, right?"

The MG swerved between two vans, sped along for about fifty yards, and jerked to a stop at a red light. They were at the Rue de Washington intersection.

"I bet you didn't know that Washington, D.C., was designed by a Freemason," Marcas said.

"No, in fact I didn't," Zewinski responded.

Marcas was afraid she was going to hit the horn again. His head was beginning to throb from all the starting and stopping. On both sides of the avenue, the sidewalks were flooded with pedestrians. And on the street, the traffic extended all the way to the roundabout. A classic Parisian traffic jam.

Jade lit a cigarette, took a long drag, and spoke again, "So where does France come in? How did your club of English buddies contaminate our country? Oh, sorry, how did they bring their light to France?"

"The English were in the midst of a war that pitted the Catholic House of Stuart against the Protestant House of Hanover. King James II, a Catholic, was forced to flee to France. He took up residence in Saint-Germain-en-Laye, where his followers came to be known as Jacobites. The Jacobites founded the first French lodge in 1726 in Paris, in the back room of an English butcher shop on the Rue des Boucheries."

"So we could have called you the free butchers."

"How enlightened of you. The Grande Loge of France was officially created but soon became the subject of a power struggle between the Jacobites and the Hanoverians, who still had strong supporters in England. The Jacobites were nobles, very attached to their privileges and also very religious. The Jacobites even sought protection from the pope before disappearing for good when the House of Stuarts failed to win back the throne of England."

The MG moved forward about ten feet.

"If the Freemasons were aristocrats, how is it that they were responsible for the French Revolution?"

"That's another legend that won't die. Let's just say that during the first third of the eighteenth century, freemasonry was taking root in France. The duke of Antin was named the first French grand master in 1738, and the order became established throughout France, drawing the elite: nobles, musicians, merchants, army officers, and enlightened clergy. As lodges opened in the provinces, diverging movements arose, the same way diverging forces emerge in political parties."

"When was the Grand Orient founded?"

All this storytelling was diverting Marcas from his headache, which actually seemed to be going away. He beginning to enjoy himself. He liked talking about Freemason history, especially the tales from the seventeenth century, when the Age of Enlightenment was starting to take hold, and absolutism was wavering for the first time.

"During a conflict of influence, the federating Grande Loge de France disappeared just as quickly as it had appeared, and in 1773 the Grand Orient de France was founded in a second attempt to centralize French freemasonry."

"Fighting among the brothers is nothing new, then?"

"True enough. That's why the myth of the great Masonic conspiracy doesn't hold water. There's never been a supreme grand master or any kind of Masonic vatican that gave orders to all the lodges."

The car behind them was honking. Zewinski had missed the green light.

"But you really were behind the French Revolution, weren't you?"

Marcas decided to have a cigarette too. He lit one and continued. "Yes and no. At the time, only the well-to-do frequented the lodges, although there were some from the third estate: artists, writers, and the petite bourgeoisie. In 1789, France had nearly thirty thousand Freemasons, but they weren't revolutionaries thirsty for blood.

The MG finally arrived at the Place Charles-de-Gaulle.

"In the vote to put King Louis XVI to death, the Freemasons were divided, nearly half for and half against. Freemasonry never promoted any kind of extremism. But it's also true that Freemason lodges supported the ideals of an egalitarian society. Still, even if there were more Freemasons in the latter group than in the former, they never deserved the blame for the Reign of Terror, which the Church and the aristocracy promulgated. They needed a scapegoat, and the Masons fit the bill."

"You've got to be kidding. I thought Robespierre was a hoodwinker, but you'd prefer to boast about having the good guys, like Montesquieu, Mozart, and Voltaire, and kept quiet about the crazies who've been Freemasons."

"History is full of depraved individuals. Should the Catholic Church be forever condemned for the Spanish Inquisitor Tomas de Torquemada?"

"Yeah, yeah."

Jade put on her turn signal.

Marcas continued. "Did you know that the Place Charles-de-Gaulle was built to glorify Emperor Napoléon and is full of Masonic allusions?"

"No wonder driving around it is so chaotic, with cars coming from every which way. What a mess," Zewinski said. She was busy trying to keep an SUV from cutting her off.

"The Arc de Triomphe celebrates Empire victories and was built by a Freemason architect. Look at it closely, and you'll see key symbols. The bas-reliefs are plain as day to any initiate. And the avenues that lead away from the Arc de Triomphe bear the names of marshals who served during the Empire. Eighteen of the twenty-six were Freemasons."

"Are there lots of places like this?"

"Yes. Go take a look at the Vivienne and Colbert arcades, and you'll find bas-reliefs of beehives and other Freemason symbols."

Jade stepped on the gas to cut off a motorcyclist and turned onto the Avenue Hoche, which she took as far as the Parc Monceau.

"Oh, and there's the Parc Monceau. Take the south alley, and you'll find a small pyramid built by a brother right after—"

"Enough already! I get it. Class over. My head is going to explode."

Just when his was feeling good again.

They turned onto the Rue de Courcelles and then veered onto the Rue Daru, where Zewinski pulled up to a small gray parking garage. She pressed the entry button and headed down the ramp to four unoccupied spaces that were marked off with faded yellow paint.

"Follow me. We have work to do."

Marcas took his time getting out of the car. Out of principle. He didn't want her to get the idea that he was jumping to her orders.

"I have what it takes to motivate you, Inspector."

"Is that so? What is it?"

Zewinski didn't say anything for several seconds. As he took his time, she stepped into the elevator. He was still fifteen feet away when she pressed the button and threw out, "I thought you wanted to see the documents Sophie had with her. I've got a copy upstairs."

Marcas swore under his breath and ran to catch the elevator before the doors closed.

28

The elevator squeaked. The paint was peeling off the walls. The carpet in the hallway was threadbare, and the musty smell grew stronger the closer they got to the office.

Marcas understood the reason for the smell as soon as he entered the spacious room. It had obviously been used for storage, and even though much of the disparate collection had been pushed to the back of the room to make space for a few desks, insane odds and ends were all over the place: identity photos, disarticulated skulls, measuring instruments, and, on one of the walls, a poster with a caricature of the devil, its talons grasping the globe, with a single word: *Juden.* Worshipful master cords and a broken stone sculpture lay in a sagging armchair. Discarded on the floor were pasteboard suns and moons. Marcas had a queasy feeling as he closed the door. The room felt like a dank tomb.

Zewinski sat down in a chair behind one of the desks and slowly stretched out her legs, crossing them at the ankle. "Impressive, don't you think? Nothing has changed."

"I thought it had all been—"

"Destroyed? No, not at all."

"How disgusting."

"The Gestapo occupied this building, and the Ministry of Defense got it back when the war ended. It doesn't have any administrative function these days. It's used mainly by black ops. As for the junk, nobody ever did anything with it."

"That can't be."

"Yep, for the most part, these are relics from the infamous anti-Freemason exhibit held in the Petit Palais in 1940. I checked."

Marcas had to breathe deeply to control his anger. He was sure Darsan had assigned them this office space on purpose—a gratuitous jab.

"How could all of this still be around?" The exhibition was infamous. Every Mason knew about it. Posters at the entrance accused Freemasons of "ruining and pillaging the nation." Inside, there were brochures, fliers, more posters, items seized from Masonic lodges, and a number of propaganda films aimed at Masons and Jews.

"I heard that General de Gaulle needed some persuading to legalize Freemason societies again," Zewinski said. "Even today, you dudes aren't all that popular. The building has some cupboards filled with bad memories from other periods too. On the second floor, there's an electric dynamo from Algeria—you know, the kind used to torture people. And there's an ingenious bathtub invented by the French Gestapo in their Rue Lauriston headquarters. It has a tipping chair. It could be that some of your buddies got baths in that."

Marcas just looked around, feeling like a lost child. Zewinski's eyes softened.

"I'm sorry. I shouldn't have. That was obscene. Really, I find it unbearable too."

"Stop!"

Her eyes hardened as quickly as they had softened. "No, you listen! I'm fed up with this stupid war between us. I have a friend's murder to avenge."

"And I, a sister's," Marcas said.

"I know. I'm tired. I can't sleep. Sophie, she was—"

The pressure Zewinski had felt since Sophie's murder was finally causing cracks in her veneer.

"More than a friend?" Marcas suggested.

The blood drained from Zewinski's face.

"Don't ever talk to me about before—"

"Before what?"

Zewinski jumped to her feet. "We're not focused. You want the documents?"

She walked over to a shelf and grabbed a pile of papers. "Here they are. And please, stop looking at my legs. Every man I meet does that."

Zewinski brushed past Marcas and spread the photo-copies on the leather-topped desk. Marcas didn't say anything. He sat down at the desk, noticing that his heart was beating much faster. Was it because of what he was about to see, or was it something else?

There were fifty or so sheets filled with signatures, seals, and diagrams. They meant nothing to a profane, but were a treasure for him. And for someone else: Sophie's murderer.

Zewinski seemed to sense his excitement. "That's not all," she said. "Sophie wrote a commentary on these documents. I... Well, I didn't give these to my superiors. Here they are, for you."

She waved the papers in front of him so he'd take them.

"This is the last thing Sophie wrote."

They looked at each other for a moment, and then Zewinski said, "I'll leave you alone. I'm going to hit the gun range and blow off some steam."

Marcas watched her leave. He felt thrown off by so much complexity. She was as solid as a rock—as tough as jade. The name fit—and she had a hard, unrelenting job. Yet was sensitive to details like men looking at her legs. He shook himself. He'd been staring at them too.

"I'm sorry, I didn't mean to—"

Zewinski smiled, and for an instant she looked shy. She walked away, closing the door behind her. Marcas settled into his chair, hoping to mentally distance himself from the nightmarish ghosts in the room and focus on the papers in front of him.

29

The train was at a standstill, having arrived at the Brussels station. The three Jews were staring at Bashir, their eyes filled with condescension, as if he were some boy caught in the act. The compartment door was closed, the curtains drawn. He was alone among potential enemies. How had these three gotten their hands on his client's code name?

Bashir's mind was reeling. Had Sol sent them? If they were Israeli agents, then they knew about Sol. Would they take the stone and kill him? But why were they dressed as Orthodox Jews, who stood out like imams in a crowded marketplace?

The only certainty was that he was more vulnerable than he'd ever been. The stone brought bad luck.

The eldest spoke. "We're here to take care of your problems. So you'll obey us calmly and quietly. You'll stay here until we reach Paris. We'll keep you safe."

Bashir didn't like the man's tone.

"Who are you? Mossad? Shin Bet?"

The three men looked at each other and laughed. The eldest spoke again, sounding more affable this time. "Do we look like Jews, my friend?"

The Palestinian looked them up and down. These guys were crazy.

"Stop jerking me around. I asked you a question."

The youngest stopped chuckling and spoke up. "Enough. We had our fun, but we've got work to do. Hans, show him."

The man closest to the door of the compartment glanced into the aisle and turned to Bashir. He removed his hat and ran his hand through his hair, taking off a nearly invisible net with sidelocks attached. He used his other hand to pull off his beard. In less than a minute, he had morphed into a smooth-faced, ordinary-looking man, were it not for his piercing eyes.

Fake Jews. At least they weren't the enemy.

One of the three spoke up. "You see, my friend, there's no need to worry. Sol sent us. When you informed him that you would be late, he told us that you were in Amsterdam. We were assigned to your security."

"I don't need your help."

The youngest turned to the others and said, "The problem with Arabs is arrogance. In the end, they get screwed by everyone. It's no surprise the Jews have been crushing them for decades."

Then he turned to Bashir, making a fist.

"Listen to me. Two pros started tailing you in Amsterdam, and one of them is on this train. He's no friend of Palestine, I can tell you that. He's probably an Israeli agent. We'll take care of him. That's why we're wearing this shit disguise."

The man sitting next to Bashir added, "Fifteen minutes before we arrive in Paris, we'll get rid of him, and you'll continue on to your meeting."

"Will I be seeing you in Paris?"

Hans was conscientiously putting his beard and sidelocks back on. "No, our assignment stops here. We'll take the next train out—in getups that are more civilized."

The two others laughed again. Hans interrupted. "Now let's play some cards to find out which of us is going to bump off the real Jew and help our oppressed Arab friend. We've got a good ninety minutes before we get there."

Bashir felt the artery in his temple pulsing. Here he was, stuck in a train compartment with three fanatical racists. He was crazy with rage over the way they uttered the words "Jew" and "Arab." Bashir was someone who made his enemies tremble, who had killed men the world over. Now he was obliged to put up with these pigs. Once he got paid for this gig, he'd avenge his humiliation.

What bothered him the most was that they had played him. And even though he had spotted the agent in the other car, he hadn't picked up the slightest scent of the team following him in Amsterdam. His senses were dulling, and he had committed unforgivable errors.

His three helpmates seemed to have completely forgotten him as they slapped down their cards and exclaimed in Dutch.

30

Missed. Zewinski lined up her Glock, planted her feet, and distributed her weight. She held her breath and pulled the trigger. The bullet shot out of the barrel at more than sixty miles an hour, piercing the bicep of the human form on the paper target. Missed. She had targeted the elbow.

Her time was up. What a crappy session. She'd hit twelve out of twenty. She was getting sloppy. She kept seeing Sophie's smashed face. And worse, she didn't believe for a minute that they would find her friend's murderer. How could they identify a killer in Rome when they were in Paris? Jade set her weapon and ear muffs on the small counter to her right and signaled to the shooting-range manager that she was finished.

On her way out, she saw a former lover, a special ops commander.

"Jade? How are you?"

"Fine. Just back from Rome, and you?"

"Shh, state secret."

"You can cut the act. I know what happened in the Ivory Coast last year. I heard you were there. It wouldn't have been you who took out those two Sukhoi planes at the Abidjan airport?"

"I don't know what you're talking about."

"Come on, right before the Ivorians bombed one of our bases, killing nine French soldiers."

"Really?"

"Too bad for you. I could have told you who took out the two Belarusians who piloted the planes. It happened in a Budapest whorehouse."

"You can't get me to talk."

"Go to hell. But give me a call if you're in Paris for a while."

"Promise. Later."

Jade watched him walk off. She missed special ops, and the more she thought about it, the more she wondered if making the switch to security had been the right decision. It had seemed like a good idea, but now she was back in Paris and couldn't get her bearings. Too many years on the road, running from her past. Her sinister offices made her stir-crazy, and her apartment felt too small.

And then there was Marcas. Every time she saw him, she wanted to slap him, just for fun. He acted so superior, and his sententious Freemason history lessons were seriously getting on her nerves. She had pulled up his file—and was sure he'd pulled up hers. He was divorced, lived alone, and appeared to be interested in only his job and Freemason history, although she did note that he wasn't averse to an occasional one-nighter.

Definitely not her type. He was pleasant enough to look at, but not boy candy. He seemed so steadfast, in a soothing kind of way. But he was a damned Freemason. Her first reaction was to run.

He brought back memories of that horrible day, seventeen years earlier.

She had skipped school to stay home and listen to the new Cure album. Her mother was a doctor and was away on a weeklong conference. Her father, a chemical-products trader who ran his own business, left early every morning.

The day had started off beautifully. Sunlight was filtering through the trees in the heavily wooded yard. She opened the door of the large, silent house to let some air in and started heading up to her room. She stopped when she heard a noise in her parents' room at the end of the hallway. She was paralyzed. She had assumed that her father was gone, but what if he was running late and was still in the house? She would be in huge trouble if he found her. He would ground her, and she'd miss that weekend trip to Normandy with her friends.

But what if it wasn't her dad? Maybe it was thieves. She panicked, ran into her room, and hid under her bed. She heard someone walking in the hallway, past her bedroom and down the stairs, toward her father's office. One person. She crept farther under the bed and tried to make herself tiny. She heard the steps again. It was her father. She was sure from the way he was walking. But then again, maybe not. She hoped he would leave soon. Things hadn't been going so well for him. Some people had come twice to take things away, and she had overheard her parents talking about closing the business.

Jade waited twenty minutes. Then a shot broke the silence. She slid out from under her bed, rushed down the stairs, and opened the office door.

Paul Zewinski lay in his old leather chair, his head to one side, his eyes wide open, blood pooling on the floor. She screamed and ran out of the house. She ran and ran until she collapsed. If only she had forced herself to crawl out from under the bed instead of hiding. If only she hadn't been so afraid. She could have saved him.

The family attorney had explained that a competitor had conspired against the family, and the court had liquidated the business to pay off its debts. The attorney added that the two people behind all of this were Freemasons. At the time, Jade didn't know who Freemasons were, but the word sounded like an insult. As far as she was concerned, her own cowardice had played as much a role in her father's suicide as the Freemasons. She dealt with her lack of courage by choosing a high-risk profession. But she still needed to take care of the Freemasons. She had a score to settle.

31

Sophie Dawes had been an excellent archivist. Each document was identified, numbered, and described in detail.

Her analysis was systematic and thorough. She had followed every lead and had run all her theories through to the finish. She was clearly passionate about the subject.

In any case, he understood why these documents had intrigued her. The first papers were ordinary: archives dating from 1801 and 1802 that had belonged to a lodge in the provinces, near Châteauroux. There were presentations, architectural plans, and internal letters, all by the same person: Alphonse du Breuil, the worshipful master of the very respectable Les Amis Retrouvés de la Parfaite Union lodge.

Sophie Dawes had done a comparative study of the lodge's name without finding anything unusual. From the beginning of the empire, lodges were founded with names related to the virtues of fraternal friendship. It was a way to move past the rifts of the revolution and celebrate a new era.

Worshipful Master Alphonse du Breuil was an archetypal Freemason of his times. He had been initiated before the revolution and in 1793 had joined the army of the French Republic. He participated in the Italian campaign in 1796 and was promoted to lieutenant after being wounded in the leg. In 1799, he took part in the Egyptian expedition as a military attaché with Napoleon Bonaparte's scientific corps. He reappeared in France at the end of 1800, having left the army as a captain. He purchased land in the Brenne region in central France and declared his support for the new constitution and the first consul, Napoleon Bonaparte.

When the Napoleonic Empire was established four years later, he sought to establish a lodge and requested approval from the Grand Orient of France, the only official Masonic authority in the country.

Marcas could see that this was where things had gotten complicated for Sophie. She had transcribed all the letters between Alphonse de Breuil and the heads of the Grand Orient de France, who were responsible for verifying every lodge. It was clear that neither side was listening to the other.

Breuil wanted to use his own rituals and create his own temple on his land in a hamlet called Plaincourault. That sounded reasonable enough, but the blueprints for the temple had shocked the Grand Orient. Breuil wanted a temple shaped like a screw—at least that was what came to Marcas's mind when he saw the drawing.

When the Grand Orient expressed its doubts, Breuil asserted that the temple was inspired by religious buildings he had seen in Egypt. Sophie had added "incoherent" in the margin.

Breuil mentioned the design in only one other letter, where he specified that the center of the temple, where there was usually a mosaic, would have "a pit with a bush and exposed roots." This pit was a key symbol, he said, because it was only in the birth of life underground that the seven heavens could be attained.

According to Sophie's research, there were no other traces of the ritual envisioned by Breuil, even though it evidently existed, because several letters from the Grand Orient mentioned the rite. In one letter, an official expressed surprise at the importance Breuil gave to the traditional bitter drink initiates were required to consume as a symbol of the difficulty of following the true Masonic path.

For Breuil, the bitter drink was a crucial element of the Masonic mystery. "The cup represents the door opening to real life. It is the path. Our rituals have strayed. We are mimicking initiation and not experiencing it in its fullness. The journey a neophyte takes is nothing more than a pale reflection of the true initiation that opens the gates of horn and ivory."

The gates of horn and ivory. Yes, Marcas remembered them well from Homer and Virgil. Both gates supposedly leading to the beyond. But he didn't know if they opened to paradise or hell.

Marcas put the pages down. He was imagining the faces of the non-Mason Soviets translating these documents. A decadent bourgeois delirium tainted with reactionary mysticism. No doubt, they had wondered why the members of this secret sect had wasted their time with such religious playacting.

He jumped when Zewinski came back in the room.

"So?"

"Your friend did a thorough analysis. But it looks like it was in vain."

"Why do you say that?" She looked disappointed.

Marcas glanced at the photocopies. "These are just wild esoteric imaginings. Nothing of real interest. A brother with a dream of renewing freemasonry. There have been many just like him. It's our messianic side."

"I don't understand."

"The papers are from an officer during the empire. He'd been to Egypt with Bonaparte, and he wanted to establish his own lodge with a new Egyptian-inspired ritual."

"What's that got to do with freemasonry?"

"Nothing, I'm sure. At the time, there was an Egyptian craze that extended to all sectors of French culture, including freemasonry. Dozens of Masons created Egyptian rites: the Sophisiens, the Rite Oriental, the Friends of the Desert, and many others."

"So did it all disappear?"

"No, there's an Egyptian freemasonry even today. The Memphis-Misraim still uses the initiation rites. But at the beginning of the empire, it was trendy. I really don't think your friend died because of these papers. There's nothing in them."

32

The train was crossing the fields north of Paris. The three men set down their cards and got up, as if someone had given a silent order.

The one who had won the game removed a large signet ring from a black pouch. It had a silver band and a fine diamond mount. Then he removed a white flask with a pipette from the pouch. He applied a small drop of the white substance to the diamond and slipped the ring on his finger.

The three men opened the compartment door and stepped into the aisle without even glancing at Bashir, as if he didn't exist.

Just before they went off, the eldest turned to him.

"When we pull into the station, take your time getting off. You don't want to miss the show."

The men left, leaving Bashir alone with his dark thoughts.

The train arrived at 11:35 a.m. at the Gare du Nord. Bashir got off ten minutes later, just in time to see two paramedics rushing along the platform with a gurney. Bashir spotted Blondie convulsing wildly inside the train. He was foaming at the mouth and shouting incomprehensibly while throwing himself at the window. Other travelers were huddled around him, gawking.

With bloodshot eyes, the man stared wildly at Bashir, who instinctively stepped back. The man was now hitting his head against the glass, a dark stream of blood flowing down his face. The bystanders outside the train groaned in shock and disgust. The train attendant pulled down the shade.

Bashir moved away, wondering what kind of delayed-reaction poison the killers had used. He shivered at the thought that he might be targeted once his assignment was completed. He'd been made and was now a potential threat. In Palestine, he could have found a safe house immediately, but Paris was hostile territory. He didn't have any contacts.

At the end of the platform, Bashir took the first escalator to the luggage counter. A guard inspected his bags before Bashir chose a locker. He would take the stone and leave the papers—an insurance policy if his client decided to bump him off after he delivered the artifact. He memorized the locker number and headed to the metro, scanning the environs to make sure he wasn't being followed.

For the first time in a very long while, Bashir felt the same sensation he had inflicted so often on his own victims: fear.

33

Jade hesitated. "That's not what she told me when I saw her in Rome," she said after a few seconds.

"What did she say?"

"Something about some Breuil dude. That he'd found a secret. It was in the papers."

Zewinski examined the documents again, looking lost. "That's all? I really thought something was going to click, that you'd find some secret formula that only a Freemason could decipher. And you're sure the crazy old geezer was nobody special?"

"No, a bourgeois who got rich on the revolution. He bought some land in—"

Marcas shuffled through the papers, his hands coming dangerously close to Zewinski's.

"...in Plaincourault, near the city of Châteauroux."

Jade pulled away.

"You're joking."

"About what?"

"That name."

Zewinski was breathing quickly.

"When I put the papers in the embassy safe, Sophie asked if we could change the code just for the night. I teased her about being paranoid, but she seemed really worried, so I said we could. She chose a word."

"Don't tell me..."

"Yep, it was the name of that village. The access code needed to have fifteen letters."

Marcas frowned. Something wasn't right. He picked up Breuil's papers again and counted each letter. He shook his head.

"There's a mistake. Plaincourault has thirteen letters."

"When Sophie put in the code, she spelled it P-L-A-I-N-T-C-O-U-R-R-A-U-L-T. She added two letters: a T and an R. She said that was the original spelling."

"What original spelling?"

"The one used by the knights of the Order of the Temple. The Templars."

Marcas let out a chuckle. "Peekaboo, there they are again. It's been a while," he said.

"What do you mean?"

"Someone always goes and brings in the Order of the Temple. It's bull if you ask me. We're back to square one. We've got two identical murders: one in Rome and one in Jerusalem. Sophie was on her way to see someone in Jerusalem, presumably the dead man. Someone—or a group of people—wanted something from them. And it's very possible that whoever it was has it in for the Freemasons. In other words, exactly what we knew before. In any case, the papers are clearly incomplete. What was she going to do in Jerusalem?"

"When I asked, she was cagey and got even more nervous. She said she'd been working with someone there."

"Did she say anything else?"

"Not really. Come on, she was stressed and paranoid. I didn't give it much thought."

"Try to remember. What exactly did she say?"

"She'd gone on and on about the secret, which had been guarded for thousands of years. I told her to take a vacation, that the occult Mason stargazing was affecting her reason."

Marcas nodded and looked back at the papers.

"Is something wrong?" Zewinski said.

"It's this manuscript."

"What about it?"

"Look here: 'Only the shadow ritual will lead to the light.'"

Marcas was quiet for a moment. "I don't like that expression: the shadow ritual," he finally said. "It sounds dodgy."

34

The hotel lobby was buzzing. A pack of photographers was milling around, and three security guards were at the entry. Bashir grumbled as he elbowed his way through the crowd.

"Contact Tuzet at the Plaza Athénée. Ask for the keys to his Daimler." Sol's message had been enigmatic, to say the least. Bashir headed toward the reception desk. At the entrance to the bar, he saw a sign announcing that P.F. Tuzet was the day's entertainment. Tuzet was apparently a French crooner who rehashed fifties ballads by the likes of Frank Sinatra and Dean Martin. A singer as a contact? Why not?

He asked for the performer. The gracious blonde hostess smiled and nodded in the direction of a man standing at the bar, next to a beautiful woman of color. She was wearing a form-fitting black satin dress, and her hair was pulled back in a bun. Bashir headed toward the crooner, eager to dump the stone and disappear.

A flute of Champagne in her hand, the woman was singing.

Gone my lover's dream
Lovely summer's dream
Gone and left me here
To weep my tears into the stream

Stroking the woman's arm, Tuzet joined in. "Willow weep for me." It was a classic that had been recorded many times over. His eyes shining, Tuzet took another sip of bourbon. What a showoff, Bashir thought.

"Sorry to interrupt your cooing, Mr. Tuzet, but we need to talk."

The singer shot him a disdainful look.

"Boy, I'm not finished with my beauty here. Call me in ten years," he said, turning back to the woman. "People are so rude today."

Bashir cut him off, his tone threatening. "The keys to your Daimler, Tuzet."

The crooner's expression changed. He grinned. "You should have said so sooner. Don't get huffy. Excuse me, my dear. I'll be right back."

Still smiling, the singer led Bashir out of the bar to a secluded spot near the elevators. He let a couple of people pass and grabbed Bashir's arm. He dropped the smile.

"Dammit. You were supposed to arrive yesterday. I hung out all evening after my gig."

Bashir pulled his arm away. "I don't have to explain myself," he said. "Here's the package. My job is done."

Bashir reached for the stone, but the singer stopped him.

"No, not here. Take the keys to my Daimler. It's parked in the garage, near the service elevator. Put the package in the trunk, and leave the keys at the reception desk."

An alarm went off in Bashir's head. He didn't like the arrangement. Parking lots were perfect for bumping someone off. He'd done it himself once or twice. The mistake in Amsterdam was one too many. There would be no faux pas in Paris.

"Sorry, buddy, but I'm not going into your garage. Take the package, and don't keep your fans waiting."

"I can't. My orders were very clear."

"I don't give a shit about your orders. I did my job."

With that, Bashir handed him the bag containing the Tebah Stone as if he were handing off a bag of garbage. He turned around and focused on vanishing.

He was sure Sol had other employees in the hotel. Three in Amsterdam, so there would be at least as many in Paris. He had no illusions. He knew that having been followed made him an unacceptable risk to Sol. Bashir would have done the same in his place.

He scanned the lobby. A man with the square shoulders of a wrestler was approaching him, looking hostile. Another man in a gray suit who had been standing near the entrance was walking toward him, as well, making eye contact with the other man. It was a trap.

All of the sudden, shouts and cries rose up from the crowd in front of the hotel. Photographers dashed toward the doors, pushing everything and everyone out of their way.

Amid the excitement, a flashy Italian actress appeared, followed by two bodyguards and three assistants, a cell phone glued to her ear. The hit man in the gray suit was caught by surprise and shoved aside by one of the star's bodyguards. Bashir rushed to the entrance, knocked down a fan, and spilled out the door.

He had gotten past the security guards but now faced a pack of screaming fans taking pictures with their cell phones. A human wall. He looked back. The two goons were still inside, trying to get out.

He took a deep breath and rushed the crowd like a bull charging into an arena. He punched a teenager in the stomach. The boy howled and crumpled over. Bashir elbowed left and right, stepping on toes and kicking shins. The cries of pain were lost in the overall hysteria. In fewer than twenty seconds, he had made his way through the crowd. But the game was not over. The others would follow his lead.

He ran across the Avenue Montaigne and flattened himself inside a porte cochère between two streetlamps. They had just made it onto the street. They didn't seem to see him. He heaved a sigh. Ten more seconds, and he would have been dead meat. He'd just wait for them to give up, and then he'd vanish.

Suddenly a voice rang out of the intercom just five inches from his head. "Sir, are you a resident or a visitor?"

Bashir jumped, glanced around, and spotted a camera above the door. An infrared detector had signaled the security guard.

The voice deepened. "You cannot loiter in front of this doorway. You must leave, or I'll call the police."

"I'm just waiting for some friends."

"Wait for them on the sidewalk. This is private property. This is your last warning."

Across the street, he saw one of his assailants pointing in his direction. It was too late.

35

Marcas had left Zewinski at the black-ops offices and was heading toward the Grand Orient headquarters on the Rue Cadet. He wanted to look into the shadow ritual. He had called ahead to tell the worshipful master that he would be coming, and the man met him at the entrance.

"Tell me, Antoine, I hear you're in charge of investigating the murder of our sister in Rome."

This was the first time the worshipful master had broached the subject of his police work, and Marcas was surprised that the man knew exactly what he was doing.

"You have eyes and ears everywhere, don't you?" Marcas said.

The master smiled. He'd headed up the judiciary brotherhood for ten years.

"I also heard a rumor about you answering to a tough-as-nails security chief who's not too crazy about you. And the interior minister has assigned Darsan to follow the case. He's not really a friend of ours either."

"What do you mean?"

"He's got a reputation as a hard ass. I think he's a bit of an anarchist."

Marcas's laugh echoed in the hall.

"Reactionary or anarchist? You've got to be kidding."

"Between the two of them—Darsan and that special agent—you've got your work cut out. Later on, I'll introduce you to one of our brothers. He's pretty high up—"

"Just how high?"

"He's the official grand archivist of our jurisdiction, Marc Jouhanneau."

"Jouhanneau, you say?"

"You know how it works. Put on your best brotherly smile, and listen attentively. He'll be here later. In the meantime, the archive conservator is waiting for you."

A few minutes later, Marcas was standing in front of hundreds of boxes on gray metal shelves in a large room on the seventh floor of the Grand Orient headquarters. Each box had a large label in black Cyrillic script. The seals on most of boxes had been broken. They had traveled from Paris to Berlin, to Moscow, and then back to Paris—an incredible journey of found memories.

Marcas returned to the doorway, where the conservator—a man in his forties, his beard speckled with white—was standing.

"It's moving to see these archives when you know their history," Marcas said. "How long will you need to go through all this information?"

"Years, probably. Fortunately, the Russians made it easier by doing an exhaustive inventory. Starting in 1953, Russian government workers studied our documents page by page, probably without understanding their scope. Perhaps they only translated the work done by the Germans.

"What were they looking for?"

"They were looking for political documents and trying to understand how lodges were organized. They might have suspected that we had our own spy network. The communists didn't like us much."

Marcas nodded. "It's not easy being a Mason. Between the Nazis and fascists, the communists, the reactionary Catholics, the monarchists, and all nature of nationalists, it's a wonder that we've managed to survive."

"Yes, it is hard to please everyone."

That was an understatement, Marcas thought. "Or anyone, for that matter," he said.

The archivist continued. "These documents have little political value. They're mostly of historical interest. And in that respect, some of the papers are priceless. Look at this."

The conservator handed Marcas a yellowed piece of paper covered in fine, old-style writing.

List of New Officers, Loge des IX Soeurs.
From the 20th day of the 3rd month of the year 1779.
Worshipful Master—Dr. Franklin

Marcas's eyes widened. "That's Benjamin Franklin's lodge. Remarkable."

The conservator smiled. "Makes you think, doesn't it. But what can I do for you?"

Marcas began by asking about any suspicious deaths similar to Hiram's murder. The conservator scratched his beard.

"You should look at the book that inventories the Russian boxes. If you find what you're looking for, give me a call, I'm in the office down the hall.

Marcas sat down and opened the binder. The inventory was a real hodgepodge, with lodge receipts from 1930, presentations from 1925, and meeting minutes from 1799. He patiently went down the list. His eyes were stinging a half hour later, and his legs had fallen asleep. That was when he found an odd listing: Dissertation by Brother André Baricof, from the Grenelle Étoilée Lodge, about Freemasons persecuted throughout history. Dated 1938. Series 122, section 12789.

Ten minutes later, Antoine had a large box in front of him. He broke the string that secured the box and took off the musty cover. Inside, he found folders containing manuscripts and tables filled with numbers. He went through them one by one until he found what he was looking for.

He took out the Baricof file and set the box on the floor next to the desk. The file was a dozen pages long. The man, a newspaper journalist, had drawn up a morbid list of Freemasons who had experienced violent deaths. Marcas went through it quickly. On page four, his heart skipped a beat.

There's been considerable concern among our eldest brothers regarding murders identical to Hiram's slaying. The first ones are said to have taken place in the eighteenth century in the Westphalia region of Germany. Twelve German brothers from the same lodge were found dead in a clearing. They bore stigmata corresponding with Hiram's death: dislocated shoulders, broken necks, and crushed skulls. Police investigators linked the slayings to a worrisome secret organization led by the Saint Vehme, which was composed of judges and army officers and dedicated to punishing enemies of Christianity. The authorities, however, never made any arrests.

I found similar murders, also in Germany, right after World War I. The first ones took place in Munich after the failure of the Spartakiste revolution, when communist extremists tried to take power in Bavaria. The Oberland, a right-wing militia led by a racist brotherhood called the Thule, retaliated. Several Freemasons were among the hundreds of people executed. The brothers were slain in accordance with the same ritual. There is evidence of another murder, in Berlin this time: a worshipful master of the Goethe Lodge who was left to die on a sidewalk with the same blows to his body. It would be interesting to know if the Nazis continued these practices, but since lodges have been banned, and detention camps have opened up, we don't have any more contact with brothers over there.

The text went on to explore the tense relationship with fascist regimes. Marcas was adding to the notes he had started in Rome. There was no longer any room for doubt. It had all started in Germany and had continued over the course of centuries. The rite was a bloody parody of the death of the most respected Freemason, Hiram.

36

Bashir sprinted past the boutiques on the Avenue Montaigne, heading toward the Champs-Elysées. Famous names—Cerruti, Chanel, Prada—flashed before his eyes. He shoved aside a group of young women. The Rond-Point Marcel-Dassault was about three hundred yards away.

The two goons were closing in on him.

Bashir dashed to the other side of the avenue as the light turned red, leaving the two men stuck on the other side of traffic. This gave him time to reach the restaurant l'Avenue, a hot spot for models, actresses, and TV personalities. At the corner he veered onto the Rue François-Ier and then onto the Rue de Marignan, which led to the Champs-Elysées. He hoped to catch a cab there, but he realized that traffic was at a standstill.

The men were closing in again. A very long minute later, he reached the wide central avenue. The sidewalk was filled with tourists. A light turned green, and engines revved, warning pedestrians to get out of the way. The vehicles started moving toward the Place de la Concorde.

Bashir had to get across the boulevard. The Champs-Elysées was much wider than the Avenue Montaigne—three lanes of cars moving in each direction. The risk of getting hit was three times higher. Bashir took a breath and dashed to the central island halfway to the other side.

A motorcyclist slammed his brakes just inches from his feet. A bus came to an abrupt stop, and a concert of honking broke out, but he arrived safely at the thin strip of concrete in the middle of traffic. It was mobbed by tourists clicking photos of the Arc de Triomphe. Bashir looked behind him. The two men were standing exactly where he had been thirty seconds earlier, blocked by moving cars.

One was smirking at him. The other was waving like a long-lost friend.

Bashir glanced the other way, at the brightly lit signs and movie posters promising thrills and adventure. He had already bought the ticket—he was running for his life. Green turned to orange. It was time. Bashir threw himself in front of the moving cars. A gray convertible banged his knee. Pain shot through his leg, but he kept running.

A scooter swerved to avoid him and skidded, crashing into a double-parked delivery truck. The honking intensified, but he reached the sidewalk.

Bashir slalomed between passersby and ran up the Rue du Colisée at full speed. Sol's men were about fifty yards behind and gaining. His pulse accelerated. His legs were burning, as if his blood were spitting acid into his muscles. He turned onto the Rue de Ponthieu and focused on his environment. An entrance to a parking garage was ten yards ahead. He looked back just as he slipped into it. He didn't see the goons.

He moved deeper into the shadows, caught his breath, and pulled an old paper napkin from his pocket to wipe the sweat off his face. He waited a good twenty minutes, savoring his freedom. Once again, he'd escaped death.

Bashir considered his options. Grab a cab to the Gare du Nord and pick up his bag? Too dangerous. Someone could have seen him leave his luggage behind. A hotel room for the night? That didn't feel safe either.

He decided on an alternative. He'd catch a train to another city. Too bad for his bag. He'd pick it up another time.

Allah was great and generous with his servants.

Bashir was eying a convertible parked nearby when unbearable pain blazed in his head.

He crumpled to the ground. He turned his head and could make out a blurry face leaning toward him.

"You really thought you could escape us?" the man asked.

Was that the Tebah Stone in his hand? Bashir's world turned black.

37

As soon as Marcas was gone, Jade called her friend Christine de Nief and invited her to a late lunch. Jade wanted to know more about the Templars but refused to ask the cop, who would have been all too happy to show off his knowledge. She had typed "Templars" into a search engine and pulled up twelve thousand pages—enough to scare anyone off. The few pages that she did read didn't encourage her to read more. They were stories of buried treasures, secrets lost since the time of Jesus, doomsday conspiracies, and secret societies of all types, including the Freemasons. Unable to separate what was believable from the rubbish, Jade gave up. Christine, however, could help her. She was a historian who worked as a television and radio consultant.

Jade arrived at the trendy Porte d'Auteuil restaurant, which was full of well-off young people. Christine had chosen it. She loved to be seen.

Jade left the keys to the MG with the valet and stepped into the crowded restaurant. She spotted Christine deep in conversation with a dark-haired man at the next table. Jade had seen that face somewhere. Christine looked up, saw Jade, and abandoned her neighbor. She waved her over.

"Darling, what a pleasure to see you. What have you been up to?"

"Shooting this morning. It was divine."

They looked at each other and laughed.

"Same old you, just the way I love you," Christine said.

Jade leaned in and whispered, "Who is that handsome man next to you? I've seen him before, haven't I?"

Christine looked serious. "You didn't recognize Olivier Leandri, the news anchor on the rise? Well, you do spend most of your time in Rome these days. Olivier and I had a thing awhile ago. I'll introduce you if you'd like. He's charming."

Jade smiled. "No, not interested at the moment. I'm working on a case."

"Darling, you're always working. At some point you've got to make time for a man—someone not so high-risk. You should try brains over brawn for a change."

"I appreciate your concern, Christine, but you and I both know that I'm not a nun. I've had my share of lovers, thank you. Maybe I'll ask you to introduce me to one of your hot celebrity friends someday. But, as I said, I've got a case to solve, and I hope you can help me. Tell me about the Knights Templar."

Her friend looked surprised. "Since when have you been interested in history?"

"I'll explain. But let's order first."

The waiter took their orders, and they started off with a glass of Champagne.

"What exactly do you want to know?"

"The basic story and then a few specific details."

"The order was created at the beginning of the twelfth century by nine knights in Jerusalem, in the ruins of the former Temple of Solomon. The order became powerful in Europe—and rich. It established hundreds of command posts. Then, two hundred years later, it experienced its downfall. The king of France, Philippe le Bel, pressed Pope Clement to ban the order, which led to the bloody persecution of its members. The order's command posts were requisitioned, its assets were seized, and the knights were imprisoned and tortured. The Templars vanished. Of course, such a tragic end has inspired wild theories and imaginative stories for lovers of cheap mysteries and esotericism. Does that answer your question?"

Christine looked at her as she nibbled a thin slice of duck *magret*.

"Yes. So how are the Freemasons linked with the Knights Templar?"

"Historically speaking, there isn't a link. There isn't a single serious historian who has proved that the two groups are linked. But Freemasons, or some of them, at least, seem convinced that there is a connection. As far as I'm concerned, they're in a parallel universe where the study of symbols and rituals counts for more than solid research."

"So all those stories of treasures and secrets are just hot air?"

"I wouldn't go that far. I'm just saying there's no proof. But who knows? Anything's possible."

Jade frowned. Possible wasn't good enough.

38

Marcas made his way down the stairs of the lodge, mentally preparing to meet the grand archivist. Grand archivist
wasn't an official Grand Orient position. Rather, it was
an honorary one, created because an increasing number
of brothers were showing an interest in Freemason history
and research. The man's role was to oversee the jurisdiction's research. Marc Jouhanneau, the Grand Orient's
grand archivist, was a specialist in the history of religion.

After the usual introductions and ritual embrace,
Marcas sat down next to the slender, pleasant-looking man
of indiscernible age. He was wearing a suit and a black
bow tie.

"Are you related to Henri Jouhanneau? Special Envoy
Mareuil gave me part of his diary to read."

"He was my father."

"What happened to him in 1941?"

"He was rounded up by the Germans because the Nazis
needed neurologists. He was sent to do research for the
Luftwaffe, Germany's air force."

"What kind of research?" Marcas asked.

"The Germans were looking for ways to increase survival
rates for pilots shot down over the North Sea. At the time, it
was impossible to last more than two hours. The SS headed
up operations, and the guinea pigs came from neighboring
concentration camps. They were dumped in icy water, and
the researchers used various methods to revive them. In
1943, my father was transferred to another camp controlled
by the Ahnenerbe and then to Weweslburg Castle, their
so-called cultural headquarters. SS physicians were doing
advanced brain research, and apparently they were quite a
bit ahead of everyone else. They were especially interested

in the various levels of consciousness. They had recruited a multidisciplinary team that even included psychoanalysts. Ironic, considering what Hitler thought of Sigmund Freud."

"It's no news that the Nazis had some crazy theories and conducted a lot of horrific experiments," Marcas said.

"I could go on and on about those experiments and theories. In the death camps, Dr. Mengele injected chemicals into people's eyes to make them blue. As for the theories, some Nazi scientists held that the Earth was hollow. There's a tale that the Germans sent an expedition to Antarctica, where they found an underground network of caves and rivers as far as thirty miles down. They were ordered to begin building a fortress there, and some claim to have made contact with extraterrestrials. Believe it or not, there were people who bought that story. We do know for a fact that the Germans sent an expedition to Tibet because of their interest in the occult."

"How do you know all this?"

"Much has been written over the years. And I have personal knowledge. My father ended up in Dachau. During his final days, he shared everything with a brother. A Jewish brother, a Freemason who forgot nothing. That man, Marek, survived. Until two days ago."

"Come again?"

"He was murdered in Jerusalem. Marek, an archeologist and expert in ancient inscriptions, was killed the same night as Sophie Dawes. He was the man Sophie was going to see in Jerusalem."

So this was the man Darsan had told them about.

"Listen, my brother, if I'm going to nail the identity of this killer—or killers—you have to tell me exactly what she was working on," Marcas said. "What was so interesting in that batch of papers? They were ordinary, as far as I could tell. All I saw were some wild imaginings of a brother with an Egypt fixation. I picked up a shadow of the Templars between the lines. But people wouldn't kill for that."

"People would kill for a secret, a secret that could have been in the temple."

"That again. You know as well as I do that our rituals have nothing to do with the Templars. Any supposed links are fabrications dating from the beginning of the nineteenth century, when scholars had access to archives pillaged during the revolution. Petit-bourgeois parvenus wanted lodges based on knightly traditions. It was a way of giving themselves a noble genealogy. Vanity. Just vanity."

Jouhanneau raised his voice. "I don't know enough to judge. Listen, I'm an old crank convinced that it's my duty to get at the truth. And that truth is the Freemason truth. I've been researching our collective memory for years. All we have are scattered fragments. We have no serious and complete scientific study of our roots."

"And therefore, of our present," Marcas said.

"That's right. Since the creation of Freemasonry, we have become one of the most listened to and sometimes most feared forces in the world. And yet nothing seems to justify this kind of reaction. Why has freemasonry become such a powerful entity in the eyes of the world? How has it survived revolutions and dictatorships? These are the questions I ask. And I'm not the only one who is asking."

"And the answer?"

"The secret! The fabled secret that no one has unlocked. We Freemasons are said to have access to this hidden knowledge without even being aware of it."

"A secret? Of course there's a secret," Marcas said. "Every real Freemason experiences it without being able to explain it. We all know that initiation changes a person. A new dimension opens, and the initiate is transformed, refined like a rough stone under an artisan's chisel. The secret lies in the ritual."

"Yes, that we agree on," Jouhanneau said, leaning forward in his chair. "But why are people killing for those papers? Some believe there's another secret. Something material. A secret lost but probably found again by the Templars."

"Here we go again, back to the quest for the Templar secret. It's a fantasy, like Jesus's son and the Holy Grail," Marcas said.

Marc Jouhanneau looked Marcas in the eye. "There's no room for cynicism here. I'm like you and prefer to leave the Templars and their great mysteries to the profane, who love esoteric secrets. But I do believe they succeeded in getting their hands on a hidden piece of information."

39

A dirt-like taste filled Bashir's mouth. His salivary glands tried to fight it off.

The room smelled of mildew and something rancid. Although it was dark, he could make out crates and broken wine racks. He was in a cold, dark cellar. One wrist was handcuffed to the wall and his head hurt. With his free hand, he felt a painful lump behind his ear.

Bashir tried to get up, but his legs refused to function, and with his hand cuffed to the metal bar, he had only four or so inches of maneuvering room.

He collapsed on the stinky mattress and tried to retrace the events: the beating, being chased by the two goons, the crooner at the hotel.

His blood was beginning to circulate again, first in his ankles and then in his thighs. But his legs still felt as though they were caught in a vise. The bitter flavor dissipated, and his eyes adjusted to the shadows. Not more than a yard away, he made out bars. He was in a cell in this basement.

He tried to get up again and felt a sharp pain in his calves. He looked down and saw that steel cables were wrapped around his knees and attached to a ring on the gritty wall. He was barefoot.

Bashir didn't persist. It was an ingenious mechanism. The more he pulled, the tighter the bonds got. At one point, they would cut off his circulation.

He searched the cell with his eyes, trying to find something he could use to break free, but other than a few shattered bottles, there was nothing useful. He settled into the prone position.

Bashir didn't understand why Sol hadn't killed him then and there, once he had delivered the stone. The three fake

Jews could have poisoned him on the train and left with it. Why wait? Why the setup at the Plaza?

He would probably have answers soon. There was no sense in torturing himself.

He heard footsteps on the other side of the bars and looked up.

He saw two men walking toward him but couldn't make out their faces. A key clinked, and the cell door opened slowly. One of the men flipped a switch, and light spread out from a bulb in the ceiling. Bashir blinked.

One of the men was grinning. He seemed almost friendly. He was medium in height, in his sixties, and had a double chin and a thick gray moustache. A canvas apron was tied around his waist. He looked like a bon vivant, with a stout middle giving away a weakness for the pleasures of the table.

Bashir recognized the man's partner. He was one of the men who had chased him.

Moustache Man approached. "Hello, I'm the gardener. What is your favorite flower?"

Bashir stared at him. He must have misunderstood. "Who are you? Free me now and tell Sol I want to talk to him."

The jovial man sat down on the edge of the mattress and tapped Bashir's imprisoned legs.

"Calm down, my friend. You didn't answer my question. What is your favorite flower?"

The man was crazy. Bashir raised his voice. "I don't give a damn about your flowers, old man. Go get the boss."

The man's eyes seemed to fill with sadness as he reached into a pocket of his apron. He pulled out a pair of pruning shears and opened the safety latch. The blades sprang open. Still smiling, he grabbed Bashir's left foot and inserted a toe between the blades.

The Palestinian stiffened. "Wait. What do you want?"

The bon vivant shook his head. "I didn't ever lie to you, did I?" he said.

Was this some kind of funny farm? The man wasn't making sense. "Lied about what? I don't understand."

He barely had time to get it out before the man snipped off his little toe, just like that. It fell to the floor, and blood squirted from Bashir's foot, splattering the torturer's apron. Bashir howled.

"I told you. I am the gardener. And an expert gardener uses the right tools. So let's not spend all day here. I'll ask my question again. What is your favorite flower?"

Bashir was struggling to free himself, but the metal restraints were just getting tighter.

"You're out of your mind. I... Roses."

The gardener gazed at the ceiling, as if he were contemplating Bashir's response. Then he looked back at Bashir and shook his head. "Wrong answer, my friend. It was the tulip."

With one slick movement, he chopped off the next toe. Bashir shrieked like a madman and nearly fainted. The second man walked up to him and gave him a hard slap. Now fear was eating away at Bashir like acid. It was stronger than the pain.

"Stop, please. I'll tell you what you want."

The gardener stood up, put the pruning shears in his apron, and pulled out a pipe from the other pocket. He took his time filling it with tobacco while Bashir's blood spurted on the floor.

"Please. I'm going to bleed out."

A smoky caramel aroma filled the room as the man took a few puffs and looked into the distance.

"I'm the gardener. I told you that, didn't I?"

Bashir felt himself becoming weaker as the blood drained out of him. The nerves in his foot were screaming, but worse, his mind was starting to go. He had to find a way to soften up his torturer.

"Yes, I know. It's a fine job."

The gardener's face lit up.

"Do you really think so? You're not just saying that to make me happy? I'm pleased. People have no respect for manual labor these days."

Bashir's vision was blurring. He was losing consciousness. He thought he had lost a quart of blood already. The man's acolyte didn't say anything, but administered a few more slaps. The gardener took out the shears again and set them down on the mattress.

"No!" Bashir cried out.

"Now, now. Calm down. We're going to bandage that up to stop the flow," he said, pulling out some gauze, a small bottle of alcohol, and surgical tape.

His assistant carefully bandaged the foot. The blood stopped flowing.

"I now have enough soil for my little protégés. By the way, you don't have AIDS or some other virus like that, do you? My flowers are very sensitive."

"I don't understand."

The gardener stood up and pulled out a trowel and a plastic bag filled with something.

"What we have here is some soil that I've enhanced, so to speak," he said, plunging the trowel into the bag. "You see, my biologist friends have explained that blood is an excellent fertilizer for my flowers. I've been testing this theory for a number of years, and to tell the truth, I'm quite pleased with the results."

Bashir stiffened. How many people had he tortured?

"I was just teasing you with my question about your favorite flower. Regardless of your answer, I would have cut off your toes. It's more poetic that way. So this is what's going to happen. You'll rest up a bit while I take care of my roses, and then I'll come back."

Bashir didn't dare say anything. He was too afraid the gardener would cut off another toe. The man touched his foot gently.

"You have another eight more toes, and then you have ten fingers, so let's make the most of it."

The two men left the cell, locking him in.

Bashir cried out, "What do you want, for God's sake?"

The gardener looked back at him as if he were a child who didn't understand.

"I don't know about the others, but I have a hundred or so roses to feed," he said.

He took a step back toward the cell.

"I wasn't being entirely honest." The gardener's voice sounded dreamy.

"I don't cut off just toes. I keep the best for last."

Bashir shrieked.

40

Marcas stood up and started pacing the room.

"Why do you think there's some secret information?"

"My father worked on experiments linked to that secret."

"What exactly? We've already established that the Nazis did a lot of god-awful experiments."

"They were looking for some way to connect with the gods. But like all doors to the infinite, it could lead to either heaven or hell."

"I'm not following," Marcas said, looking at his watch.

"Imagine a celestial drug that would allow you to communicate directly with the origin and power of life, with what we Freemasons call the Grand Architect of the Universe. And imagine what the Nazis could have done with that. For them, it was the soma, a Vedic ritual drink. It was an Aryan grail. That substance was believed to be an integral part of a lost Freemason ritual: the shadow ritual."

"That's crazy," Marcas said. "A secret lost in antiquity, a kind of ecstasy to the power of—"

"To the power of infinity."

"No, I don't buy it."

"I don't expect you to understand, but my father died for this secret, and Marek consecrated his life to the quest—he had vowed to uncover it to honor my father. Last month he found an engraved stone, the Tebah Stone, which mentioned a substance similar to the one the Nazis were looking for. He was murdered, and the stone is gone."

"Okay, let's go over it again. We're talking about an ancient secret, a kind of philter, a drink that people knew about and then lost. It was the famous soma of the ancients, the drink that makes you resemble the gods."

Jouhanneau smiled. "That's right. Since time immemorial, we've known that certain plants—well, the molecules in the plants—reveal things about the human soul."

"And do you know which plants were in this drink?"

"Sophie identified one of them in a document we got back from the Russians. The first person to have access to the formula could, in theory, produce a one-of-a-kind elixir that would open new doors of perception, as Aldous Huxley called them. And it would be good or evil, depending on who performed the ritual."

"Okay, so tell me the ingredient that you know about."

"Have you heard of Saint Anthony's fire?

"No."

"In 1039, in central France there was an epidemic of 'holy fire,' as it was called, and hundreds of farmers went crazy, suffering unbearable hallucinations."

"What caused it?"

"*Claviceps paspali* or *Claviceps purpurea*. It's an ergot fungus that grows on cereals including rye, wheat, and barley. In 1921, scientists isolated hallucinogenic alkaloids from this parasitic fungus. In the nineteen forties a chemist purified them and came up with lysergic acid diethylamide, also known as LSD, the drug of choice for hippies in the nineteen sixties and seventies. It's very powerful. In the Eleusinian Mysteries dedicated to Persephone, the Greek goddess of hell is represented with a sheaf of wheat."

"And Sophie's discovery?"

"After finding the first archives that mention ergot as part of the lost ritual, Sophie alerted me, and we refocused our research. I contacted Marek, and he made the connection with what my father had told him about the Nazi experiments. A month later, Sophie found the coveted Breuil Manuscript and realized that it held information about the other ingredients, and at just about the same time, Marek found the Tebah Stone. Sophie headed off to visit a chapel in a place called Plaincourault, and then she boarded a plane for Rome. I never saw her again."

41

"You know, there are still mysteries about the Templars that haven't been fully explored," Christine said before they said good-bye. "Who knows? Maybe there is some key to be found."

Jade's cell phone buzzed as she was about to slide behind the wheel of her car.

"Antoine here."

"I don't know an Antoine. Sorry."

"Antoine Marcas. Remember?"

Jade grinned. He didn't look like an Antoine.

"Sorry, Marcas, but I never connected you with a first name. Maybe one day. So?"

"I checked out the archives and spoke with an official from the lodge. We need to make a trip to Plaincourault."

"No kidding. Got any real news?"

"Well, pack a bag. I'll find a hotel where we can stay."

"Make sure it's two rooms, buddy."

"In the meantime, we'll need access to Interpol and anti-terrorism files. I'll get on it with my contact at the ministry."

"You mean Jaigu?"

"Listen, we need him. Don't make a fuss. There's more, too. We may have a lead on who ordered the kill and why."

"Go on. Spill the beans."

"It's a long story. I suggest that we meet at the office. See you in an hour, okay?"

"Fine. Listen, I wanted…"

"What? Hurry up, I've got to go."

"Nothing. I was almost going to be nice."

Marcas was silent for a few seconds.

"Be careful," he finally said. "If you keep that up, I might think you want to become a Mason or something."

She changed her tone. "I'd rather die. Go to hell."

She ended the call and headed to her apartment to pack a bag, not all that unhappy about letting him take the lead.

42

Nobody on the upper floors could hear the Palestinian's shrieks and wails. The soundproofing and overall calm gave the manor house a cocooned feel. The little Plessis-Boussac château, nestled in a charming valley just south of Paris, harbored the headquarters of the French Association for the Study of Minimalist Gardens. The few curious souls and botany enthusiasts who called the telephone number that was listed always got a message. Those who peered through the gates could see people gardening and taking care of the surrounding fields. A small team of volunteers regularly ordered supplies from the neighboring village and always held an open house to show off the superb greenhouse next to the château, which was known for its exotic plants and magnificent roses.

The association's president, a rose specialist who appreciated the good things in life, always made donations to the local Red Cross. Everyone in the area called him the gardener, which made him happy. He was from South Africa and had settled in the region at the end of the nineteen eighties, after a handful of nature-loving European investors bought the château. From time to time, some of them would arrive for a retreat.

Those would be higher-ups in the Orden, who used the manor house as a stopover when they were in transit to other countries. It was one of the lesser houses that Orden owned.

The tower had been entirely renovated. The large guest room was on the second floor. It was filled with Empire-style furnishings, including a canopy bed and a sumptuous carved desk.

The Tebah Stone sat on a red-velvet stand, which brought out the rock's black luster.

Sol was contemplating it. Finally, it belonged to him. This was the beginning of a new life. He weighed the stone in his hand and ran his fingers over the Hebraic letters that were thousands of years old. The stone seemed to vibrate with energy. It hypnotized him.

He broke the spell and looked at himself in a small mirror on the desk. Eighty-five years and counting. His body was declining, but his mind was as sharp as ever. How much longer did he have on this planet? Five, ten years at most. But his life was going to change radically. The words on the stone and the documents he had kept for so many years were finally going to lead to a door that opened to an astonishing power—the power of the gods.

He ran his hand through his hair and adjusted his collar. He felt a dull rumbling—a tractor going out to the fields—and a distant memory rose to the surface. A memory from another country and another life.

Sol closed his eyes. He recalled the man he was, the dashing Obersturmbannführer François Le Guermand. He remembered his last night in the bunker before the mission that would change his life. Those marvelous nineteen forties, when blood pulsed in his veins. Having enlisted well before he was of age, he had been heady with excitement, too young to understand the risks and possible consequences.

During his years of exile in South America and other friendly countries, he watched the world change and progress, but he never felt the excitement of those years of iron and fire, when his adopted country—Germany—came that close to building the most powerful empire the earth had ever known.

The thought brought him back to more mundane concerns. He speculated that the Palestinian had already gone through the gardener's hands, or rather, his pruners. Sol didn't especially like torture, but he recognized its effectiveness. The gardener's protocol always worked, even on the toughest victims. The combination of absurd behavior, violence, and meaningless chatter disoriented the victims, pushing them into an extraordinary state of submission.

Sol picked up the Tebah Stone again and took a long, deep breath, as if he were trying to communicate with its ancient soul. Then he gently set it down and rose from the desk.

He needed to talk to Joana. A piece of the puzzle was missing, and the Freemasons had it.

How he hated that lot.

François Le Guermand owed his life to the Thule, as did so many other former members of the SS. After the war, the network had saved him, giving him a new identity and setting him up in Argentina and then Paraguay. He had married and taken over an electronic-parts company that belonged to a member of the Orden. He was a sleeper agent. He was awakened in the nineteen fifties and ordered to coordinate a freemasonry-watch unit. Over time, he took on increasing responsibilities until he was playing a central role in the Orden.

Le Guermand had witnessed the Cold War, rockets to the moon, the fall of communism, and inventions he could have never imagined. And now, at the end of the road, he was finally going to achieve what he had most longed for.

Le Guermand had been ordered to steal the ultimate secret. The seed of the world. And he was on the verge of success.

43

Joana had been staked out on the Rue de Vaugirard since morning. She'd tossed Zewinski's apartment to no avail and was now waiting for her to return. She had just ordered coffee at the café across the street when her phone buzzed. It was Sol.

"Any news?" he began without any greeting.

"Nothing in the apartment. I'm waiting for her. Did you get the Palestinian?"

"Yes, he's in the gardener's hands now."

"Why are you torturing him?"

"I need the old Jew's notes and documents. And I need to make sure he didn't talk to anyone. This supposed professional got himself tailed by the Israelis when he crossed the Jordanian border, just like a beginner. Fortunately, we started watching him in Amsterdam."

"Why was he followed? Do the Israelis know you're after the stone?"

"No, a border patrol recognized him. He's a wanted Palestinian activist. The Jews are eager to identify his network in Europe."

Joana sipped her coffee as she surveyed the street.

"How do you know that?"

"My dear child, we kidnapped the agent that was following him as soon as he arrived at the Gare du Nord. Two nurses picked him up after he had a sudden attack of epilepsy."

"I suppose our gardener friend got him to talk."

Sol chuckled.

"We can't hide anything from you. Alas, our friend of the plants doesn't like Jews much. I'm afraid he may have gone overboard. All of the man's extremities went under the shears. The Palestinian will balance things out nicely. Nobody will accuse us of taking sides in the Israeli-Palestinian conflict."

Joana could hear him snickering over the phone. She prayed that she would never fall into the gardener's hands.

"Now let's talk about your orders. Go get the woman from the embassy, and bring her here. We've lost enough time as it is. I need those papers to finish what I started."

"And then?"

"She'll meet the gardener."

Joana knew Sol was in a hurry, but she had a question. "Why did you want me to kill that woman with those three blows?"

"Good-bye, my dear," he said, ending the call, "Make haste."

44

Jade parked her car down the street from her place and hurried along the sidewalk. It was midafternoon, and the sidewalks were crowded. At one point she had to elbow her way around a woman wearing heavy perfume who was paying no attention to where she was going. The bitch had even scratched her. Welcome back to Paris, Jade thought.

Jade couldn't decide how she felt about Marcas. The man irritated her but intrigued her, too, with his strange mix of smugness and mystery.

Argh, she was coming off like a Harlequin heroine.

The stories of esoteric Freemason murders perplexed her. There were so many gray areas in the case, nothing could be eliminated. And Marcas was like a fish in water when it came to secret societies. There was no trusting him. She couldn't even be sure that her contacts in intelligence weren't connected with the Freemasons. The hoodwinkers were everywhere.

Pure paranoia. It was hard not to be paranoid. But her orders were clear. She had to work with Marcas. Sophie's face wasn't so clear anymore. Her murder felt like nothing more than a bad dream. Yet her tortured body lay in a cold tomb in the suburbs of Paris. It was very real. Sophie never should have joined those tricksters, with all their hocus-pocus. Jade had one more reason to hate the bastards.

But orders were orders.

She started to cross the avenue and hadn't made it half-way when her head began to spin. She could see the other side, but her senses were dulling. The sidewalk seemed to go on infinitely, like the horizon. She stumbled along like a sleepwalker. She was having trouble breathing. She could hardly keep her eyes focused.

Jade panicked. Controlling her body was vital to her job, and the slightest change in perception turned on all the alarms. She tried to apply the advice her instructors had repeated time and again during her training: breathe deep, empty your mind, chase away the fear.

She had panicked once before. It was during a dive simulating an underwater commando attack. When she had set a fake magnetic explosives on the hull of a ship, her regulator had malfunctioned, and she couldn't get any oxygen. It was the nightmare of nightmares. She was losing consciousness in slow motion, knowing full well the inevitable outcome. The instructor had saved her in the nick of time.

But today, in the middle of the fifteenth arrondissement, surrounded by a bustling crowd, nobody was offering any help.

Her leg muscles were slowly stiffening. Her arms were numb. She didn't have any feeling in her mouth either. Anxiety, moreover, was paralyzing her ability to think, as it had in the dark, muddy waters off Normandy. She couldn't control herself. She was failing. She was going to collapse on the concrete, and nobody would lift a finger.

As she struggled to reach the sidewalk, she felt a supportive arm slide around her back and clutch her side. A miracle. Someone in this anonymous crowd had seen that she was in trouble.

"Don't worry, miss. I've got you."

It was a woman's voice. Friendly, warm. She had to get control again. She saw a café just across the street.

"Help me get over to that café. I'm just a little tired."

The woman propped Jade up and held her tight to keep her from falling. She couldn't see her guardian angel's face. All she perceived was a sweet-smelling perfume, a vaguely familiar fragrance. The panic receded. She felt safe.

The voice was smooth. "Lucky for you I was right behind you."

Cars were honking. Jade and her rescuer were in the street, blocking traffic. Jade vaguely perceived a taxi driver angrily gesticulating at them.

She let herself be led. Saved at the last minute. What luck. She'd have to get the woman's address to thank her. Who would believe it: the special ops commando fainting in the middle of Paris. What a joke.

A young man with a thin strip of a beard approached them. "Do you need some help? Your friend's not looking so good—"

Jade wanted to answer, but the woman was faster.

"No, it's nothing. She's diabetic. I have to give her some insulin. I'm parked right over there. Thank you for offering."

Then the woman addressed her directly. "Come on, Jade, help me out here."

Jade's mind was reeling. Who was this stranger who claimed to be a friend and knew her name? And what was the bullshit about being diabetic? She tried to talk, but nothing came out.

A wave of terror rolled through her body. She was as vulnerable as an infant. She saw the young man walk off. She watched the café tables begin to recede. She wanted to reach out and grab a chair, but they were too far away.

"Le… Let me go. I—"

Her body wasn't responding. She'd been drugged. All she could sense was the heavy perfume.

That perfume. The woman she had elbowed her way around. The scratch on her arm. A classic maneuver.

"Don't worry, Jade. Everything is going to be all right. I'm going to take you to a place where you can rest. We have so much to talk about."

"I… I don't know you… Leave me…"

Passersby were scowling at her, as if she were drunk. The door of a black car opened, and she was pushed into the backseat. She was now entirely paralyzed and couldn't make out colors or shapes anymore. Everything was becoming a grayish blur.

The woman's sensual voice resonated in her head. "Rest assured, Jade. The drug will take you away to dreamland."

She felt a kiss on her forehead. A wave of panic rolled through her paralyzed body. The perfume was making her queasy.

"Sleep well. Oh, I did forget to introduce myself. I'm Joana, your new friend. I hope we'll get along during the little time you have left."

Jade fell into an ink-black sleep.

DEBIR

The holy of holies
on the western side of Solomon's temple,
where the Ark of the Covenant was kept

~~~

I sent my soul into the invisible,
Some letter of that after-life to spell.
And by and by my soul returned to me
And answered, "I myself am heaven and hell."

—Omar Khayyam, The Rubaiyat

45

Death. A quick one, to be done once and for all with this unbearable suffering of his flesh and soul. The gardener's third session was the worst. The torturer started on his remaining fingers, one at a time, tip first, multiplying the torment. His left hand was nothing more than an open wound, covered with a makeshift bandage offered by the gardener in his great mercy.

And then Sol showed up. He hadn't pictured an old man like that, with hair as white as snow and ramrod-straight posture despite his age. He wanted to know if Bashir had picked up any documents with the Tebah Stone, and if so, where they were.

Exhausted and out of his mind with pain, the Palestinian was ready to confess whatever they wanted to hear so that the persecution would end. He told him the locker number at the Gare du Nord, hoping for some leniency. In vain. Sol promised that the gardener would not disturb him anymore, but his life would end in this cellar.

If, however, he had a final wish before dying, Sol would try to oblige. Bashir asked for something to ease the pain, along with a brew of the magic mushrooms he had purchased in Amsterdam, which were hidden in the double lining of his luggage. He was given a light morphine derivative that did not relieve his suffering.

A few hours or minutes later—he no longer had any notion of time—Sol returned with a scalding liquid that Bashir drank to the last drop, holding the cup with his right hand.

"Wait until the mushrooms take effect before you kill me."

He was short of breath, but he had enough strength to add, "You bastard, I did my job, and this is how you pay me."

Sol patted Bashir's sweat-soaked hair. "The Jews followed you. The risk was too high. It's nothing personal. I have a lot of admiration for the Palestinian cause."

"Stop the bullshit! You're just a damned Nazi."

Sol rose to his feet without answering. Bashir didn't have the strength to hold up his head anymore. A final question was tormenting him. "Why did you have me kill that man in Jerusalem with three blows?"

Sol looked at him and smiled. "It would take too long to explain. Let's just say that our victim belonged to a group that has been an enemy of ours for a very long time. It was a calling card meant just for them. I have to leave you now. If it's any consolation, a woman will be at your side when your hour of deliverance comes. She'll be in the cell next to yours. I hope that she will bring you some comfort. May you quickly reach your paradise and enjoy the pleasures that Mohammed promised. In my religion, unfortunately, we don't get that kind of welcoming committee."

Bashir watched him walk toward the door of the cell. His head was spinning from the mushrooms. Soon he would plunge into a parallel universe. He realized he was experiencing his final seconds of awareness and murmured, "What religion?"

The old man's voice echoed in the basement. "Power."

46

Marcas reread the Grand Orient archives Jade had given him. Either the Breuil Manuscript was pure nonsense, or there was something worth paying attention to, and the allusion to the Templars could point to it. In any case, someone had Sophie murdered in Rome for these papers and had Marek murdered in Jerusalem at the same time, presumably for a stone related to the papers.

Breuil had spent time in Egypt and was focused on building a new kind of temple. Instead of a mosaic in the center, this temple would have a bush with exposed roots. Breuil also alluded to the bitter beverage drunk by Freemason initiates and the shadow ritual, keys to gaining access to the Great Architect of the Universe.

Breuil's ideas contradicted traditional Masonic teachings. Freemason temples were generally designed to symbolize the development of an initiate's inner temple—knowledge of universal harmony. Spiritual growth was seen as a step-by-step process. An initiate became an entered apprentice, then a fellow craft mason, and then a master, and that was just the beginning. Some lodges had a number of higher designations. Patience and humility were the crucial pillars required to reach higher levels of knowledge.

Marcas hadn't paid attention at first, but now it leaped out at him. Breuil was claiming that his ritual could open the door to a state of all-encompassing awareness. It was a direct line to God. And that was blasphemy—if such a word could apply to the Freemason universe.

Marcas put the papers down and massaged his neck. Sophie had gone to the Templar chapel in Plaincourault, according to Jouhanneau. What message would he and Zewinski find there?

He looked at his watch. Thirty minutes late. That didn't seem like her style.

Then there was the question of how Plaincourault was spelled: thirteen or fifteen letters?

He glanced at his watch again. What would she be wearing: pants or a skirt? He started imagining her legs—and stopped himself. He had more urgent things to think about. Sophie's murder was becoming something bigger than an investigation. It was starting to feel like a quest.

What he had found in the archives was troubling. And then there were those slayings that mimicked Hiram's death: not only the ones that had been committed recently, but also the ones that had been committed over the course of many years. A long-standing conspiracy to kill Freemasons? But why? It seemed that some invisible enemy was crossing through time.

He looked at his watch a third time. Had Zewinski forgotten him? He called her number and got her voice mail. He left a sharp message.

She was definitely irritating him. Her hostility to Freemasons was more than just the usual distrust of the uninitiated. He wanted to know where that hostility was coming from.

47

It was the smell that woke her up. It was heavy, nauseating, and it filled every inch of the room. Death. She'd experienced it at a hospital in Kabul. A women had developed gangrene after delivering a baby, and her flesh was rotting away. But the Taliban wouldn't allow her to be treated by hospital physicians because they were all men. Jade had risked her life by sneaking in medications provided by two volunteer doctors. Still, the woman had died.

Jade emerged slowly from her torpor. Her head felt tight, as though it were in a vise. Someone was speaking in Arabic. She knew the language, but she had no idea who was talking. The person was moaning between sobs, pleas, and declarations. Where was she?

"*Bvitti*, I climb on the stone… My nails reach for my cursed flesh… *Bvitti*, the sky is red with blood. An eye is watching me. I must leave…"

She tried to get up to make out who it was, but she couldn't. Her legs were tied down. She looked around and realized that she was in a cell.

"I see it. It's wonderful, but the stone is keeping me back… Go away. You're the demon…"

The man shrieked.

"You're the devil… You're tempting me. Curse you. Nothing escapes the All Powerful."

Jade turned her head to the right and saw a man who was also being held prisoner. He was thrashing around, as though he were possessed. Even in the darkness, she could tell that his hands and feet were covered with bloody bandages. That was the smell. The poor man had gangrene. No one had taken care of it, and he was going to die. Beyond a certain stage, antibiotics couldn't help.

Jade panicked. "Is anyone here?" she shouted. "Come quick. There's a man who's dying."

She stopped when she realized the shouting served no purpose. Her kidnappers knew perfectly well what state the man was in. They had done it to him.

She took deep breaths in an effort to get her fear under control. They don't want to kill me, she told herself, or else I wouldn't be here.

"*Bvitti...* Root of the sky... The eye has also turned black, and tears of blood are flowing. It's wonderful. I am one of those tears..."

Jade tried to get the man's attention.

"Who are you? Can you hear me?"

The man turned toward her. He was soaked with sweat and drooling.

"I am the one who is... the abyss."

Thank God he was tied up too and couldn't attack her. As soon as she thought it, she acknowledged the absurdity. He was too weak, and his hands and feet were useless.

The man continued his monologue, but the words became less distinguishable. Jade turned away and tried to recall how she had been kidnapped. It was a professional job. She had been drugged and abducted in broad daylight in front of hundreds of people. The woman who did this was most likely in cahoots with Sophie's murderers. In fact, they could be one and the same person. Jade felt a wave of blinding rage.

Her attention shifted to the man's words.

"The stone is my ladder! Me, divinely impure."

The smell was unbearable. He wouldn't last long. She had to do something quick.

"Who is your God?"

"The Very Great One... The Veiled One. Nobody knows his true words."

"Do you?"

"I saw the golden face of the Very Saint when he blew his soul into the stone. He spoke... in the middle of the languages of men. And the sacred word is their destiny."

"What men?"

Mad laughter filled the room.

"The impious have unearthed the stone and reaped destruction. In the cloud of words, God engraved the one that would reduce them to slavery."

"What impious ones?"

"The sons of Zion that have not recognized the Real God. Today the stone will speak. It will say the sacred word. *Bvitti. Bvitti. Bvitti.*"

She turned away from him and would have jumped, had she been able. A man with a bushy moustache was staring at her, a pipe in his mouth, a hand in his apron. He was smiling. She responded with a snigger.

"Can't you see that he's dying?"

A second man approached. He looked more threatening. He was staring at her too. The first one opened the door of the other cell, and they both entered.

"You're right. We're going to calm him down right now. Hans?"

The second man pulled a pistol out of his jacket and placed it against the dying man's temple.

The detonation rang through the cellar.

"No," Jade screamed as a geyser of blood and flesh hit the wall. The vision of her father flashed in her mind, with his head on the armrest, the puddle of blood on the floor. The nightmare all over again. A bullet in the head.

But she wasn't a little girl now, and the fear wasn't paralyzing her. She was furious. It was an icy rage that emanated from a dark place that would always be there.

"You sons of bitches!"

The man with the moustache entered her cell, sat down beside her, and patted her thigh. He was wearing a strange expression. He shook his head, set his pipe on the floor, and, with a mischievous look in his eye, said, "I am the gardener. What's your favorite flower?"

48

Marcas took the steps two by two. He'd gotten Zewinski's address from Darsan. His irritation with her had given way to anxiety. He had a bad feeling about her being late. Now he was almost in a panic. He couldn't get up the steps fast enough, and when he reached the third floor, his heart started pounding. Her apartment door had been pried open. He advanced quickly, back against the wall, his service revolver in front of him. He used his foot to push the door all the way open and immediately saw the place had been tossed. After a quick check to make sure all was clear, he pulled out his phone.

"Alexis?"

"Antoine, great to hear from you. I'm back in Paris, you know.

"Can you get your buddies to locate Zewinski's cell phone?"

"Have things gone that far already? Really, you should take it slower with a broad like that."

"Look, she's disappeared and she's not answering her phone."

"Don't take it so personally."

"I'm serious. Her place has been tossed, and it looks like some nasty folks are behind the Dawes murder. Locate Zewinski for me. Now."

"Okay, okay. I'm on it. Anything else I should know?"

"Yeah, check with our contacts in Israel. Find out if any known traffickers have left the country. I also need to know about any developments in the investigation of the murder at the archeological institute?"

49

"Who are you?"

"I told you. I am the gardener."

The man did look the job. Jade sat up and saw him searching through his apron pocket.

"Why am I here?"

"I don't know. I just want to know your favorite flower."

"I hate flowers. Too bad."

The man pulled a small pair of pruning shears out of his pocket and waved them in front of her eyes.

"That's impossible. Everyone loves flowers, especially women. I'll have to teach you some manners."

He applied the gardening tool to her big toe. Jade understood the dying man's bandages. She didn't even tremble as her training kicked in. She had learned all the ins and outs of torture: sensory deprivation, drugs, electricity, and all manner of instruments for delivering pain. Inflicting repeated violence on a subject was an age-old practice and often highly effective. It had been favored in Pinochet's Chile and General Videla's Argentina, with a little help from the CIA.

The Arab's death had served as a preview, preparing her psychologically for what lay ahead. But there was no way she would let this bastard with a mustache see any fear. If he planned to cut her up, he wasn't going to take any pleasure in it. She knew the pain would be horrendous, but she conjured up an image of Sophie and focused all her hate on the henchman.

"Before you start your gardening, I want to ask you a question."

The man stopped what he was doing and looked thrown off.

"Um… Okay."

"I've heard that torturers like you are impotent. I read a study. They enjoy inflicting pain because they can't get it up. Is that true in your case?"

The blood drained from moustache man's face.

"Hans, leave us," he said, waving the assistant away. "I need to have a little talk with this young lady. She has some wayward ideas that could use a trim. I think her cries might be too much for even you."

He looked her up and down, biting his lip.

"A woman who doesn't like flowers and doubts my virility. For once, I'm going to innovate and start with the ears."

He slowly aimed the pruners at her head, but Jade didn't struggle. She knew her torturer was waiting for the first sign of fear. She plastered a smile on her face, trying to upset the balance of power.

He opened the metal blades and slipped them gently around her right ear, almost like a caress. Jade closed her eyes and tightened her fists to concentrate her energy.

The man leaned in. She could smell his sour breath tinged with the acrid odor of pipe tobacco.

"In five minutes, you will beg me to stop, and I won't."

Just as he was about to apply pressure to the shears, a woman's voice rang out. "That's enough, gardener. Leave her alone."

The man straightened and looked at the bars. The sadist was now clearly angry. "How dare you interrupt me? I have explicit orders."

The woman on the other side of the bars raised her voice. "Mine are more important. Sol wants me to bring her upstairs so I can take care of her personally. Get out of here now. And take your gorilla Hans with you."

"Nobody talks to me that way, young lady. Do you know who I am in this organization?"

"Yes, and I don't give a crap. Do you want me to tell Sol that you disobeyed?"

Fuming, the gardener put his pruners away. "I only have your word for it. Just this time. She'll eventually get what she deserves. I've never tried a woman's blood on my little protégés."

He turned and smiled at Jade. "I'll be back soon."

He opened the cell door and left with his man. Joana walked in and sat down on the mattress.

"Just in the nick of time. You owe me one."

Jade looked at her with disdain. "You won't get any gratitude from me. I know who you are. You killed my friend in Rome."

"Yes. She was a little too easy for my taste. You, however, are a much more interesting target. We have things to talk about, the two of us, but I must take some precautions."

Joana took out a small leather bag and removed a silver ring with a pointed mount. She put it on her index finger. Before Jade could react, the killer pressed the ring against her bare foot. A drop of blood rose at the puncture wound.

"You're lucky, Jade. Gallons of blood have been spilled in this cellar. But today, not a drop of your blood will go on the floor. You're going to sleep for fifteen minutes while I take you upstairs."

Jade felt her head spinning again, as it had when she was kidnapped. She wanted to say something, but she was already elsewhere.

50

They'd localized Zewinski in the Chevreuse area about an hour southwest of Paris. More, actually, because Marcas was stuck in a traffic jam leaving the beltway—commuters heading home. It was the wrong time of day to get kidnapped. Dammit, Zewinski!

He called Marc Jouhanneau as he drove.

"Did Marek say anything about the stone?"

"Just that it was clearly authentic, and he was decrypting it. Sophie thought it might have one of the ingredients or something else related to the ritual. In any case, the stone is in enemy hands."

"Enemy hands?"

"They are everywhere."

"What do you mean by that?"

"They killed Sophie and Marek. It's a very structured organization that has been persecuting us for a long time. They want to get their hands on the secret that belongs to us."

"Who exactly are they?"

"You'll find out soon enough. Before and during the war, they were called the Thule. They may go by another name now. But they have the same signature and kill in the same way."

Marcas hesitated a moment and then said, "Do you know of similar murders?"

"My father was killed in Dachau in the same way."

Yet another Hiram murder, Marcas thought. He was losing count.

Jouhanneau cleared his throat. "Yes, the Beast is still here, hidden, and has struck again. It's us against them. Evil is lurking near the temple doors, brother. You must stop them. The message is clear. Go to Plaincourault, and you'll understand."

Marcas ended the call. First to Chevreuse, he said to himself, then to Plaincourault.

51

An aristocrat in the late eighteenth century had to be the one responsible for the still-intact décor of this room. During the final years of the reign of Louis XV, libertine nobles had filled their mansions with highly elaborate and ornamental furnishings in a style called Rococo. It lent itself to sensual pleasures of all sorts. Estates in pastoral valleys had quickly mimicked the châteaux in Paris and Versailles. Far from the court and the fashionable salons of the capital, the owners of these rural mansions could feel that they weren't isolated, but instead part of a sumptuous culture where any enjoyment could be had.

But the pleasures of the luxurious lifestyle were short-lived. The blood of the French Revolution swept them away. Many of the homes disappeared, victims of history and an expanding real-estate market. Only a few remained, bearing silent witness to a period when freedom of the body accompanied an independent spirit.

This mansion was one that had survived. The French windows overlooked sumptuous grounds, and the louvered shutters let in thin strips of sunlight that sparkled on the polished wood floor. Lovers had most likely enjoyed the delicate play of light on their alabaster skin. A Venetian mirror hung above the veined marble chimney and took in the entire room. Women's clothing was strewn on sensually rounded armchairs. A stiletto pump had ended up under the mahogany desk. Its mate lay on the bed. A white linen scarf was draped over a plaster bust.

In the back of the room, curtains opened to a dark alcove. A canopy topped a bed that held the sleeping prisoner.

Joana was on the sofa, contemplating the woman she was going to kill. She got up and walked to a window. The grounds were calm. The estate's employees had finished for the day. There was nobody on the expansive lawn. No one would bother them.

She looked back at the bed. Jade had moved her head. What dark world had she been in? Slivers of sweat had formed under her armpits. Joana had never seen anything so erotic. When she had brought Jade into the room, she'd given in and undressed her before attaching her with wire to the bedposts. Now she was waiting for her victim to wake up.

Although Joana hated weakness, she was ambivalent about her own occasional lack of discipline. She looked over at the desk. Inside a plastic box were two mushrooms. She'd only used a little when Sol ordered her to brew them for the Palestinian to help him pass to the next realm. She had enough left for her own fantasies.

52

Jade moaned softly. She was cold. Her hands were asleep, and pain was shooting up her legs. She wanted to move, but nothing happened.

"No sense trying," a woman said.

She had to open her eyes.

"A real Sleeping Beauty, except the wait for your Prince Charming will be long. Eternal, in fact."

The woman assassin was sitting in front of her, staring. Her eyes were cloudy.

"He's not coming at all. So…"

The woman stood up. "Don't make me torture you. Think of your body." She leaned over Jade. "Such a fine body, delicious without anything covering it. You must have known a lot of pleasure in your short life."

Now the woman was on the bed.

"Your friend was beautiful. I kissed her before killing her."

Jade wanted to scream. "Tell me what you want."

Joana inched closer. Her blonde hair brushed Jade's skin. "Me? Oh, many things, but first…"

Jade stiffened.

"Is my doll afraid? Do you prefer your cop friend?"

"What about my cop friend?"

"Seriously. You disappoint me. With a cop? I would have thought more of you if it had been with—what was her name again—Sophie?"

"Bitch."

"If you want, my dear. In any case, you are going to die. Don't hold back."

Jade took a deep breath. "No, there's nothing between the cop and me. He's not my type."

The woman's voice seemed to lose its lilt. "He's not?"

"No."

"So you did prefer your girlfriend, then."

"What do you think?"

The woman leaned in closer yet.

"What if I don't like guessing games?"

"My hands. Sophie loved when I used my hands."

Joana stood up and swayed.

"Your hands! Your hands. Do you think I'm an idiot?" She snickered.

"I can prove it to you."

"So prove it," the assassin said, shuffling through the papers on the desk and pulling out a letter opener. "One hand. Only one. Make the slightest—I said the slightest—wrong move…"

She shoved the letter opener under Jade's throat.

"…and I'll slit your throat."

An image of Marcas flashed in Jade's mind. Why him? Why not her father? Or one of the men who had loved her? Why him? He was nothing to her. Here she was on her deathbed—literally—a woman with more than one lover but no one she had loved, and oddly, she was thinking about that dude with a ridiculous first name: Antoine.

Her jailer finished releasing her right wrist and grabbed Jade's hand.

"Now pleasure me."

53

"Wait. First, tell me where you're from."

"Croatia. A lovely country. You should see it someday. Oh, sorry, you won't be able to."

Jade was coming out of her drug-induced haze and calculating her chances of escape. With one hand and her feet still tied up, the killer had a big advantage. She didn't want to give into the lunatic's whims, but she didn't have much choice, given the letter opener at her throat.

"I'm waiting."

The woman's voice was becoming throaty, and Jade felt more pressure on her neck. Desperate to get out of the bad-movie scenario, she remembered the words of the unfortunate dead man.

"I know about *bvitti*," she said.

Joana let up on her throat a little. "Bvi... What?"

"*Bvitti*. I need to see your boss. I know about the stone."

"That damned stone with some crap about a mind-altering substance that could 'seed the mind with prophesies.' We got the archeologist's papers, and we're on top of it. Actually, that stone's just one item on our shopping list."

"Tell your master I know more about the Freemasons. They're one step ahead of you."

While trying to keep Joana distracted, Jade was feeling around with her free hand. She found the shoe on the bed and slowly brought it closer as Joana leaned in.

"I want your hand now," she said.

The stiletto, with its metallic tip, made a perfect arc before striking the Croatian's temple, knocking her to the side of the bed. The killer cried out and collapsed on the floor. The letter opener had only grazed Jade in the process.

Jade grabbed the blade and cut herself free. She wasn't out of trouble yet. The house was probably full of the gardener's friends. The woman was curled in a fetal position on the rug. Jade pressed down on her carotid artery to slow the flow of blood to her brain and prolong her state of unconsciousness but stopped short of killing her. She tied her up and gagged her.

Adrenaline was pumping through her now, and her mind was crystal clear. She walked across the room and looked out the window at the deserted grounds. She was on the second floor.

Jade headed toward the door and gently cracked it open. Music was coming from the end of the hallway. Too risky. She didn't have much time. She'd try the window.

She dug through Joana's handbag and took out her identity papers, undoubtedly fakes, and her cell phone, which would have key information about her contacts. She got dressed quickly, then went in the bathroom to splash some water on her face. The reflection in the mirror was frightening. She looked like an escapee from an asylum.

She didn't have time to make herself more presentable. On her way back across the room, she picked up the letter opener. Everyone would understand. How could a moral compass hold up in the face of people who tortured and killed without remorse? She pointed the blade at Joana's belly. A few inches, and the bitch's life would be over. Sophie's laughing eyes flashed in her mind. The hate was brewing. It wouldn't take much more to get her revenge. Jade had killed before in the line of duty, but never anyone who was powerless.

She pulled herself together. No, she wouldn't become a killing machine. She was better than that. But frustration lingered in her mind.

Jade looked around and saw a stone sculpture on a side table. It was some sort of stylized column. She weighed it in her hand—at least ten pounds. She raised it above her head and slammed it down on the woman's right wrist.

Joana came to with the searing jolt of pain. She screamed into her gag. Her eyes filled with tears. She twisted her body in an attempt to get free, but Jade sat on her legs.

"I have a dark side, too. I'm not a nice little girl. You'll be a cripple the rest of your life. I'm not quite done, though."

She immobilized the broken wrist with one hand, and brought the sculpture down on Joana's fingers. She was methodical and precise. The woman's eyes filled with hate.

"You'll never use your hand again. In case you wondered, one of my instructors taught me that little trick. He learned it from a Congolese army officer. It's customarily used to punish thieves."

Before she got up, Jade slapped the woman's face.

"And that's just to humiliate you. The problem with us girls is that we're taught to repress our urges. It feels good to let go from time to time, don't you think? Adieu, bitch."

Zewinski checked the bonds to make sure Joana couldn't escape and then went to the window and climbed out. The grounds were silent. She grabbed the cornice and in less then a minute landed softly on the gravel. Two men, probably armed, were walking along the gate, blocking the way out.

Jade slipped toward the greenhouse and crawled about three hundred feet under the windows. When she reached the other side, she raised her head and peeked through a window. The gardener was inside watering a strangler fig. He was talking to it. The image of the poor tortured man came to mind, and the taste of anger filled her mouth. She didn't have time to kill him. She needed to get out of there and reach Marcas.

The gardener interrupted his monologue and turned toward Jade. Her heart skipped a beat. He looked in her direction for a while, his ears pricked, and then went back to watering his plants. Jade let out a sigh of relief and stole into the woods at the edge of the property.

54

Marcas's phone vibrated. The screen indicated an unknown number. He answered and heard a woman's voice.

"Marcas, I need you to come get me right away."

"I know, Jade."

"What do you mean you know?"

"You think I've just been waiting around for you? You stand me up and don't answer my messages. I check your place, and it's been trashed. Your car's on the street—with a parking ticket, I might add—and you think I'd go back to the office and sit on my hands until you whistle for me like I'm some chauffeur?"

"I was kidnapped by Sophie's killers."

"I had your cell tracked. We located the estate where they took you, and I'm watching the gate right now. The cavalry's on the way. At first I saw only two guards, but things are definitely picking up in there. Where are you, Jade?"

"In Dampierre. It's a nearby village. It looks completely deserted. Good thing I memorized your number. Hurry. They're going to be after me."

Her tone was urgent.

"I'll be right there."

"Marcas?"

"What?"

"You called me Jade."

"Chalk it up to the adrenaline rush."

55

The gardener looked down at the tied-up woman, his eyes full of disdain. What incompetence. She had endangered Orden. His men had searched the estate, in vain. The prisoner had fled into the woods, and the chances of getting her back were slim. He had just three men to secure the château, not enough to organize a search party. And he had more urgent issues to tend to. Orden would have to erase any trace of its presence before the police arrived.

Each of Orden's properties had an emergency evacuation plan. The staff here did a timed test run twice a year. Phase one: retrieve any papers from the safe and activate the fire system. Phase two: take out the six bodies kept in freezers, and put them, along with their fake identity papers, in the bedrooms. Phase three: leave the grounds, using the station wagons parked in a garage. In the last drill, the team had accomplished everything in exactly twenty-five minutes.

The gardener freed Joana.

"That bitch destroyed my hand! Give me some morphine."

The man didn't respond. Had it been up to him, he would have put a bullet in her head—the usual procedure for incompetents. She was responsible for bringing down a house of Orden and letting a hostage escape—someone who could identify those in the mansion, including him. But she was one of Sol's protégés, the daughter of a board member. Untouchable.

"Hans will bring you a shot. We leave in fifteen minutes. I'll report your failure. Because of you, Orden is losing a precious base, and I'm losing my little dearies."

~~~

Joana's hand was killing her.

"Your dearies?"

"My darling plants. They'll die in the fire. I'll never get over it. I'm very sensitive."

Joana fell back, looked at the ceiling, and let out a laugh.

"You're a madman. You cut people up with pruning shears and cry over your damned plants."

The gardener glared at her and turned to leave the room. "Fifteen minutes, no more," he shouted. "That's when the fire starts."

Joana pulled herself up. The gardener wouldn't spare any details in his report. She knew her errors wouldn't be forgiven, and her injuries would keep her from doing what she liked best: killing. She didn't expect any pity from Orden. Only weak people showed pity. That was what Sol preached. Her only chance of salvation lay in her father.

56

Marcas could never sleep well in a hotel, and this night was no exception. He had spent the better part of it smoking and thinking. If you could call it thinking.

His mind was torn between the information he had to process and the woman with bruises on her wrists and ankles sleeping in the room next to his.

Now he knew what was written on the Tebah Stone. Jade had told him about the dying man's delirium, and his repeated mention of a stone and the word *bvitti*. They would never know who the man was, but he had contributed a significant piece to the puzzle. Then there was what that female assassin had added about the archeologist's report, about it being a substance that could "seed the mind with prophesies."

Bvitti. The word was familiar. He'd read it somewhere, but where? He pulled out his laptop.

It took him a good half hour to find an article on a site on African religions. French ethnologists had studied initiation rites practiced in a village in the jungles of Gabon. The village was in a large area belonging to the Mitsogo tribe.

Bwiti was both a religion and a science that enabled its initiates—who underwent a secret three-day rebirth ceremony—to enter another spiritual dimension where they could communicate with their ancestors and come to understand the relationship of the earth and the beyond.

To experience Bwiti, an initiate would ingest the root bark of a sacred plant, *Tabernanthe iboga*. The sacred chemical substance was ibogaine, a psychoactive alkaloid. It had powerful hallucinogenic properties and purportedly didn't cause dependency. In fact, it had been used in the

West since the mid-nineteen eighties to treat cocaine and alcohol addiction.

Jouhanneau would be thrilled. He would have the second ingredient.

As Marcas read the article, a shiver ran up his spine. The coincidence was troubling.

There are striking similarities between Bwiti and Freemason initiation rites. Ultimately, the outcome is the same: knowledge of the mystery of the beyond, which Freemasons call the sublime secret. More surprising, however, is that the Freemason ritual uses three strikes of the mallet in memory of the assassination of Hiram, the architect of the Temple of Salomon, because of his refusal to reveal the sublime secret.

The researchers noted that during the Bwiti ceremony, "the initiate was struck three times on the head to free his spirit."

It was almost too much for Marcas to take in. How could the Bwiti practice find itself inscribed on a Hebraic stone several centuries old? Perhaps via Egyptian merchants who had contact with African tribes or perhaps via Ethiopian traders, which also sent expeditions into deepest Africa.

His imagination was running wild. Did Sheba, the queen of Ethiopia conquered by King Solomon, offer this plant to the Hebrews?

His mind exhausted, he closed his laptop and went to bed. In the morning, his eyes were red, and his face was pale and hollow. He'd hardly gotten three hours of sleep.

Marcas stretched and walked over to the window. Dawn was chasing away the final scraps of night. He couldn't get the Thule off his mind. Who were these people who could kidnap a trained army officer like Jade in the middle of Paris to drug and torture her for some fantasmagoric secret? The same people who had killed his brothers in other times and places?

He picked up his phone and called Jouhanneau again.

"Marcas here." He quickly briefed Jouhanneau on Zewinski's kidnapping, her sequestration with the dying man in a state of delirium, and her flight and rescue. He told Jouhanneau that they had taken refuge in a hotel run by a brother.

Then he shared his discoveries about Bwiti.

"You've caught up with the Thule," Jouhanneau said. "Now you need the third ingredient and the dosage. Go to Plaincourault, where that eighteenth-century Freemason du Breuil wanted to create the new ritual."

"The shadow ritual."

"One of the keys to the ritual is in the fresco. You both have to get to Plaincourault as soon as possible."

"Hold on, brother. We're not trying to make this drug. We're after killers."

"Did you catch anyone?"

"Well, no. By the time the police arrived, they'd burned down the estate. I'm presuming the bodies in the ashes weren't theirs. We need to track them."

"Sophie was in Plaincourault before she went to Rome. She left me a message about an extraordinary fresco in the chapel. I'm sure it holds a key."

"Listen, our priority is—"

Jouhanneau's voice hardened. "A lot is at stake. The fresco is apparently a representation of the original sin. Eve's temptation. The missing link—and maybe a code, a formula—is in there. Call me when you get to Plaincourault."

Jouhanneau ended the call.

Marcas sipped his hot chocolate. He thought about the Breuil papers and how the man had insisted on a pit with a bare-rooted bush in the center. Was it coincidence that some people referred to the iboga as the Garden of Eden's tree of knowledge?

They were getting closer. But closer to what? They had two ingredients: iboga and Saint Anthony's fire. Just one more ingredient and they'd have the mind-blowing cocktail. But Marek had found something on the stone, something relating to a substance that "would seed the mind with prophesies." The danger was evident. The wrong dosage could mean the difference between heaven and hell, between the gates of horn and ivory.

Marcas pushed his hot chocolate aside. It was all too much, and none of it seemed to be getting him any closer to the reason he was here in the first place—finding Sophie's killers.

57

Frozen fries dumped in a burning-hot vat of oil of indeterminate age and origin, with greasy sausage on the side. Jade dabbed some ketchup on the fries to give them a pop of color, then scowled.

"Who eats this stuff?" she said.

Marcas looked in the rearview mirror and changed lanes to pass a camper. A little girl in the camper stuck out her tongue. Zewinski made a scary face in return, and the girl screamed and turned away. The parents glared. Marcas sped up, and the fries fell on Zewinski's pants.

"Careful. This damned junk food just stained my pants."

Marcas smiled. "Send the cleaning bill to Darsan. He'll be thrilled."

"You really couldn't find anything more suitable to eat?" she said, holding up a limp fry. "This is an insult to gastronomy in general and potatoes in particular. And I won't even mention this soggy thing they call sausage. It even stinks."

"There wasn't anything else at the service station. No sandwiches, no salads, nothing. And you were sleeping. Just another hour, and we'll be there. We can find something to eat then."

Zewinski put the food back in the paper bag and tossed it in the backseat. She made herself comfortable. They drove by forests, followed by monotonous fields that she found reassuring.

By the time Darsan had gotten his team to Chevreuse to arrest the Orden members, smoky ruins were all that was left. The firefighters had found six bodies, and everyone in the area sincerely lamented the loss of the people at the French Association for the Study of Minimalist Gardens, especially the nice Dutch gardener.

Zewinski hadn't reacted at the news of the fire. Darsan wanted to see them for a debriefing, but she had agreed to go along with Marcas's plan. She told Darsan that they were following a new lead and wouldn't be back until the next day. Zewinski was thinking about the crazies who had held her hostage and were now running free. A human life was nothing to them, nothing more than an opportunity to practice their absurd doctrine.

In her line of work, Zewinski had seen harsh, compassionless human beings who carried out summary executions, terrorist attacks, and revenge killings. But only once before had she seen such cruelty. That was under an Afghan warlord, General Abdul Rashid Dostum.

These memories were eating at her. Adding to her unease was the fact that she had gotten closer to Marcas in the last several hours. Marcas—why was she surprised? She had always had a thing for men who put themselves on the line.

"Don't you find something completely off about this story of archives and the Templars?" she asked.

"Off?"

"Yeah. Hunting for an ancient secret that might not even exist at a time when the world has more pressing issues: dictatorships, disease, hunger..."

Marcas just looked at her.

"And here we are, taking a drive in the country on some occult treasure hunt. If it weren't for the murder and kidnapping, it would be ridiculous."

"Correction. Two murders, counting Marek—three, if you include your cellmate," Marcas said, lighting a cigarette. That wasn't counting the other Hiram-like murders he'd heard about. "And to answer your question, no, I don't have a problem with our 'occult treasure hunt,' as you call it. When you accepted that job offer at the Rome embassy, did you think you'd be taking medicine to sick kids in Africa? Sorry. You're not working for UNICEF. I'm not either. I'm a cop doing my job. And right now my job's tracking down those killers, who happen to have an agenda."

"True enough. But I'm trying to put all this in perspective. With you, I have the feeling that I'm chasing a ghost, running after the wind, trying to grab a fantasy. Indiana Jones chasing the Holy Grail."

Marcas took a drag on his cigarette and exhaled.

"So you'd really feel more comfortable in a commando operation, where the enemy's right in front of you with submachine guns, and you've got yours pointed back. A modern-day OK Corral, right?"

"You took the words right out of my mouth."

"Well, nobody made you come along. Last I heard, you agreed to this. I can drop you off at the next train station, and in two and a half hours you'll be in Paris."

Marcas looked bullheaded now.

"Well excuse me for not liking arcane mysteries. I never read your code book. I don't understand why people get so worked up about Templars, astrology, healers, and the like. It's fairy tales for adults. And let's not even get into your Freemason enigmas. There are deadly sects out there that get pumped on that crap."

"Don't be so simplistic. It's easy to enter most sects and very hard to leave. It's the opposite with the Freemasons. You can leave anytime. And you can choose what you believe. A large number of Grand Orient members don't have the slightest interest in esotericism. Some are Masons purely for the fraternity and even share your opinion. Other lodges explore symbolism without ever getting into anything related to magic or the supernatural. In any case, there's a virtue called tolerance, and every individual is free to believe what he or she wants."

"Not in obscurantism."

Marcas frowned. "If only you knew how much Freemasonry has fought obscurantism. Did you go to school?"

"Of course I've gone to school. I don't see the connection."

"The connection? Public school, founded in France by Jules Ferry and open to everyone without class distinction, was inspired by Freemason ideas. The legislators who voted for that law were hoodwinkers, as you call us. The same goes for public education in the United States—it was a Freemason-backed initiative. Freemasons in France created the first collective health insurance system for workers. And Freemasons all over the world are working on programs that improve the lives of millions of adults and children: scholarship programs, disaster relief, hospitals, libraries, museums—you name it."

"Okay, okay."

Zewinski watched. The man was getting angry. Finally—he had dropped his well-behaved demeanor. She liked him better this way. She decided to push a little further.

"I get the social interest and all, but there aren't a whole lot of working-class folks in your lodges. They're full of doctors and businessmen and politicians. Regardless of the generation and the regime, you guys always side with power."

Marcas's fingers were turning white as he gripped the steering wheel.

"You're probably right about our membership. But it's absurd to say we're always on the side of power. Did you ever wonder why all totalitarian systems in the world have systematically forbidden freemasonry?"

"Yeah. Hitler and Mussolini did that, but they banned every kind of organized group, from labor unions to Catholic organizations."

"Add to that Pétain in France, Franco in Spain, and Salazar in Portugal. Freemasons have been persecuted in practically all communist countries and have had troubles in democracies, as well. Freemasonry, moreover, is prohibited in all Arab countries except Lebanon and Morocco."

"Thanks for the propaganda—tinged with paranoia, if I might add. But you haven't bothered to mention all the ordinary people like me who believe you Freemasons have something suspicious up your sleeves."

Marcas pulled onto the berm and hit the brakes. He turned to her.

"That's enough. Let me be clear. I'm not a spokesman for freemasonry, and just like any other group, Freemason lodges have their share of bastards. You're convinced we're all corrupt. That's fine by me. Your choice. But I'm not proselytizing, so would you quit busting my balls?"

Zewinski smiled. She had won the match. And he was almost attractive when he was annoyed.

"I suggest that you start driving again. It isn't safe to stay parked on the side of the highway like this."

"No, I won't start driving again. Not until you explain why you're so hostile to Freemasons."

Zewinski shifted in her seat.

"I'm waiting."

Zewinski sighed and told the story of her father's suicide and the role played by the Freemasons, who had forced him to sell his company at a price that was far lower than its value. When she finished, tears were rolling down her cheeks. Her father and her close friend, Sophie. Both dead because of Freemasons. That was enough to inspire a lifetime of animus.

Zewinski sensed that Marcas wanted to console her, and she almost wished he would reach for her hand. Instead, he waited quietly until she was done crying and passed her a clean and neatly folded handkerchief. He started the car and gradually accelerated as he pulled off the side of the road.

"Not another word until we get there," Zewinski said, staring out her window.

58

The five men and two woman were sitting on a bench overlooking the rocky bay. They were absorbed in their thoughts. Memories of their last meeting were still fresh in their minds.

The man with steely eyes and gold-framed glasses spoke first. "Sol called earlier. He was still in France. We should start with our regular business, and when he arrives, he'll fill us in on the Hiram operation. Be brief. Let's begin with Heimdall."

Every member of the board had taken a Nordic name at the time of initiation. Heimdall, an attorney who worked in a large practice, pulled a document from his briefcase.

"Our assets in the Miami-based pension fund and the consortium in Hong Kong have reached five hundred million euros," he said. "Investments in some of our other funds have dipped, but the Paxton steelworks, which we recently purchased, is doing well. Now I have a recommendation. I would like the board's approval to invest in an Israeli company."

The other members murmured their disapproval. The man smiled.

"I know we've been ethically opposed to investing in anything owned or managed by Jews. But this is an investment I endorse. The company's performance has been subpar over the last few years, but its holdings have great potential. I propose buying the company and selling off its assets at a considerable profit."

The man with steely eyes spoke. "It's out of the question. Anything else? No? Your turn, Freya."

The woman with short blonde hair cleared her throat. She was a well-known Swedish doctor whose work in cloning had nearly won her the Nobel Prize.

"There's not much to report," she said. "We've made no progress in prolonging the life of human clones. I don't see any improvement for the next couple of years. Our incubator in Asuncion is full of embryos. I propose that we sell them on the black market for medical research."

The other members agreed. The head of the group then pointed to a stocky man. "Thor?"

"Twenty representatives from political groups in both Eastern and Western Europe attended our most recent seminars on the progressive nature of our social program. The trainees seemed to be concerned about high unemployment, which the world's democracies can't seem to check. They left with a better understanding of our solution."

"Is that all?"

"No. We're having trouble with our white supremacy friends in the United States. The Ku Klux Klan, White Power, and Aryan Nations, which is closer to our movement, are bickering with each other. I recommend additional funding for the latter group."

The other woman, who was sixtyish and had piercing eyes, spoke up. "No. Why should we keep giving money to those crazies who tattoo swastikas all over themselves, giving our cause a bad name? We got rid of those Nazi symbols years ago. We should jettison the Americans with their portraits of the Führer. Here in Europe, we've been successful in furthering our own brand of populism coupled with xenophobia. We hurt ourselves by reconnecting with anything having to do with Hitler."

The man with hard gray eyes nodded. He had taken the name of Loki, the Nordic trickster god. "You're right," he said. "We'll cut them off. Thor, you'll go to the United States and take care of it. And you, Balder?"

A corpulent man shifted on the bench. "As you know, Sol was in France, at our residence in Chevreuse.

Unfortunately, the mansion had to be evacuated because of serious mistakes made by one of our female members. The gardener, one of our most capable South African colleagues, called to fill me in. Some of the team members have gone to London. The woman's with Sol at a hotel in Paris. Sol will tell us more when he gets here."

The man called Loki heard the grave tone in Balder's voice. That woman was his daughter. He knew that Orden statutes were clear: the punishment was death.

59

Marcas and Zewinski were driving through the Brenne region, the land of a thousand lakes. In fact, this region had some twenty-five thousand acres of ponds and lakes. After Mézières-en-Brenne, they took a local road for about six miles and then headed toward the park headquarters, where they would collect the keys to the chapel. Marcas knew the area well. He had dated a woman—a sister—from this area. She was the head of the historical monuments society. He had called her to get authorization to visit the chapel.

The parking lot was half full. Marcas and Zewinski stretched their legs, happy to be out of the car. The sun was still hanging over the large lake beyond the parking area, and a group of people with cameras and giant lenses were taking pictures. Jade walked around the car.

"Look at the paparazzi. Who's the star?"

"Here the stars are the whiskered tern, the little bustard, the common pochard, and the Eurasian bittern."

"Bustard sounds like something I'd call you," she said with a grin.

"So you're drawn to wild things," he responded with a wink. "You'll like this preserve. It attracts birdwatchers from all over Europe."

They walked toward the park headquarters. A group of kids ran by. Marcas frowned. He missed his son. They entered the building, which also housed a gift shop and a restaurant.

"Take a seat," Marcas said. "Order us some fried carp. It's a local specialty. I'll add a bottle of organic cider. I'll go get the keys."

Marcas returned just as the waitress was bringing over their food. He sat down and waited for her to walk away. "Now I'm going to tell you what we're really looking for in the Plaincourault Chapel."

60

A gigantic cloud of starlings circled above the Étang de la Mer Rouge, the largest lake in the region. The ballet lasted a good twenty minutes. Then some scouts split off from the flock, and the mass of birds broke up, as if by magic, settling in the surrounding trees for the night.

The sun, master of the dance of dusk, disappeared in the west, and evening took over. Tourists and inhabitants also retreated, leaving no trace of human presence in the immense aquatic space.

The car sped toward the southwest, heading for a village called Mérigny, where they would find the chapel.

"So correct me if I'm wrong," Jade said. "According to some enlightened Jouhanneau dude, top-tier illuminati of the Grand Orient, the secret to Sophie's documents lies in this chapel lost in the middle of nowhere, and we'll find it in a fresco painted in the Middle Ages."

"Yep."

Zewinski opened a tourist brochure on the chapel. "Here it says that Plaincourault was built in the twelfth century and belonged to the Knights Hospitaller of Saint John of Jerusalem, who later became the famous Order of Malta. They exercised authority all around the chapel, and until the fourteenth century, only knights were allowed in."

Zewinski stopped reading. "I don't get it," she said. "Sophie told me this was the Templar chapel."

"I was wondering the same thing," Marcas said. The answer's in the Breuil Manuscript. In the thirteenth century, two Templar dignitaries went over to the Hospitallers. Today we'd call them renegades. They became commanders. Breuil found documents confirming this. They were probably the two commanders who had that fresco painted.

In any case, the relationship between the Templars and the Hospitallers isn't all that clear. In Jerusalem, they were at war with each other, but members of the two orders in Europe formed alliances. We do know that when the Templars fell in 1307, many of the knights took refuge with the Hospitallers."

Zewinski continued to glean information from the brochure. "During the French Revolution, Plaincourault, like all other church assets, was seized by the state and sold to the people. The chapel was turned into a barn and started falling into ruin. In January 1944, a Vichy government worker responsible for historical monuments classified the chapel as a national monument. The building remained locked up and prey to the elements for more than fifty years. Then, in 1997, it was restored. Specialists spent three years returning the frescos to their original state. The chapel's now part of Brenne National Park."

They arrived half an hour later, after two wrong turns. The chapel stood on an overlook at a turn in the road. It was next to a field and a large farmhouse.

They parked on a dirt track running all the way around the building.

The site was deserted. The headlights had frightened away two rabbits. A dog barked in the distance.

"Here we are," Marcas said. He got out of the car and headed toward the entrance without waiting for Zewinski. He pulled out a large metal key, slipped it into the lock, and turned.

"Slow down," Zewinski called out. "I'm coming too."

He was already inside and could barely hear her. He flipped a wall switch, but nothing happened. He pulled out a flashlight and swept its beam back and forth.

Zewinski caught up, and they slowly walked past the rows of benches, taking in the paintings, silent witness to the time when Christianity was the most potent force in France and an integral part of the lives of both humble field workers and aristocrats.

On their right, Saint Eloi, wearing a halo, was striking a horseshoe with a hammer under the watchful eyes of two craftsmen. Farther along, angels with blurred faces were gazing at other saints. On the left, near the third row of benches, there was a Middle Age bestiary, with two fighting leopards, their claws splayed. One was wearing a crown.

The flashlight beam revealed a rich palette of colors—yellows and reds, nuanced grays, bluish touches, and alabaster green.

"Marcas, look at this."

Higher up on the wall, a beaming fox was playing a medieval musical instrument, perhaps a viola, for a hen and her chicks. Next to it, like a scene in a graphic novel, the fox was slitting the hen's throat.

"I get it," Zewinski said. "The fox is playing the woman. He's out to get himself some fresh meat. Those knights had a dark sense of humor, didn't they."

"Some sense of humor," Marcas said. "But the fresco we want is over there, near the altar."

They walked past a small black railing that marked the entrance to the apse. Marcas angled the flashlight to illuminate the ceiling and the frescos. It created a play of shadows, making the pictures on the ceiling dance.

Jade grabbed the light. "Let me find out what doesn't fit," she said.

At first, nothing jumped out at them. A Byzantine-inspired Christ Pantocrator presided over the apse. His right fingers pointed to the sky, and he was surrounded by a traditional tetramorph, four allegorical representations of the evangelists: a lion for Mark, an eagle for John, an ox for Luke, and a man for Matthew.

On either side were frescos about six feet high, separated by narrow windows.

"What's that?" Marcas said. "Let's see what I can remember from catechism. Here is a crucifixion, there the Virgin Mary with child, a whole bunch of souls, and over

there, to the far right, Adam and Eve surrounded by…
Well, well, what is it that I see? It's a—"

Marcas let Zewinski say the magic word.

61

The wind had been picking up since nightfall. The forecast was storms over the Adriatic. Boats were returning to port. Lightning flashed in the distance, followed by thunder.

Fascinated by the show of unbridled elements, Loki was sitting on the bench at the edge of the overlook. He was holding a cell phone to his ear and talking to his master, Sol.

"A good omen. Thor is wielding his hammer. The board isn't happy with your explanation regarding the Hiram operation, except perhaps Freya. They respect you and would never dare to question your word, but—"

"But what?"

"They belong to another generation. They share our political ideas and love the organization's power, but remain deeply skeptical. They don't think Operation Hiram will yield anything. And the loss of one of the order's houses galls them."

Loki looked out at the rumbling sea. Sol's voice grew stronger.

"But they were initiated. They know that the spiritual side is most important. If Operation Hiram succeeds, we'll be at the dawn of a new era. The Thule will be back. Don't they understand?"

"In theory, yes, but discussing anything related to the divine is too abstract for them. Heimdall even wondered if you were getting senile."

Sol was shouting now. "They'll see if I'm a crazy old man! When I think about what their forefathers sacrificed. They're gutless wonders, every one of them. Their entitlements are all that they care about. None of them would have made it into the Waffen SS, like I did. They've lost the taste for blood. I made a mistake giving them power.

We need to replace the board. You'll do that for me. I need to finish Operation Hiram. When it's all over, we'll be witness to a new night."

"A night?" Loki asked, watching dark clouds roll over the coastline. Sol's voice sounded like a metallic echo.

"A night of long knives. Like the Führer's. More pleasures await your Iron Maiden. I have to go now. I'm meeting some very interesting people. And by the way, your daughter says hello."

He ended the call.

62

"A giant toadstool."

Marcas nodded. "A superb *Amanita muscaria*, or fly amanita," he said.

Jade and Marcas stepped closer to the mural to get a better view.

Adam and Eve stood naked, their hands covering their genitals. Between them, five long-stemmed mushrooms rose from a single spot. A snake was wrapped around the central stem, its head toward Eve.

Jade leaned in. "Amazing. A shroom instead of an apple tree. That's an intriguing depiction of the original sin. It must have been a shock for the worshippers."

"Maybe not. The worshippers weren't ordinary people, you know. This chapel was forbidden to commoners. It was used exclusively by the Knights of Hospitaller for two full centuries."

Marcas pulled out his phone and started taking pictures of the mural while Zewinski examined the details.

"What's this got to do with the Breuil Manuscript?" she asked.

Marcas put his cell phone back in his pocket. "Remember, Breuil bought this chapel and the land around it, so he must have seen the mural. He came back from Egypt and wanted to create a completely new ritual, change the bitter initiation wine, and dig a pit in the middle of the temple for a bush. Take a good look at the mushroom. Doesn't it look like a fruit tree?"

"It looks like a mushroom to me."

"Yes, but Breuil, like many other Freemasons, was skilled at using parables and symbols. I think he wanted to use this mushroom in his ritual. It's the missing ingredient."

Zewinski shrugged. "Why this mushroom?"

"It's not just any mushroom. It's a magic mushroom. It's known for its hallucinogenic properties. Many religions and other belief systems have used mushrooms since ancient times to commune with the divine. So according to this painting, Adam and Eve were chased out of paradise for eating a mushroom, not an apple."

"I've heard of South and Central American cultures that have cults based on sacred mushrooms."

"Shamans in many cultures rely on psychedelic mushrooms. The psilocybin mushroom was an integral part of Aztec religious ceremonies in Mexico because of its hallucinogenic properties. They called it *teonanacatl*, which means 'God's flesh.' And as far back as 1,000 BC, there was a Mesoamerican mushroom cult in what is now the Guatemalan highlands."

"How do you know all this?"

"I listened to one of our brothers, a botanist, give a brilliant presentation on the role hallucinogenic mushrooms played in Central American religious ceremonies. He suggested that the visions recounted by Christian mystics were identical to hallucinations experienced by Mayan and Aztec priests."

Zewinski smiled. Finally, a rational explanation from a Freemason. Maybe she could even like him someday.

"Did he have anything to back up his theory?" she asked.

"He talked about experiments conducted in the nineteen sixties in the United States. A Dr. Walter Pahnke gave psilocybin to Christian theology-student volunteers. After absorbing a purified form of the mushroom, three of the ten said they had experienced intense mystical visions. They had the feeling of being one with Christ and the Virgin Mother. They really saw Jesus and Mary."

"How'd that work?"

"The molecules in the plants have a chemical structure similar to neurotransmitters. They basically replace the brain's neurotransmitters, causing what you might call a big bang in the head."

Zewinski looked at the mural again. "Is there anything else to discover?"

"Sophie came here and found something else. But what? It must be in the details. There must be some coded formula or a partial one, probably in numbers."

Zewinski stared at the wall. "For the code to the safe at the embassy, Sophie insisted on using the Templar spelling of the word Plaincourault. She added two letters to get fifteen."

Marcas bit his lip. "What if we focus on the number fifteen in this mural. There are five mushroom caps atop five stems."

Zewinski shook her head. "No, look. Two other thinner stems branch off from the central trunk and support the main cap. That's five caps and seven stems."

Marcas scratched his head. "Five and seven. We don't have fifteen."

Jade grinned. "I know. Five plus seven plus three equal fifteen. So three would be the number. Look, the snake is wrapped around the stem three times."

"Congratulations. A-plus in symbolism."

"So why three numbers?"

"My turn now. In Freemasonry, every grade or degree is symbolized by a number: three for the entered apprentice, five for fellowcraft, and seven for master."

"I gather that each ingredient gets a number: three for one, five for the other, and seven for the third. But which ingredient gets which number?"

"Good question, but what I want to know is this: where's the pit? Breuil underscores the importance of the pit, where the roots take hold. It was only in the birth of life underground that the seven heavens could be attained. The key enlightenment lay in the earth, or the womb, or something of that nature."

"Could three, five, and seven help us find it?"

Marcas and Zewinski began counting steps from the base of the mushroom in various directions, testing different combinations of the numbers.

"Maybe the numbers have nothing to do with it," Zewinski finally said. "You and your Freemason symbolism bull are getting us nowhere."

Marcas moved back to the mushroom and started feeling the wall.

"Hold your horses," Zewinski said. "You may be a cop, but this is historical property that belongs to the people of France, and you're getting your greasy fingers all over it."

Marcas smiled but continued working on the flagstones at the base of the fresco. "Look, one is crooked. Give me a hand."

Zewinski looked around the chapel for a tool and found a candle snuffer. She gave it to Marcas, and he pried the stone up, using the snuffer's long handle. Something in a dirty canvas-like cloth was under the stone.

"Well, look at that."

Marcas unwrapped two wax-sealed vials containing a murky liquid.

"Do you suppose that's the God brew?" Zewinski asked.

"Anything is possible."

Marcas sat down on the step beneath the altar. The heat collected in the building's thick stone walls during the day was dissipating. Zewinski sat down next to him, and he became very aware of her presence.

Jade was looking at the night sky through one of the narrow windows. It was dark inside, except for the glow of the flashlight on the floor.

"What a perfect place for this mysterious crap," Jade said. "I can just see the knights in their long capes kneeling before this heretical painting." She shivered. "And we're still no closer to finding Sophie's murderer."

Silence filled the chapel. Marcas put his arm around her. Jade took his hand and moved closer.

No sooner had she done this than a voice rang out in the darkness. "Look at that. Adam and Eve back together in front of the Tree of Knowledge. What a scene."

63

Marcas and Jade shielded their eyes from the harsh light the man was aiming at them.

"Fly amanita grows in round formations called witches circles," the man said. "This region has always been known for its witches. Leave the vials where they are, and put your hands up. Now slowly move away from the painting."

Four threatening figures moved toward them, one limping. Marcas regretted leaving his gun in the glove compartment of his car.

The group stopped in front of them, where Marcas and Jade could make out their faces. In the middle was an older man with white hair and an expressionless face. Jade recognized the person to his left: Joana, who was waving her bandaged hand. On the other side of the leader was a younger man with short hair and a detached look in his eyes. He was pointing a MP5 submachine gun with a sound suppressor in their direction. The fourth man stood in the shadows. The leader lowered his flashlight.

"I happened to overhear your fascinating conversation about the amanita. Its nefarious reputation as a poisonous mushroom dates to the beginnings of Christianity. But before Christianity took root, it was considered the plant of immortality. It was used as early as the latter part of the Paleolithic Period. You mentioned God's flesh. Shamans and pagan priests venerated each mushroom as a little piece of divinity on earth. But when the Church took power, these mushrooms became witches ware. Did you know that Saint Augustine wrote a text denouncing the use of these very special plants? But I'm digressing. Klaus, can you hold my flashlight?"

Rubbing his hands together, the old man stepped in front of the fresco.

"Absolute blasphemy. A hallucinogenic mushroom replacing the apple. The knights were taking a great risk during the Inquisition."

"Who are you?" Marcas asked.

The white-haired man continued to contemplate the painting. "My name is Sol. That name means nothing to you, but the name of my order should."

"The Thule, right?"

The old man turned around. "Good. Very good. So there really are a few Freemasons who know something about world history. For that matter, I want to thank you, Inspector. We started following you after your tête-à-tête at the Interior Ministry. What interesting meetings you've had, especially at the Grand Orient Lodge. You were such an easy target. We stayed on your tail, even when you were picking up your charming friend not so far from our compound. If it hadn't been for you, we wouldn't be here having this nice little chat. And I wouldn't have found what I was looking for."

Sol picked up the vials, his eyes glistening.

Marcas spoke in a matter-of-fact tone. "So you weren't surprised by the presence of this mushroom."

"No, I figured it would be one of the ingredients in the brew. Fly amanita contains ibotenic acid and muscimol, long-range missiles that directly target neurons. I was hoping to know how much of each ingredient to use, but now, because you're so clever, we have something even better: the actual mixture. Hans, take it to the team and have them make up a fresh brew."

Sol turned back to Marcas and Jade. "All we need is to do now is lay the groundwork for the ritual."

Joana interrupted, "Leave the girl to me. I'll take care of her."

The old man raised a hand. "Later. We'll keep our Adam and Eve together for a moment. I still need the Mason for the ritual. We'll be having a very special ceremony."

Marcas interrupted. "Then what? Will you kill us? Like Hiram?"

Sol's lips curled into a smile. "Perhaps. But we're not there yet. Let's go."

The bodyguard moved toward them.

"Who are you, really?" Jade's voice echoed in the chapel.

"My real name? It's François Le Guermand, once French, like you."

"And now?"

"Nationality is of no importance. Only race counts."

64

Jade and Marcas were in the back of an SUV, their hands and feet bound. After about an hour on the highway, the vehicle turned onto what felt like an unpaved road. Centuries-old oak trees cast ominous shadows under the moonlight.

"Where are we going?" Marcas asked.

Sol turned around and looked at him. "The Orden has a small property in the Perigord-Limousin Natural Park. I think you'll find it quite comfortable."

A two-story stone house stood at the end of the forest road, next to a tumbledown dovecote. The brown shutters of the house were open, and the lights on the first floor were on. A man in a hunting jacket drew back the curtains and waved. Jade stiffened when she saw him.

The bodyguard, who had been driving, parked the vehicle in front of the porch. He hopped out, made his way around the car to open the door for Sol, and then opened the back, untying the bindings around Marcas's and Jade's feet. The man emerged from the house and started down the grassy path. He was smoking a pipe.

"Look, our friend the gardener is coming to say hello," Sol said.

Joana made a face. "How kind of him. I could have done without."

"Now, now. Be nice. He's prepared the house for us."

"What devotion."

The gardener reached them and greeted Sol. He ignored Joana.

"I'm happy to see you again. I've prepared a buffet, and rooms are ready for you and our honored guests."

"Thank you. I'll be sure to mention your efficiency to the board. We won't be here long. Bring our guests in for dinner."

The man rubbed his stubbly cheek. "Really? I thought I would spend a little pruning time with them."

"Do as you're told."

"What about her?" the gardener said, pointing his chin at Joana.

"She's seconding me in this operation. Consider her your superior."

Joana snickered. "Did you hear that? Do your duty. Bring the prisoners."

The man glared at her. "We'll see once this mission is over. Believe me."

He stepped aside and let Sol and Joana enter the house. Then he took Marcas and Zewinski in. The walls of the entry hall were filled with stag trophies, and under each mount was a copper plaque indicating the year the animal was bagged. Some were more than a century old.

The gardener freed their hands.

In the main room, a man was adding two place settings to the table. The walls were hung with paintings of local squires in eighteenth-century hunting gear. The landowners were staring into the room, looking suspicious of any visitors. Farming tools were laid out here and there, adding a finishing touch to the rustic look of the room. Sol sat down in one of the carved chairs and looked around. He pointed to two empty chairs.

"Come, my friends. Join us for something to eat."

Marcas and Jade looked at each other, then sat down in silence. Large platters full of carrots, beets, lettuce, chicory, radishes, and tomatoes were lined up next to a soup tureen filled with an orange-colored liquid and a large bowl of boiled potatoes.

Marcas helped himself to some vegetables. "I'm surprised. You're not much of a carnivore."

Sol was serving himself generously. "True. Meat is forbidden. I haven't eaten any in sixty years. It's a secret to longevity."

Jade wasn't touching any of the food. She looked at Sol. "You do know what happens when law-enforcement officials are kidnapped in this country, don't you? Every police officer and gendarme in France will be looking for us. You won't get away."

"Shut up," Joana interrupted. "One more threat and I'll kill you. Slowly."

"With just one hand?"

Joana shot up and grabbed a knife with her left hand.

"Enough," Sol bellowed.

Glaring at Jade, Joana held her position a few seconds. Then she slowly sat down again.

Sol turned to Marcas. "Yes, we were talking about meat. It contains toxins that cause disease. Fruits and vegetables, however, are extraordinarily nutritional. I recommend the pumpkin soup to your right. It's excellent."

"Is that what the Thule teaches?"

"Among other things."

Marcas observed the old man and then said, "Since you honor us with such fine food, would you also be kind enough to shed light on some obscure points?"

"Why not? I rarely have the opportunity to talk with Freemasons. I usually kill them."

"What is the Thule's goal?"

"That is an exhaustive subject, but in short, our goal is preserving the superiority of our bloodline. I'm honored to be part of this organization, which is focused on stopping the invasion of blacks, Arabs, Jews, Chinks, Japs, and mixed breeds of all kinds."

"Oh, so the Thule's a kind of animal-rights organization," Jade said. "Although I wouldn't put you and the Fund for Animal Welfare in the same league."

"How did you find out about the Freemason archives?" Marcas asked.

Sol waved his hand. "I prefer to tell you about our order. Perhaps you'll understand better, but considering the group you belong to, I doubt it. Take a look at the bust behind you."

Marcas and Jade turned around and saw the sculpted head of a man with a receding hairline, double chin, and long, straight nose. The stand it was on was decorated with a circular swastika atop a dagger.

Sol lit a cigar. "That was Rudolf Grauer. We owe him everything. You'll find his bust in each of the order's properties. He created the Thule society long before the birth of the Nazi Party. He was a genius, and he changed the face of the world. Compared with him, Hitler was a no-account. Grauer was born in 1875, the son of a locomotive engineer. As soon as he was old enough, he became a merchant sailor. In 1900, he settled in Turkey, where he made a considerable fortune before returning to Germany, certain of his path in life. He was quickly adopted by the aristocracy and became Count Rudolf von Sebottendorf. At the time, a nationalist movement was afoot in Kaiser Germany, embodied by various patriotic and anti-Semitic groups given the general name *völkisch*."

Marcas was listening carefully. "Anti-Freemason too, I suppose?"

"What do you think? At the time, our founder was part of the Germanenorden, and he rose quickly in the ranks. He left for Munich in 1918 to found a lodge called the Thule-Gesellschaft. In less than four months, he managed to recruit the elite and start two newspapers, including the *Beobachter*, which the Nazis would later use. He was quite influential, and he used the same operational approach as the Freemasons, which, of course, he had studied carefully. But his was based on Norse paganism."

"And that's your symbol?" Marcas asked, pointing below the bust.

"The Thule's emblem incorporates a circular swastika— the Thule was using that swastika when Hitler was begging people to buy his paintings on the streets of Vienna—and a dagger of revenge."

"How interesting. The same kind of weapon is sometimes used in Freemason ceremonies."

Sol went on. "Very quickly, Sebottendorf dictated the first and only commandment: the white race must rule the world. He was a visionary with one word as a credo: *Halgadom*."

Jade was shifting in her seat.

Sol went on in a soft voice. "*Halgadom* means sacred temple. You Freemasons want to recreate the Jewish Temple of Solomon, and we want to build a temple for all the people descended from the Aryan Thule race—Nordic, Germanic, Saxon, Celtic, and, well, French. All those with blood in their veins from the migrating Germanic tribes, the Goths and the Francs."

"Our temple is one of fraternity, equality, and all humanity."

"Right. Your lodges are as elitist as they come," Sol said, pouring himself a glass of water. "Sebottendorf knew that only the proletariat could renew the Aryan race, and he wanted to spread his ideas through the working class. One of his associates, Karl Harrer, founded a group for that. In January 1919, Anton Drexler rose to the top of the German workers party, which Adolf Hitler would later join and turn into the Nazi Party."

"Hitler prospered on the ruins of the armistice, because of endemic unemployment and heightened nationalism," Marcas countered.

"Yes, but the Thule was in the background. Although we had no direct control of Hitler, we did infiltrate the ranks of his dignitaries and others close to him. Hess, Rosenberg, Himmler, and others. Do you think Hitler would have risen to power without financing from German industrialists? Many were members of the Thule. But Hitler failed because of his megalomania. We overestimated him."

"Millions of Jews were reduced to slavery and exterminated," Jade, her cheeks flushed with anger, spit out. "That was a fine program you had."

Sol nodded to his bodyguard. "Miss, do I need to have my bodyguard shoot you in the head?"

Marcas touched Jade's thigh to calm her. He picked up the conversation.

"But you're French. What are you doing mixed up in all that?"

The old man smiled. "It's very simple. I joined the Waffen SS during the war, and members of the Thule chose me for initiation. I was sponsored, like a Freemason."

Marcas's face hardened.

Jade spoke up before he could say anything. "Perfect. Just like a game of Happy Families. In the Nazi family, I want the grandfather, the French SS officer. How many woman and children did you kill?"

Joana stood up and slapped Jade with her good hand. The bodyguard grabbed Jade's arms to keep her from retaliating. Sol's eyes filled with disdain.

"The Charlemagne Division fought at the front and defended Berlin. We had nothing to do with the concentration camps. It was because of my bravery that I earned the rank of *obersturmbannführer*."

"And then?"

"My mission consisted of hiding Freemason documents pillaged from France. They were highly prized by the order. Do you understand now?"

"But why?"

"One of the Thule branches in the SS, the Ahnenerbe Institute, was doing research on Aryan India and discovered the existence of the sacred drink, the soma. Very soon thereafter, they conducted experiments with hallucinogenic plants at the Westphalia castle. They had recruited archeologists and biologists to figure out what was in the soma. It was tested on Russian prisoners. The mixtures had spectacular effects."

Zewinski guffawed. "What a bunch of crazies. You just wanted to get high."

Sol slowly put down his cigar and turned to her. "You do know that in the nineteen fifties and sixties, the CIA was doing the same experiments, don't you?"

"The Americans?"

"The CIA financed advanced research on LSD. A certain Dr. Sidney Gottlieb headed up the experiments. Gottlieb and select associates laced fellow researchers' coffee with LSD to test their reactions. Later on, he expanded his research to include prostitutes, prisoners, drug addicts, and mental patients—people who wouldn't be believed if they told their story. Some of the subjects reported that they felt like their flesh was dropping off their bones."

"The flesh falling off the bones," Marcas said in a half whisper.

Sol looked at him. "What is that, Inspector?"

"Those experiments ended a long time ago," Marcas said. "So you're after some mind-control drug. Is that it?"

"Oh, Inspector Marcas, you so underestimate the power of the soma. With it, the Thule will be reborn, and the Aryan race will rule again."

Jade rolled her eyes. Marcas kicked her under the table before she could speak.

"What does this have to do with the Freemason archives?" he asked

"We'd been looking for the Freemason secret for a long time. Then, in the archives from France, researchers at the Ahnenerbe found a document that referred to a ritual based on a divine drink."

Marcas pursed his lips. "The shadow ritual."

Sol lit another cigar. "That's right. The Ahnenerbe had a French neurologist and Freemason, Henri Jouhanneau, transferred to Berlin to go through the archives lifted from Paris. He found scattered fragments of the ritual. There was a study on rye ergot and a manuscript by a man named Breuil."

"Where do you come into this?"

"In 1945, my convoy ran into a Red Army roadblock, but I managed to escape with a handful of documents, including part of the Breuil manuscript that mentioned three ingredients, one being a plant from the East. In it, he described a trip to Egypt. I hid the papers under the altar of a church in a ruined village, and I headed for Allied lines. When Jouhanneau's son got that call from the Jewish archeologist in Israel, we were ready."

"The Tebah Stone?"

Sol nodded. "Yes. Then you did the work for us. I never will be able to thank you enough for the chapel."

"And now? What are you going to do?"

Sol yawned and stood up. "Joana here is quite impatient to take care of your girlfriend, but I still need the two of you. I'm tired now, and I need my rest. We'll see each other in the morning, and we'll discuss the ritual then."

A vestige from another era, Sol was looking very old. Marcas asked one more question.

"Why the name Sol?"

"It comes from the sun god revered during the Roman Empire: Sol Invictus—the unconquered sun. It relates to the winter solstice, December twenty-first, when the sun is reborn, and the days get longer. Christians turned the solstice into a celebration of the birth of Jesus. Like the sun—and unlike Jesus, who was crucified—I will go unvanquished."

65

The bodyguard ushered Marcas and Zewinski into a bedroom, sat them down in chairs, and bound their hands and feet again. Then he left.

"What do we do now?" Zewinski asked.

"I don't know yet," Marcas said. "I suppose we should get some rest too."

They sat in silence.

"What do you think about this secret mystical drink?" Jade finally asked.

"Freemasonry isn't about magic for me or about power. What counts is the work that you do in the lodge. There's no elixir, no secret potion, no single key that gives access to the divine. The light comes from understanding the beauty of symbols, knowing how to find traces of overall coherence in the human world."

"The rest is just fantasy then?"

"As with a lot of things, people think the Freemasons have much more influence than we really have. Take the seal on the dollar bill. You've seen the pyramid with the eye at the top. It's recognized as a Masonic symbol, and, indeed, many of the founding fathers were Masons. It's not likely, though, that they had any big scheme in mind. At the bottom of the seal, there's a Latin expression, *novus ordo seculorum*, which means 'new order of the ages.' Some people think there's some mysterious message in this. But the phrase probably refers to the establishment of a democracy in the new world—that's all."

"But what's all the secret mumbo jumbo then?"

"It's about ritual, ritual that hasn't changed since the eighteenth century. The initiation ritual, for example, has the candidate being purified—symbolically—by the four elements: earth, water, air, and fire. Since ancient times these elements have represented both man and the universe, and they symbolize stages in a person's journey toward truth. As you go through the ceremony, you move from chaos to the road of creation. Earth is the place of preparation for the trials ahead, a place of passage; water, the origin of life; air, the quest for knowledge; and fire—"

"You're doing it again."

"What?"

"Being pedantic. Meanwhile, we're tied up with crazy killers down the hall."

"Yeah. I hadn't forgotten that."

They spent the rest of the night shifting fitfully in the chairs, dozing on and off.

When the first rays of sunlight came through the window, they heard movement in the hallway.

"Hey, anyone out there?" Jade shouted.

The door opened, and the guard came in.

"I need to go to the bathroom," Jade said. "Do you understand?"

The man shook his head. "*Nein, nein.*"

Jade put on her meanest look and shouted, "Sol, *schnell.*"

The man hesitated, then left the room, locking the door behind him. Marcas turned to Jade.

"Is that the best you've got? I mean, doesn't embassy security implant some secret GPS emitter in the heel of your shoe or something like that?"

"Yeah, right. And you, don't you have some telepathic connection with the Grand Architect of the Universe who could alert your brothers?"

"What a couple we are," Marcas said. He looked at Jade and saw how pale she was. He didn't want to think about how ghoulish he looked. He needed a shave, and he probably had dark rings under his eyes.

The key turned in the keyhole, and the door opened. The guard appeared with Joana.

"Sol is still resting. I'm here. Talk," she said, walking over to Jade, who reared back.

"We want to go to the bathroom and wash up," Marcas said.

Joana took cutters out of her pocket. "We're not monsters. Klaus will go with you, but first, I will borrow one of your girlfriend's little fingers. The gardener's not entitled to all the fun."

Before Jade had time to react, Joana clipped off the finger. Jade shrieked in pain. Marcas fought to free himself.

"Stop!"

"Shut up, dog. That is nothing, compared to what she did to me," Joana said, holding up her crushed hand. "Soon enough, when we are done with you, she will beg me to kill her."

Jade kept screaming in pain.

66

The candles illuminated the small crypt under the castle. Loki was contemplating the piece of black marble engraved with a circular swastika. It was used in the solstice ceremonies. He hadn't had any news from Sol in twenty-four hours and was beginning to worry about his daughter. His fellow board members had been looking at him oddly since his last conversation with Sol. It didn't matter. He'd be rid of all those incompetents soon enough.

Heimdall had wanted to speak to him alone.

Loki heard heavy footsteps echo in the stone stairwell. He turned and saw Heimdall with a security guard.

"I thought you were coming alone."

"Loki is the trickster god. I never forget that. Operation Hiram is canceled."

Loki moved closer to the altar. "How is that? Sol will be furious."

The two men came toward him. "The board took a vote earlier."

"Impossible. I wasn't there."

"You are no longer part of the Thule."

Loki regretted not having a weapon with him. "That can't be."

"Your cell phone was tapped. We're aware of Sol's intentions: the night of long knives. You can understand our displeasure."

He heard other footsteps. Two armed men entered the crypt. Loki held onto the altar.

"You don't understand. Operation Hiram is vital for the Thule."

"Sol is a senile old man chasing ghosts, and he nearly got us made by the French police. He has committed too many errors. These Freemason assassinations are stupid. As for his Palestinian killer, it wouldn't have taken much for the Israelis to connect him to us. Have you forgotten von Sebottendorf's principles? Our strength lies in our invisibility. That is how we prosper and remain untouchable."

"I know that better than you."

"Enough. Orders have been given to get rid of Sol and your daughter, as well as their prisoners. As for you, we're going to take you to see your friend."

Loki stared at him, uncomprehending.

"A maiden."

"You can't!"

"The Iron Maiden."

67

Sol came in next.

"I'm hoping you'll be amenable to talking now."

"You're animals," Marcas said.

"Joana, show him our merciful side, would you? Bandage up the woman's hand." Then Sol focused on Marcas. "The original plan was to organize a full Orden solstice ritual in June, but our schedule has been bumped up. I need your input."

"Never."

"My brother—if I may call you that—how much would you like to see this woman of yours suffer?"

Marcas glared at him.

"Our friend Breuil talks about a temple with a pit and a plant. Where do you think we can find that?"

Marcas had already given this some thought, but he was still confused. He glanced at Jade. Her eyes were pleading. He turned to Joanna, who was fiddling with the pruners.

Marcas looked Sol in the eye. "Okay, let's go over what we know. In Breuil's ritual, there was a bush with exposed roots, something about life coming from underground to reach the heavens. And we have the brew. That's not a lot to go on."

"I'm sure your advanced Masonic knowledge will help you find the answer."

"There wasn't anything else about the ritual per se, but he did pay attention to the bitter drink. If I recall, he said that initiation had become a parody."

"Initiation?" Jade managed to say.

Marcas looked at her. Something clicked. "Yes, initiation. That's it. The four elements are key to initiation: fire, air, water, earth. Fire, Saint Anthony's fire, ergot; air,

Amanita muscaria, the fly amanita; and water, the primordial element. In the *Bvitti* cult, iboga led initiates back to the roots of their existence."

"And earth?" Sol asked.

"Earth would be the place of preparation and passage."

"So we dig a pit?" Joana said.

"The pit was symbolic," Marcas answered. "You'd want some sanctuary, a temple, or, I suppose, a cave. Prehistoric people used them for religious rituals. Some scholars believe painted caves were sacred spaces reserved for connecting with another dimension, like our temples."

Sol was smiling now. "So we need a cave-temple. And as I'll be communing with the gods, I want the best possible cave-temple. What do you suggest?"

Marcas was drawing a blank.

"Well?" Sol said. He turned to Joana, "You may be in for some more fun."

Marcas's eyes darted from Jade to Sol and Joana as he tried to come up a cave-temple. "You said we're in Perigord?"

"Not exactly, but close enough."

His mind was racing: Perigord, southwestern France, truffles, foie gras, Sarlat, Dordogne. "Lascaux," he finally said.

Sol's eyes gleamed. "I was right about you, Inspector. Lascaux is perfect. It's the Sistine Chapel of prehistory. A singular place, ideal for testing the soma of the gods."

68

The convoy was ready. There had been some commotion in the afternoon, when Hans came and went again. Sol had decided to delay their departure until evening. He wanted to avoid the tourists and Lascaux workers. He needed privacy for his ritual. Sol was wearing a satisfied look as the prisoners, still bound, were brought outside. He nodded at Klaus, the guard, who freed Marcas's hands and then pointed a gun at Zewinski.

"Don't try anything stupid, now," Sol said, handing Marcas a cell phone. "Call one of your Freemason contacts and get us into Lascaux. I want the real caves, not the tourist replica."

Marcas punched in the number for the worshipful master of his lodge and, keeping his voice as calm as possible, politely inquired about the weather. "I'm so sorry to hear it's raining in Paris. I'm in Dordogne and I'd like to visit Lascaux—the real cave—this evening. Can you pull some strings at the ministry for me? If that doesn't work, call my buddy Jaigu. He's always trying to fix me up with women. Maybe he knows a good-looking blonde at the Committee for the Preservation of Lascaux. That's right. Tonight. Nine p.m. There will be two of us."

Marcas ended the call, and Klaus bound his hands again.

"I'm looking forward to the drive. We haven't finished our discussion," Sol said. "But first, let's thank our host, the gardener, for his hospitality."

Klaus pushed the gardener in front of Sol. The man's face was covered with blood.

"Our protector of plants and flowers had a strange notion to kill us while we were resting last night. Fortunately,

Klaus was watching over us. I suppose he received his orders from the board. Joana, would you take care of him?"

Joana, knife in hand, walked up to the gardener. She plunged the knife into his lower abdomen and pulled it up and to the right. Shrieking, the man collapsed. Sol marched to the SUV without looking back.

"Amazing how much dexterity that girl has even in her left hand. I'm pleased our Joana hasn't lost her touch. It'll take about twenty minutes for him to die."

The gardener was twisting on the ground like an earthworm cut in half.

Klaus pushed Jade and Marcas into their seats in the back. Sol and Jade took the middle row of bucket seats, and Klaus slid behind the wheel. Sol whistled as he studied a road map.

Marcas decided to start the conversation again. "You didn't tell us how the war ended for you."

Sol looked back at him. "It was quick. I escaped from the French patrol that intercepted me, and I made it to Switzerland to contact our Odessa network.

"Odessa?"

"And here I thought you knew your history. The SS and Thule realized well before the Battle of Stalingrad in 1943 that defeat was coming. Of course they set up an evacuation network to neutral countries. Mostly South Africa, but also Syria and Egypt."

"Odessa was the operation's name?"

"Odessa for Organisation der Ehemaligen SS-Angehörigen, or Organization of Former SS Members. The SS had used its war booty to buy businesses in the countries that would take in the ex-officers. Bank accounts had been opened in respectable places like Switzerland, naturally.

"So I guess Hitler didn't know about the plan," Jade said. "If he had, he might have opted to spend a pleasant post-Reich retirement in some obscure South American village instead of killing himself."

Sol smiled, "You are so right. Hitler was a criminal. We had no desire to help him save his own skin."

"What?"

"Our precious blood was spilled in that war. Millions of Aryans died because of him."

"You're joking, right?"

Sol smiled again, as if he were talking to a child too young to understand. "Of course you don't share my point of view. The Thule had no direct power over the Führer, and at best could only influence certain decisions. The Thule had even less influence when madness took hold of him."

"And you?" Jade asked.

"I started another life, and I rose in the Orden ranks. When communism fell, we recovered the few Masonic papers that I had hidden, and we analyzed them."

Sol's eyes were glistening. "That was when I understood how priceless they were."

"But for what?" Marcas exclaimed. "Do you really want to contact God?"

"Not your God, my friend, but mine, which is infinitely more powerful."

69

They were parked in the center of Montignac, the small town closest to Lascaux. Marcas and Zewinski, still tied up in the back of the SUV, said nothing. Outside, Joana hung up her phone. Sol rolled down the window.

"They picked him up this afternoon, and he should be here shortly."

Marcas shot Zewinski a questioning look.

"Who?" Marcas asked.

Sol stepped out of the car and stretched his legs, ignoring the prisoner. "Marcas and I will go on ahead. You and Klaus wait here with the lady. When our friends get here, have them drive you to the caves. Klaus, give me the package Hans dropped off."

The bodyguard handed a small bag to Sol and yanked Jade out of the car.

"Let go of me, dammit," Jade said, shaking off his grip. He had a gun at her back. "I'll stay here. What the hell else would I do?"

Klaus hustled her toward Joana, who took up a position in the shadows, near a tree.

Sol climbed into the driver's seat. "Klaus, make sure Joana doesn't get carried away—not until I say so," he said as he drove off.

~~~

A cool wind had risen with the stars. The conservator of the cave was standing at the entrance, giving the unexpected visitors a final look-over. Visits were usually scheduled months in advance. The few people who received permission to see the actual cave—and not the replica created for tourists—had to slalom past a multitude of administrative obstacles before the Ministry of Culture would approve the visit. The process was long, and he, as conservator, followed procedure. Nobody entered Lascaux without clearing all the flags. And everyone who made it to the end, mostly eminent researchers and high government officials, was aware of what a privilege—miracle even—it was to be there. They entered this sacred space with both humility and childlike expectation.

These visitors did not fit the bill. One was an arrogant-looking old man who appeared to be well past the age of retirement. He was wearing a dark trench coat, and a wool scarf was wrapped around his neck. He was carrying a walking stick and a small gray bag. A younger man had a muscular build and a full head of black hair, but he hadn't bothered to shave. He face was drawn and tense. They didn't seem to be important researchers, and they didn't look like government bureaucrats.

Whoever they were, they apparently had some clout, and the conservator had to let them in, no matter what he thought. Four local boys had found the cave and its paintings in 1940, and after the discovery, as many as a hundred thousand people poured into the underground space every year. That was until the early nineteen sixties, when it was closed to the public because of the damage done by artificial lighting and carbon dioxide exhaled by the visitors. Destructive layers of algae, calcite crystals, and bacteria had formed on the walls. The cave was restored, and entry was limited.

Sensors had been placed throughout the galleries. They were connected to a computerized system that constantly measured humidity, temperature, and carbon dioxide. Lab techs working some distance from the site would know immediately if an unauthorized man or animal entered the sanctuary.

If it had been up to the conservator, anyone who entered would be forced to wear space suits. As it was, they were required to wear sterile caps, gloves, and coveralls.

He had received a fax from Paris that evening. The conservator was ordered to be at the cave at nine and to show two men in. He was to leave them alone when he asked to go.

"And what time should I come back for these unexpected visitors?" he had asked, emphasizing the word "unexpected." As far as he was concerned, this visit was blasphemy, and he was having a hard time concealing his anger.

"When you are told to!" was the only response.

The conservator had ended up calling the Périgueux police prefect's office. He was worried and asked the prefect's chief of staff what he thought. They'd known each other for years.

He got a quick answer. "My dear friend, remember that we are simply government officials. That's all."

At nine precisely, the conservator handed the visitors their sterile gear and opened the security entrance to the cave.

70

Sol and Marcas were following the conservator.

"The main cave is nearly seventy feet wide and sixteen feet high. There are several smaller galleries. We're now in the Hall of the Bulls. To the right is the passageway that leads to the nave and the apse and then to the Chamber of the Felines."

Marcas saw Sol tighten his grip on the pouch. Then he looked around, his eye catching a long line of aurochs and horses. There was a frieze of bulls and what looked like a bear. A whole bestiary in bright colors that looked like it had been painted the day before.

"Magnificent!" Sol said.

The conservator seemed to relax a little. "Lascaux is unique, a masterpiece of the Magdalenian period some eleven thousand to seventeen thousand years ago."

"How can you be so precise?" Marcas asked.

"Researchers collected more than four hundred tools and bone fragments in the cave and carbon dated them."

"Incredible. Are there only animal representations?"

"No. That's what makes Lascaux so mysterious. Look, there's a unicorn near the entrance."

"A mythical animal?"

"Yes, the Magdalenians dreamed, just as we do."

Marcas recalled the tapestry *La Dame à la licorne* at the Cluny Museum in Paris. Biologists specializing in plants of the Middle Ages had suggested that some of those depicted in the tapestry might have had hallucinogenic properties.

"What's most intriguing are the geometric symbols. There are several hundred of them, like checkerboards or grids. We don't know what they represent."

"Could they have some spiritual significance?"

"Perhaps. They don't appear to correspond with any-thing tangible, like animals. Not all scholars agree, but they could well relate to ritual ceremonies held here."

"Do you think that Lascaux was some kind of sanctuary?"

"I personally think it was a temple, yes. I'll show you why."

The conservator guided his visitors down a gallery to a semicircular area and then through a narrow passage that led to a deeper area.

"This is the Shaft of the Dead Man. Look at the scene."

On the wall, a man with what looked like an erection was sprawled out in front of a bison.

"He has the head of a bird. It's quite possible that this was a shaman," the conservator said.

"A shaman?" Marcas asked.

"Yes. Prehistoric humans most likely came here to commune with the spirit world. The shaman was their intermediary."

Sol was examining the man with the bird head. "But he looks dead."

"A death preceding a spiritual rebirth. That's what the bird symbolizes. The shaman's life force has been freed to journey into the beyond."

Sol looked totally absorbed.

"We have come a long way since theorizing that Lascaux was simply a place where men came to make art," the conservator said. "I, as well as many others, believe that the humans who did these paintings were infused with a sense of the sacred."

"What do the animal representations mean?"

"Some researchers hold that these creatures were visions or hallucinations seen during ritual ceremonies."

They headed back toward the Hall of the Bulls.

"What's over there?" Sol asked, pointing down a dark tunnel.

"The Painted Gallery. It has the great black bull, bison, ibexes, and a—" The conservator looked at his watch. "Listen, it's getting late."

"And a what?" Sol asked.

"Excuse me?"

"You said 'ibexes and a—.'"

The conservator was close to the exit. "And a horse," he said. "An upside-down horse. It's coming out of a crack, as if it has crossed through a wall. Perhaps another vision."

"Leave us now," Sol said.

The conservator hesitated.

"Now," Sol growled, and the man left.

Marcas heard the door close with a click. He turned around. The paintings shone brilliantly against the pale limestone walls. Sol was pointing a gun at him.

71

"So here we are, Inspector. A perfect place for the shadow ritual. Remember, no funny business. You know how Joana feels about your woman. They should be here soon. If you want to see Ms. Zewinski alive again, you'll do what I say."

Marcas felt entirely cut off from the world and about as insignificant as a dust mote in this cave haunted by the ghosts of humans who had lived some fifteen thousand years earlier. Even during his Freemason initiation, when he was by himself with the ritual skull, he hadn't felt so alone. The bulls and bison on the walls would survive long after his own bones were gone. And that could happen sooner rather than later if he didn't find a way to control this madman and his sidekick Joana.

Sol was waving the gun at him. "Go on. Prepare the ritual."

Marcas set out to recall the details in the Breuil Manuscript. The basics were like any other Freemason ritual. Then the image of Sophie Dawes's body flashed in his mind, followed by the list in his notebook of the ritual slayings of his fellow Freemasons. Anger was boiling up inside.

"No dawdling, Inspector."

Marcas unfolded the map of the cave the conservator had given them and found the east, which he marked with a stone. Opposite it, he placed two other stones symbolizing the pillars Jakin and Boaz, marking the entrance to the temple. Using another stone, he drew a rectangle in the middle, as indicated by the Breuil Manuscript. He used the same stone to scrape out a small pit.

"In theory, you need to leave behind any metal before entering the temple," Marcas said, looking at the gun.

"Nice try," Sol said, still pointing the weapon at him. "Over there."

Marcas stepped aside as the old man walked toward the pit, opened the pouch, and pulled out the old vials they had found, along with two matching new ones.

72

The on-call tech flushed the toilet and pulled up his zipper.
His shift would last another hour. He was tempted to leave
now, as the probability of an incident in the Lascaux cave
was as close to absolute zero as you could get. In the eleven
years he had been monitoring the sensors and maintaining
the instruments, he had never once experienced an alert.
Well, there was that time in the Hall of Bulls. A government
minister and his mistress, on a tour with other dignitaries,
had ducked into the hall for a quickie. The sensors had
immediately picked up the rise in their body temperatures
and the cave's carbon monoxide level, but because the tryst
was over as soon as it started, the heavy breathing hadn't
harmed the bulls.

The technician went back to his office and continued
to take apart one of the sensors he had been working on.
With a little luck, he'd be able to change the diode and test
it before his shift was up. He was opening the instrument
with a Philip's screwdriver when an alarm rang out in the
control room. He set down his tools and opened the sliding
door. He walked over to the control panel, cut the alarm,
and checked the parameters. The carbon dioxide measure-
ments indicated that several people were in the cave. A VIP
tour. He had been notified. But he had been told that only
two guests and the conservator would be in the cave. He
clicked on the application to convert the carbon dioxide
units into the number of visitors.

The number seven flashed on the screen.

He located the visitors. Two were in the shaft, while
the others were walking in that direction. The technician
swore and turned off the computer. He was always the last
to be told. A guided tour for two turned into one for several

more and nobody had bothered to say anything. Well, too bad. He wasn't about to put in any overtime watching a half dozen VIPs on yet another magical mystery tour.

73

Loki fought back with all his strength, but the Russian cuffs hindered his hands and feet, giving him no room to maneuver. The guards were carrying him like a sack of potatoes. He begged for mercy, even though he knew it would make them even more contemptuous. Like them, he had never felt the slightest compassion for anyone.

The sound of the waves slapping against the cliffs rose in the starry night, mixing with the song of nightingales perched in the yew trees that lined the overlook.

The small group made its way to the chapel, the scene of so many horrors, the walls soaked with the memory of countless torture victims.

Loki hoped the maiden would be set for a quick death.

Under the crucifix, the board members formed a half-circle around the bloody maiden. Loki was placed in the device. He held back his tears and spoke to his companions. "I take responsibility for my actions and remain a loyal servant of the Orden. I worked all my life for *Halgadom*. Grant me a quick death."

The group moved in closer. Heimdall was the first to speak. "Do you recall the leniency you extended to our brother from London the last time you officiated at a ceremony with this instrument—an instrument that you yourself placed in this chapel?"

"No! He embezzled from us!"

"He was a good friend. I didn't say anything to save him, because Orden comes first. But in his memory, you will meet the same fate. Think about Sol and your charming daughter, Joana, who is already in Valhalla if the gardener has carried out his orders. We will remove all traces of Operation Hiram and become what we were meant to be:

invisible, working in the shadows. And then the day will come when we reveal ourselves to humanity."

The metal creaked as the guards closed the cover on Loki.

Through the crack between the lid and the maiden's side, Loki saw the pious move in even closer, and he heard Heimdall's final words.

"You have twenty minutes to live. Experience the maiden's bite to the fullest."

Darkness filled the space around him.

74

There was a commotion at the entrance. Marcas looked up and saw Joana pushing Jade in front of her and Klaus with another man. Marcas tensed and stepped toward them.

"Inspector, this is a Glock 19, and it's still pointed directly at you," Sol said. He turned to the new arrivals. "Welcome. Did you have any trouble getting in?"

Joana pushed the two captives next to Marcas, "Not at all. Klaus knocked the conservator down the stairs leading to the entrance and we took his keys."

The newcomer turned to Marcas. "I'm sorry, my brother, for dragging you into all of this. I fear it is raining hard."

Marcas nodded. He had used the term himself. "Raining" was Freemason code for imminent danger.

"My brother, I'm the one who involved you." Marcas turned to Sol. "Let him go. He's got nothing to do with this."

But Sol had Klaus bind the man's wrists.

"Oh, but he does, more than you imagine. We've been watching him for years now—the son finishing his father's work. When you met in Paris the other day, he did tell you all about it, didn't he? Mr. Jouhanneau knows so much about us, Inspector. It would be a shame for him to miss the finale. And besides, do you really think I would try this without a guinea pig?"

Jouhanneau looked at Marcas. He nodded but said nothing. Jade glanced at him, grimacing. Jade's face was drained of all color. Her hand had to be hurting. And Marcas knew Sol would kill them without giving it a second thought.

Joana led Jouhanneau to the center of the temple and forced him to sit. Marcas started to struggle, but Klaus kneed him in the stomach.

Jouhanneau turned to Marcas. "This is my path, brother."

Sol opened one of the new vials and brought it to Jouhanneau's lips, pulling his head back by the hair and forcing him to drink. The man choked, then swallowed. Sol unbound his hands and helped him lie down on the cold ground as everyone else looked on.

Marcas felt he had reached the end of a long journey. He could see no escape.

Nothing happened for a few minutes, and then Jouhanneau began to jerk. He looked around, his eyes wide with fear. He cried out and seemed to be trying to lift his arms and legs. But he couldn't.

"I can't... I can't..." His whispered words became a shriek of alarm. "The flesh falls from the bones."

75

The group stood in silence for a long moment, until Jouhanneau coughed and moved. Everyone stared at him as he sat up without any sign of emotion. He lifted his arms and formed a triangle in front of his lips. He was smiling.

Sol walked over and stood in front of him.

"What is it like to fuse with the gods?"

Sol nodded to his guard, who pushed Marcas and Jade against the wall. Joana stood back.

Jouhanneau was as still as a statue. He didn't seem any different, but something had changed in his face. His eyes were emanating a dull energy. Marcas had trouble looking at him.

Sol apparently hadn't noticed. He grabbed the second vial and waved in front of his guinea pig. "Your silence doesn't matter. The bad side effects of the drug seem quite limited. I, too, will complete my quest in this sacred place, built by pure men who believed in the forces of nature not yet contaminated by the God of the Jews and his bastard son."

Jouhanneau turned to him. "You know nothing about what is, what was, and what will be," he said in a toneless voice. "The veil of knowledge will not rise for you."

"Is that so? We'll see about that."

Sol poured the liquid down his throat. He licked his lips, then coughed and closed his eyes. A twisted smile formed on his face.

Marcas and Jade inched closer together.

Seconds later, Sol opened his eyes, grabbed his walking stick, and pointed it at Jouhanneau.

"On your knees, Freemason."

Jouhanneau's voice rang out. "No. A free man kneels before no one."

Sol gave the guard the signal. A shot rang out, echoing in the cave.

Jouhanneau collapsed, clutching his stomach.

"You bastard," Marcas roared.

Joana pistol-whipped him. Marcas stumbled against the wall. Jade tried to help but her hands were still tied.

Sol stood over Jouhanneau. "I feel an incredible force rising in me, as if I were young again." His faced was a mask of cruelty. "I am an SS again, marching for the glory of the West. Tell me, Mason, before I do away with you for good, what did you feel? Did you see your God?"

Jouhanneau stared at him.

"You couldn't understand. I saw myself. That is all."

"You're lying, dog."

Sol raised his stick and brought it down on Jouhanneau's shoulder.

"No!" Marcas shrieked.

But Jouhanneau did not scream. Sol seemed possessed.

"In prehistoric times, shamans sacrificed animals to win the favor of the gods," Sol shouted. "It's all here in the paintings. You're just an animal. I'm burning up. My strength is taking over."

He brought the stick down again, this time on Jouhanneau's neck. Marcas and Jade both struggled to free their hands as Sol shrieked, "Are you going to tell me what you experienced?"

Jouhanneau was lying on the ground, straining to hold his head up. Marcas could tell he was gathering his last bit of strength for the final blow.

"I will die like my father and like my master before him, Hiram. It is an honor. As for you, you could never understand. You must have a pure heart, or…"

The grand archivist stretched out his hand.

"Antoine, my brother. I am not afraid. That is the secret of the shadow ritual. If you knew, Antoine… I crossed through the darkness, and then there was… No, not the Grand Architect, no, just me. I am no longer afraid. Never again."

Sol was laughing like a madman. He raised the stick the final time and brought it down on Jouhanneau's skull.

"Why? Why him and all the others?" Marcas cried out. "Why the same way Hiram was killed?"

Sol strode over to him.

"It's an ancient custom. Nobody knows who devised this blood ritual. The founder of our order, Count von Sebottendorf, called on us to use it. When the Thule chose to become invisible during the rise of Nazism, we decided to send a chilling message. Maybe no one could see us, but we were there, in the shadows. What finer way to demonstrate our secret power than to kill you Masons the same way Hiram was slain? But I'm wasting my time. I have much to do. I'm fulfilling my destiny."

He staggered and looked drunk. Klaus reached out to support him, but Sol pushed him away. Joana moved toward him too, but the old man spit at her feet.

"It's nothing. I'm going to sit down now. Take care of those two. I am no longer afraid. That's what he said. 'I am no longer afraid.'"

Before anyone could act, Sol keeled over. He twisted on the ground and foamed at the mouth. His voice was filled with anguish, "No! Not them! They're all around me. Not that! Can you see them? Can you see them? Don't let them get near me. Get back. I'm an SS officer. You must obey me. No!"

Joana rushed to Sol. His henchman pulled out a gun and pointed it at Marcas and Jade.

Marcas turned to Jade. "I'm sorry," he said. He shoved her out of the way and closed his eyes. "I'm no longer afraid."

A shot rang out, then another. Marcas collapsed on the ground. His last image was Sol writhing nearby, like a rabid beast.

THE ORIENT

76

At the Hospice de la Charité outside Paris, the old man in the padded room suffered day and night. The nurses pitied him. Like a child afraid of the dark, he begged them to keep the lights on. He cycled between uncontrollable anguish and tears of despair, when he would say "I'm sorry" over and over. Even the strongest anti-anxiety medication couldn't calm him. The psychiatrists had no cure.

The nurses had put him in a straightjacket to make sure he didn't harm himself.

77

He woke up with his mind muddled and his vision blurry. He blinked. Jade's face appeared above him.

"Don't move."

"Where am I?"

"Safe in Bordeaux, at the Arche-Royale Clinic. You got lucky."

"I'm thirsty."

Jade handed him a bottle of mineral water. He poured it down his throat as if he hadn't had a drink in days. An agreeably cool sensation filled him. He wanted to sit up, but pain shot through his right side.

"I told you not to move. The bullet almost sent you to the beyond. The docs have ordered two weeks of rest in this room and then a month of convalescence."

"What happened?"

Jade wiped his forehead.

"We owe our lives to your friend Jaigu, as hard as it is for me to say that. Somehow, Darsan found out we were at Lascaux. How do you damned Freemasons always know everything?" she said with a smile.

"Ah, yes. You see, we're not all bad. When I called my worshipful master to see if we could get into the cave, I gave our code word for danger and let Jaigu's name slip."

"Darsan sent Jaigu, since he had been in on the mission from the start. When he got there, he saw us go into the cave with Jouhanneau. He followed and killed Klaus just as he got a bullet off."

"And Sol?"

"Captured, with Joana. She was transferred to a special-ops prison, where she's being interrogated for information on Orden and its network. Sol is in a psychiatric hospital."

"Why?" Marcas said, feeling himself drift away and Jade's voice become distant.

He fell asleep.

78

The Hospice de la Charité-Dieu had grounds that no gardener had domesticated. Century-old trees spread their branches alongside the building. There were no bars on the windows. Most of the patients were harmless, lost in their silence or their imagination. The real world was little more than a distant memory.

A linden tree, planted when the hospice was built, had branches reaching to the second-floor rooms. In the coolness of evening, the scent of the flowers filled the silent halls. After climbing through the window, a man took a white lab coat out of his bag, put it on, and clipped on a hospital identification badge. Now he just needed to find room 37.

When he did, he smiled at the patient's name: François Le Guermand. The past always caught up with you. As did Thule with those it had sentenced to death.

79

Antoine Marcas walked into the room just as a nurse was preparing the body to be taken away. The hospital director had immediately informed Darsan, who had contacted Marcas.

The man who had called himself Sol lay on the bed. Marcas could make out his emaciated body under the sheet. His hands were strapped to the sides of the bed. An unpleasant odor was rising from it.

The worker blushed. "I'm sorry," she said. "I haven't finished. Are you family?"

"No."

"You understand. They can't take care of themselves."

Marcas nodded. He showed his badge. "Call the head doctor, please," he said.

The nurse hurried out while Marcas contemplated the former SS officer's face. It had stiffened into a grimace. His eyes were still open, fixed on the ceiling, as if in terror.

The doctor, a young man, walked into the room.

"What did he die from?"

"Are you familiar with his file?"

"A little bit."

"The patient suffered from obsessional psychosis due to irreversible brain lesions."

"What kind of psychosis?"

"Fear, sir."

The nurse was back. She tried to close the patient's eyes but couldn't.

The doctor shrugged. "Some go into death with their eyes open. If we can't get them closed, we cover them with a headband."

Marcas went outside. The warm air under the trees felt good. He took out a cigarette, but his hands were trembling.

"You shouldn't smoke."

He turned around. Jade was sitting on a bench under the linden tree. Its leaves were rustling in the breeze. Marcas put the pack back in his pocket.

"How did you know I was here?"

"Darsan told me."

He looked at her, and refrained from asking *why* she was there. He just smiled.

She stood up, and they started walking toward the gate.

"I have a question," Jade said.

"Yes?"

"What's the secret of the shadow ritual?"

Marcas's eyes wandered over the hospital walls.

"The soma takes fear away."

"Is that all?"

"That's more than all. We humans are born afraid to leave our mother's belly, and we die afraid to leave this life. Now just imagine a life without fear. Nothing would hold us back. We'd be absolutely serene. Jouhanneau smiled when Sol killed him. He wasn't afraid."

Jade looked at him. "But why didn't the drug have the same effect on Sol?"

"He didn't have a pure heart."

"But..."

"So he suffered. He experienced something he had never felt before: guilt. We all have it in us—the good and the bad. Maybe the true Masonic secret is in the practice of ritual and initiation, in facing yourself through the efforts you make to reach the light. It's the path, not the destination. All Sol did was try to steal a fix, like a drug addict. He got high on the gods he envisioned—the gods of retribution and anger, and they made him suffer."

Jade slowed down.

"Would you want to experience it?"

"No, I'm vain enough to think I can continue on the path of knowledge without a drug, no matter how celestial it is. That said, the questions raised by this mixture are astonishing. If sacred and religious experiences are the result of disturbances in the brain caused by external stimuli, then God is simply a drug. Divine light is little more than a neuronal big bang. But..."

"But what?"

"Perhaps this substance really does have the power to put us in touch with something bigger than we are."

"I actually love it when you get that sententious look. It's too funny. You chase away the Mason, and he comes running back."

Marcas laughed.

In front of a newspaper stand, a delivery man was dropping off a shipment of magazines. A gust of wind blew one onto the sidewalk. Marcas stopped it with his foot and picked it up. On the front page were a compass and square, the Freemason symbol.

Revelations
Freemason secrets unveiled
Exclusive interview

Marcas paged through the magazine to the article. "A pharmaceutical startup has announced the launch of a new plant-based antidepressant, Somatox. Makers of the drug claim it will revolutionize the antidepressant landscape."

Marcas felt like tossing the magazine into a garbage can, but he returned it to the pile where it belonged. Just let it go, he said to himself.

He looked at Jade. "So tell me. Do you still think we're all a bunch of nasty hoodwinkers?"

"Hmm. Let's just say, I know now that all the apples aren't bad."

"I could introduce you to some more of us. You might actually like a few."

"Don't press your luck, Inspector."

Marcas stopped grinning and took her hand. "I'm so sorry she did this to you."

"Don't sweat over it," Jade said. "I still have nine. And the last time I checked, they were all working. It changes the balance when I shoot, but it's no big deal."

She smiled at Marcas again, hardly the hard-as-stone security chief he had met a lifetime ago. She held his hand and intertwined her fingers with his. In the distance, the sun was rising above the deserted street. To the Orient.

Thank you for reading Shadow Ritual.

*We invite you to share your thoughts and reactions on Goodreads and
your favorite social media and retail platforms.*

We appreciate your support.

Sorting Facts from Fiction

This book is of course a work of fiction but also based
on true historical facts. If you want to know more, visit the
following page:

www.lefrenchbook.com/shadow-ritual-facts-fiction

About the Authors

Eric Giacometti, studied biochemistry and genetics in Toulouse, France, before going into journalism. Then, at the height of his career as an investigative reporter, he was contaminated by the thriller virus. His life took on another dimension: journalist by day, writer by night. That is when he and his childhood friend Jacques Ravenne created the Freemason police inspector Antoine Marcas. "Writing escapist fiction was a perfect antidote to the depressing stories of scandals and corruption I faced every day. Having one foot in reality and the other in fiction is incredible, but it's key not to mix the two." In 2013, he left his full-time reporting job with a French daily newspaper to work freelance and write. He teaches journalism and writing.

Jacques Ravenne is a high-level French Freemason. He is also a literary critic, known for his work on the writers Paul Valéry, Yves Bonnefoy, Gérard de Nerval and Stéphane Mallarmé. In addition to his academic work, he was also a local elected official for a number of years, and contributes regularly to Freemason publications. He discovered the Marquis de Sade's château in 1985, beginning a long fascination with the man, which has resulted in an anthology of his correspondence and a novel based on Sade's life.

About the Translator

Anne Trager loves France so much she has lived there for over a quarter of a century and just can't seem to leave. What keeps her there is a uniquely French mix of pleasure seeking and creativity. Well, that and the wine. In 2011, she woke up one morning and said, "I just can't stand it anymore. There are way too many good books being written in France not reaching a broader audience." That's when she founded Le French Book to translate some of those books into English. The company's motto is "If we love it, we translate it," and Anne loves myteries and thrillers.

Discover more books from

Le French Book

www.lefrenchbook.com

Paris Homicide Mysteries by **Frédérique Molay**

An edge-of-your-seat mysteries set in Paris, where Chief of Police Nico Sirsky and his crack team fight crime in the French capital. Already translated: *The 7th Woman, Crossing the Line,* and *The City of Blood.*
www.parishomicide.com

The Winemaker Detective Series
by **Jean-Pierre Alaux and Noël Balen**

A total Epicurean immersion in French countryside and gourmet attitude with two expert winemakers turned amateur sleuths gumshoeing around wine country. Already translated: *Treachery in Bordeaux, Grand Cru Heist, Nightmare in Burgundy, Deadly Tasting, Cognac Conspiracies,* and *Mayhem in Margaux.*
www.thewinemakerdetective.com

The Consortium Thriller Series
by **David Khara**

A roller-coaster ride that dips into the history of World War II, then races through a modern-day loop-to-loop of action and humor. The series juggles with time and place in a potent mix constructed around flashbacks that allow readers to piece together key events. Already translated: *The Bleiberg Project, The Shiro Project* and *The Morgenstern Project.*
www.theconsortiumthrillers.com

CPSIA information can be obtained at www.ICGtesting.com
Printed in the USA
BVOW08s0553090315

390611BV00003B/4/P